F A T E D

Crystal managed to elude Brent for a moment, but she discovered that the creek bed was slippery. A startled shriek escaped her as she lost her balance and started to tumble backward.

In an instant, Brent was there to save her. He lifted her up in strong arms and kept her from being drenched. He held her child-like against his chest as he carried her out of the creek.

"You've rescued me again," Crystal said breathlessly.

"That seems to be my fate lately," he acknowledged with a half grin.

"You are always there when I need you most—"

Once they were on solid ground, Brent stopped and gazed down at her. Gone were all thoughts of revenge for the soaking she'd given him. The only thing that mattered to him now was holding her close and kissing her again.

"Do you need me now?" he asked quietly.

"Oh yes—"

HUNTER'S MOON

BOBBI SMITH

LEISURE BOOKS NEW YORK CITY

A LEISURE BOOK®

July 2003

Published by

Dorchester Publishing Co., Inc.
276 Fifth Avenue
New York, NY 10001

ISBN 0-8439-5155-9

Visit us on the web at www.dorchesterpub.com.

To Charlotte Parry, David Sebastian Martinez, Michelle Oglesby, Randi Howell, Syl and Lorraine Borel, and the whole gang at the Book Bug in Sikeston, MO—Joyce and Merlin Hagy, Glenna Swilley, Brenda Fowler, Valonna Fowler and Mike Belk. You're wonderful!

ACKNOWLEDGMENTS

I'd like to thank Barbara Fey, Jean Phillipe, Steve Fine, Jim Brown and Diana Tucker for all their help with research.

"Hi" to all the gang at my Curves who work out with me at 6:30 a.m.—Jill, Cathy, Tina, Karen, Sharon, Karen, Pam, Kelly, Charlotte, Marsha, Ginna, Diane, Pam, Stacy, Tina, Debbie, Marilyn, Vicky, Carol, Sherry, Sandy and Pat.

HUNTER'S
MOON

Chapter One

Half-Moon Ranch
Texas Hill Country, 1870

The distant sound of a gunshot split the quiet of the early afternoon.

Brent Hunter heard it and reined in. He frowned as he cast a quick, suspicious glance around. "That sounded like it came from the direction of the house."

"Why would anybody be shooting there?" asked the ranch hand who was riding with him.

"I don't know, but I intend to find out," Brent replied, growing uneasy. He knew his mother was home alone. The hands were all out on the range working stock, and his father had gone into town on business. His eight-year-old sister, Abby, had ridden in with their father. She had been invited to spend a few days there with friends.

Spurring his horse to a gallop, Brent raced toward home, leaving Hank to follow. As he topped the low rise that overlooked the ranch house, he was surprised to see his father's thoroughbred stallion tied up out front. He had thought Jack Hunter was going to stay in town another day. Other than that, nothing appeared out of the ordinary. But though everything seemed quiet enough, Brent had learned in his twenty years to trust his instincts, and they were screaming, *Trouble.*

Brent rode in and stopped before the house. He dismounted and hurried up the porch steps.

"Ma," Brent called out as he walked in the door. "What was the shooting all about?"

The scene that greeted Brent shocked him to the depths of his soul. His mother lay on the floor unmoving, the bodice of her gown soaked in blood. His father was standing over her, swaying drunkenly. He held a gun in his hand, and his clothing was stained with blood.

Jack Hunter was startled by his son's unexpected intrusion. He stared at him. "Brent—"

"Ma!" The word was torn from him as he ran to his mother's side. He was frantic to help her, desperate to save her. When Brent knelt down beside her, though, he knew immediately there was nothing he could do. The wound had been fatal.

2

"She's dead, Brent." Jack was so drunk his words were slurred.

"What happened?" Brent demanded.

"I don't know. . . ."

"What do you mean, you don't know?" Brent stared up at him in confusion.

His mother had been shot. His father was holding the gun.

Why?

Their family had been going through some rough times, but as far as he knew, their troubles weren't anything they couldn't have overcome with hard work and determination. It was true that his father had taken to drinking more heavily than ever lately, and his parents had been arguing more about his drinking and money, but Brent had never thought things were bad enough to lead to something like this . . .

"I don't know how it happened." Jack stared blankly around himself, then let his gaze drop to his dead wife. "Oh, God . . . She's dead, and it's all my fault—"

"*Your fault?*" Brent raged in disbelief. "Did you do this? Did you shoot her?"

He looked at his son, the vile accusation repeating in his mind: *Did you do this? Did you shoot her?* Slowly, knowing he could do nothing else, Jack nodded in response.

Disbelief filled Brent; then fury unlike anything he'd ever felt before erupted deep within him. Not caring that his father was still holding the gun, Brent launched himself at him. He tackled him and knocked him to the floor. The gun flew from Jack's grip. He was so drunk that he offered little resistance as Brent pummeled him mercilessly.

Hank had just reached the house when he heard the sound of a crash inside. He ran in to find Jack and Brent locked in a brutal fight, and Beth Hunter dead on the floor.

"Brent!" Hank ran to separate the brawling men. He was a big, burly man, but even so, it was hard for him to haul Brent off his father. "What are you doing?"

Brent fought against Hank's powerful hold. He wanted to be free to take out his rage at his father.

"He killed her!" he rasped.

"Boss?" Hank looked at Jack.

Bloodied and unsteady, Jack got slowly to his feet, but he didn't respond.

"You shot her?" Hank pressed, waiting for the answer in disbelief.

Jack's face was battered and his expression was bleak as he looked at the ranch hand. He nodded only once.

Hank was stunned. Brent tried to break free from him again, and this time Hank let him go.

"I'll go get the sheriff," Hank offered numbly. Then glancing at Beth, he added, "And the minister."

Brent straightened and ordered, "Take him with you. Get him out of here."

"Son, T . . ."

Brent turned his back as Hank went to help Jack. He didn't watch his father stagger drunkenly from the house with the hired hand. Brent didn't care if he ever saw his father again.

He cared only that his beloved mother was dead.

"May she rest in heavenly peace. Amen," Reverend Crawford intoned, solemnly concluding the prayer service over Beth Hunter's grave.

"Amen," echoed the family, friends, and ranch hands who'd gathered at the graveside.

The reverend closed his Bible and looked up at the Hunter children. The pain of their loss was etched in their faces. The three young men—Brent, Quince, and Matt—were stoic, but young Abby was clinging to Brent, crying her heart out. Quietly, Reverend Crawford went forward to express his condolences. He knew what a tragedy this was for the family. They'd lost not only their mother, but their father, too.

"If you need anything, anything at all, you have only to ask," he told them, shaking Brent's hand.

"Thank you, Reverend," Brent answered.

In truth, Brent wanted to ask him to bring their mother back. But he knew the painful reality, and he said nothing.

Their mother was dead.

She was gone from them forever.

They would never see her again.

Brent kept a sheltering arm around Abby. It had been hard telling Quince and Matt about their mother's death when they'd returned to the house that day, but going into town to find Abby and tell her the news had been the most difficult thing he'd ever done in his life. Abby was sweet and innocent. She didn't deserve to have her whole world torn apart this way. Brent had wanted to protect her from harm, to shield her from hurt, but their father had ruined all that. He could only try to make things better for her in the future, and he and his brothers were determined to do that. He led his trembling young sister away from the small family cemetery and back toward the house.

The rest of the day passed in a blur for Brent.

Edmund and Iona Montgomery, his parents' long-time friends, were there to help console Abby and offer their support. Though he had never much cared for Edmund, today Brent needed all the support he could get. He needed to be strong to deal with what lay ahead.

Brent went outside onto the porch for a moment of quiet away from the crowd indoors. He wanted some time alone to think. He was now the head of the family and in charge of his nineteen- and seventeen-year-old brothers, Quince and Matt, and little Abby. It wasn't going to be easy, but somehow he would find the strength to hold everything together—he had to. He had no choice.

"Brent?" Edmund called out from the doorway.

Brent had been standing back in the porch shadows, where he'd hoped no one could see him, but Edmund had found him.

"I'm here," he answered in a flat voice.

"I saw you come outside and I wanted to make sure you were all right," Edmund said as he came to stand beside him.

Brent cast him a sharp glance. He doubted that he would ever be all right again. Nothing was ever going to be the same in his life—nothing. "I'll be fine."

Edmund must have heard the strain in his voice, for he smiled understandingly. "I know this is a difficult time, but I had to ask you . . . Have you spoken to your father since—"

"No," Brent cut him off in disgust.

"Well, I wanted to tell you that I went by the jail to see him as soon as I heard the news. I thought I might be able to help him in some way."

Brent glanced at him, but said nothing. He didn't know why anyone would want to help his father after what he'd done.

"I tried to get him to talk to me, but he wouldn't. He just told me to leave," Edmund went on. "Do you know what went on that day? Why on God's earth did he shoot your mother? I've known your parents since before you were born, and none of this makes any sense."

"I don't know a thing."

"He didn't explain it to you?" he pressed. "He didn't make any excuses?"

"No."

"I know they were having trouble. Now, don't look surprised that I would know. Your parents and I have known each other since we were younger than you. Whatever the problems were, they didn't seem important enough to warrant what happened. Maybe you should go visit him at the jail and try to get him to tell you about it. It's been a few days. Maybe he'll talk to you now," Edmund urged. "It's important that we find out."

"I know what happened."

"But you don't know why."

"All that matters is that he killed my mother." Brent had no desire to speak to his father again. In fact, he would have preferred to disown him altogether.

"I'm sorry, Brent—so sorry. But think about it. You need to know what your father was thinking. Your mother was a beautiful, loving woman. She didn't deserve this . . . to be shot down—"

Brent cut him off before he could say anything more. "No, she didn't."

Edmund stared at him for a moment, looking away only when Brent stared back at him. He went back indoors, leaving Brent alone with his thoughts.

Brent did not follow him in. He was in no mood

to talk with anyone. Confusion, sadness, and anger tore at him.

A driven man, he left the porch and returned to his mother's grave. He stayed there until the last of the visitors had gone. Only then did he return to the house.

"Well, we're almost there," Brent said to Quince and Abby as he drove the buckboard slowly through the streets of Diablo the following afternoon.

Brent had thought long and hard about what Edmund had said to him the night before. As uneasy as the man made him, he'd realized that in this case the banker was right.

He needed answers, and he needed them now.

Brent had told Quince what he planned to do, and Quince had insisted on accompanying him. No one knew where Matt was. He'd left the ranch after the funeral and hadn't been seen since.

When Abby had heard what was happening, she'd told them they would not be leaving without her for she wanted to see her papa again.

"Good," Quince said tightly. "I want to get this over with as fast as we can."

"I wish Matt had come with us." Abby was growing a bit nervous now that the actual confrontation was drawing near. She would have liked to have had all three of her big brothers with her for support. "Why did he go away?"

"Who knows what Matt was thinking?" Brent was

still angered by his youngest brother's disappearance. Matt had always been the undependable one, the wild one, but at a time like this, the whole family should have been together.

Brent thought back over the weeks and months just past. He remembered how his father's drinking had increased dramatically and how his parents had seemed more and more at odds with each passing day. Sometimes they barely spoke to each other, and at other times they argued heatedly. As difficult as things seemed to have been for them, though, Brent would never have suspected that the situation would end in tragedy.

"But maybe Papa didn't really do it," Abby said. In her innocence, she was clinging desperately to a last thread of hope that this was all some horrible mistake.

Neither Brent nor Quince responded to her. There was no point. Brent just hoped that she wouldn't be hurt any more deeply by what was about to transpire.

"Ready?" Brent asked when he reined in before the sheriff's office.

"As I'll ever be," Quince said in disgust. He jumped down and went to tie up the horses.

"Brent . . . I'm scared." Unlike the absent Matt, Abby had never been inside the Diablo jail before.

Brent took her hand in his to reassure her. "Quince and I will be right here with you. You won't be alone."

Her chin quivered a little as she fought to keep from crying. "All right. I'm ready."

Brent wished he could say the same.

Quince helped Abby down, and when Brent joined them, the two brothers shared a steadying look before they started into the sheriff's office.

At the sound of the door opening, Sheriff Miller looked up from his desk.

"Sheriff Miller," Brent began as he led the way inside, "we were hoping to see our pa."

"Sure."

The lawman stood as Brent and Quince walked in, but he frowned slightly when he saw that Abby was with them. He'd known the Hunter boys would show up eventually, but he hadn't thought they would bring their little sister along. This was hardly the place for a young girl. Still, he couldn't refuse to admit her to see her father. Fortunately, Jack was his only prisoner. He noticed that Matt wasn't with them.

"Let's go on back," Sheriff Miller said as he opened the door to the cell area and went in, leaving them to follow.

"Jack, you got company," the lawman announced, standing aside.

Jack Hunter had been lying on his cot, one arm across his eyes. At the sheriff's announcement, he sat up. His children were standing there looking at him through the bars of the jail cell—all of them except Matt.

"I'll leave the door open in case you need anything. I'll be right outside at my desk," the sheriff told them as he left.

"What are you two doing here?" Jack demanded coldly as he glared at Brent and Quince. "And why did you bring Abby?"

"Papa . . . I wanted to—" Abby began in a soft voice.

"She doesn't belong here." He cut her off without acknowledging her. Even at so tender an age, Abby greatly resembled her mother, with dark hair and green eyes. Pain stabbed at Jack as he thought of Beth and all that had happened. He was sober now, and being sober only made everything worse.

"Abby needed to see you—and we wanted to talk to you," Quince said.

"Where's Matt?" Jack asked harshly, standing up and looking past them to see if his youngest son was still in the outer office. "Going over old times with the sheriff?"

"Matt didn't come with us," Quince answered him.

Jack's eyes narrowed. "Why not? I've hauled him out of here often enough before, what with his drinking and whoring and carrying on." He glanced at Abby as if to say it was time she knew what kind of brother she had.

"The truth is, he's gone. We don't know where," Quince said.

"Gone?" Jack repeated in anger. He glared at

Quince for a long moment. "I should have figured."
He turned his cold-eyed regard on Brent. "Get out
of here—all of you."

"No, Pa," Brent said. "We're not leaving until we
get some answers."

"You want answers?" he demanded.

"That's right," Brent went on, determined not to
be denied. "Why did you do it, Pa? Why? We want
to understand."

"You want to understand? How can I make you
understand, when I don't understand how it happened myself? I was drunk. We were arguing. The
next thing I knew, she was dead."

"That's your only explanation? That you were
drunk? That the two of you were arguing?" Brent
challenged angrily. "That's not good enough."

"It's going to have to be. Your mother's dead. I'm
guilty! What don't you understand about that? Go
away and leave me alone!"

"Papa!" Abby ran to the bars, tears streaming
down her face.

"Get out of here, and don't come back!" Jack ordered, turning his back on them. "I don't want to
see any of you."

"Abby . . . come on." Brent said, as he and
Quince went to their little sister and drew her away
from the cell and into the outer office.

Brent closed the door behind them, shutting their
father out of their lives.

One Month Later
The Diablo State Bank

Brent stared down at the legal documents Edmund had spread on his desk, trying to come to grips with what he'd just learned. Edmund owned the only bank in Diablo, and he had summoned Brent to discuss the Half-Moon's financial situation.

"You're serious about this?" Brent asked.

"Absolutely," Edmund answered. "Look, I'm just being honest with you. I'm not trying to hurt you. Your father took out these loans using the Half-Moon as collateral. Now that he's in prison, I may have to call them in."

Brent was shocked by the news that the ranch was so deeply in debt. He'd had no idea his father had borrowed this heavily to buy the thoroughbred stock he'd wanted so badly. "But you can't—"

"I can, and I will—if you don't make the payments on time."

Brent looked up at Edmund, wondering how the man could have changed so much in such a short time. At the funeral he had seemed supportive, but now he was threatening to take the ranch from them. They had already lost their mother and father. The Half-Moon was all they had left, and he had no intention of losing it. It was their home.

"You know what a difficult time this has been for us," Brent argued.

"This isn't personal, Brent," Edmund explained

smoothly. "This is about money. This is business. I made these loans to your pa in good faith. Now that you've taken over running the ranch, they are your responsibility."

Brent was chilled by the banker's manner.

This is business. . . .

Brent had thought things were difficult before, but discovering his father had gone in debt—almost to the point of losing the ranch just to finance his dream of raising thoroughbred horses—left him stunned. "I'll take care of it."

As he spoke, Brent looked down at Edmund. The banker stared up at him with the hard, cold eyes of a predator. The coldness was as shocking as if he'd pulled out a gun and aimed it at Brent's gut.

"I can count on your being on time?" Edmund asked.

Brent matched his coldness. "You have my word."

He turned and walked out of the bank without saying anything more. There was nothing left to say. He wasn't sure how he was going to break the news to Quince that they were on the verge of losing everything. Matt, too, if he ever showed up again. They were all going to have to work damned hard to make the Half-Moon a paying proposition, and according to Edmund, they didn't have much time.

Brent knew he could count on Quince. He couldn't say the same where Matt was concerned.

Brent had given Edmund his word that the loans

would be repaid on time, and he would do it. The Half-Moon meant too much to him. He would not lose the ranch because of his father's debts.

Somehow, some way, he would save their home.

Chapter Two

Long Horn, Texas, 1880

"What are you going to do about the money you owe John Hall, Dan?" Crystal Stewart asked her brother as they found a moment to talk in private at the Palace Saloon. Dan was a gambler who liked high-stakes poker games, and he'd just lost a big hand to the other player. "You owe him a lot."

"I know what I owe him!" Dan seethed, his anger hiding his desperation. "If you'd helped me the way you were supposed to . . ."

Crystal was his shill. Dan had trained her to work the saloon like a bar girl and to signal him and let him know what the other men at his table were holding in their hands. Tonight, however, the other gamblers had been very careful not to let anyone

17

get a look at their cards. And Dan had lost badly.

"I tried, but it almost seemed that they were on to me," Crystal said. "I'm tired of doing this, Dan. I don't like trying to cheat people. It's wrong. We need to find another way to support ourselves."

"I'll worry about finding another way to support ourselves right after I figure out a way to pay off Hall," he said in a snarl.

Dan was tired of her talk about quitting. He knew she didn't like helping him, but he didn't care. She was a pretty woman with her blond hair and curvaceous figure. She could distract the other gamblers and help him win. That was all that mattered. They had a good thing going, most of the time, and he planned to keep it that way.

Dan went on, "I told Hall before he left that I'd meet him later tonight with the cash."

"But you don't have it!"

"I'll get it somehow. How much do you have on you? What have you made in tips tonight?"

"I'm not sure—a few dollars."

"Give me what you've got."

"We need this money for food and to pay our hotel bill."

"I'll figure out a way to take care of that later—after I get Hall off my back."

Crystal was disgusted as she handed over what cash she had. "I'm going back to the hotel."

"Fine."

As Crystal left, Dan returned to the poker table

with her money. He hoped his luck would change. It had to. He needed to win back enough to pay his debt.

If he didn't . . .

Dan refused to think about the possibility. Instead, he concentrated on the hand he was dealt.

Crystal sought out the quiet sanctity of her small room at the hotel. It had been a very long night. She undressed and donned her simple cotton night-gown, more than ready to seek the solace and peace of sleep. At least when she was sleeping, she didn't have to worry about Dan.

She went to the washstand and for a moment studied her own reflection. The woman looking back at her seemed almost a stranger. Dan always insisted she wear face paint to make herself seem older and more sophisticated than she was. The reflection in the mirror looked worldly and mature and very tired.

Crystal scrubbed her face clean, wondering how she had come to live like this—working in saloons, helping her older brother cheat at cards—but she knew the answer. Their parents had died when she was only sixteen and Dan twenty; they'd had no relatives or family friends to help them. Dan had always been the wild sort who fancied himself a good gambler, and he'd planned to make his living that way. At first he'd resented having to take care of her, but when he'd realized how pretty she was,

19

he had bought her some fancy dresses and trained her to help him.

It had been nearly four years now, and Crystal had had enough. She didn't like cheating people.

She made up her mind that tomorrow she was going to tell Dan he was on his own. The decision filled her with a great sense of relief as she went to bed, and she fell asleep quickly. Soon this life she'd been living would be over.

Crystal wasn't sure what woke her, but she sat up in bed and was startled to see the shadow of someone in her room. It looked like a man, and he was closing the door behind him.

"Dan?"

The man didn't answer as he locked the door.

"What are you doing?" She started to get up, still thinking it was Dan. "Is something wrong?"

"Oh, no, honey, everything is just fine."

Crystal went still at the sound of the leering, horrible voice. The man moved close enough for her to recognize him. It was John Hall.

She grabbed her blanket and clutched it to her breast, but she knew it offered little in the way of real protection. Dan had often encouraged her to keep a derringer with her, but she'd always refused. Now she wished she had a gun to defend herself.

"What are you doing in here? Get out!"

"Now, that's no way to greet me," Hall said in a lecherous voice as he slowly crossed the room toward her. "Your brother sent me to you."

"What?" Shock radiated through Crystal.

"I just left Dan. He didn't have my money, but he said you'd work it out for me. I was watching you all night. You are one pretty woman, and a piece of you might just settle up what he owes me—if what your brother says about you is true. He says you're still a virgin." Hall loomed before her, tall and threatening.

Panic seized Crystal. She was trapped. Dan wanted her to play the whore to settle his gambling debts!

"There must be a mistake—" Crystal started to protest.

"No, Crystal, there's no mistake. You're mine for the rest of the night, and Dan said you'd be real good to me."

Hall reached out and grabbed Crystal by the upper arms, dragging her up to him. She struggled to break free, but she was no match for his strength. He held her easily.

"I like feisty women." He laughed in her ear. "Come on, honey, fight me some more."

His words chilled Crystal. He tore the blanket from her grip and pawed at her breasts through her nightgown. She began to tremble as he crushed her tightly against him.

"Stop it! Let me go or I'll scream! My brother would never send you here!"

"Go ahead and scream. Ain't no one going to hear you," he breathed in her ear.

His mouth covered hers, and his tongue plunged into her mouth in a vile kiss.

"No!" Crystal shrieked, jerking her head away to avoid his nauseating assault.

Again Hall laughed at her. "Yeah, you're going to be fun to ride."

He pushed her.

The side of the bed hit her at the backs of her knees, and Crystal fell backward. Moments before, she'd thought the bed was her safe haven, but now it had become an instrument of this man's terror.

Hall loomed over her. He stripped off his shirt and started to unbutton his pants.

"Let's find out if Dan was telling me the truth about you." His voice was filled with lust, and drool slicked his lips as he leaned down toward her. "I think one night with you ought to pay some of his debt to me—if you make it worth my while."

Hall grabbed the neckline of her gown. In one harsh pull he tore the soft garment down the front, baring her lovely body to his gaze. He started to unfasten his pants. He was ready for her and determined to have his pleasure.

Crystal had never been so frightened in all her life. She twisted to the side just as he would have fallen upon her. She couldn't believe her own brother had done this to her!

Reaching out, Crystal groped in the darkness, searching for something—anything—she could use as a weapon. Her hand touched the lamp on the nightstand beside the bed, and she knew what she had to do. Crystal grabbed it just as he snared her other arm.

Hall had been ready to throw Crystal back down on the bed. He was thinking only of parting her thighs and thrusting deep within her. He was hard with wanting her, and nothing was going to stop him from having her. He jerked her toward him.

Crystal swung out at him with all her might and brought the lamp crashing down in his face. The glass chimney shattered on contact, and Hall collapsed. He lay half on top of her, a deadweight.

Frantic and frightened, Crystal fought to escape. She shoved at him with all her might, and he slid, facedown, to the floor. She scrambled off the bed and then cowered, frozen, on the far side of the room, clutching her torn gown together, fearing that at any moment he would get back up and come after her.

But Hall didn't move. Crystal waited, expecting the worst. Still, he didn't move. Terror of a different kind filled her. Had she killed him? Was he dead?

Horror ate at her as she crept toward where he lay. She tried to see if Hall was still breathing, but in the darkness she could discern no movement of his chest. Blood covered his face and pooled beneath his head.

Crystal knew in that moment what she had to do. She had to flee.

There was no one she could turn to for help. Dan wanted to make her a whore. He had sent this man to her to settle his own debts. Her only brother had betrayed her in the most horrible way.

Crystal knew she could never trust Dan again.

She knew, too, that no one in town would believe she'd killed Hall in self-defense. Hall was an influential man in these parts, and she was only a dance-hall girl. If she were going to save herself, she had to run away that very night. She was on her own now, and she was a wanted woman.

She stripped off the remnants of her ruined nightgown, then quickly dressed. She stuffed what clothing she could fit into one bag. Then she grabbed up her mother's jewelry and the little cash she had kept hidden from Dan in her room. It wasn't much, but she hoped it would get her out of town.

She had only a few hours until dawn.

She had to move quickly.

Chapter Three

San Antonio, six months later

"All right, everybody, quiet down!" ordered Bill Clark, the bartender and owner of the Six Gun Saloon. "It's time for Miss Opal to perform!"

A rousing cheer went up.

The men had been waiting all evening for just this moment. They all turned and eagerly faced the stage at the back of the room. They were more than ready to see the blond beauty whose reputation had spread far and wide in the few months she'd been working at the Six Gun. Even the saloon girls turned their attention to the stage.

Everyone loved Miss Opal.

The curtain parted. An expectant hush fell over the crowd. And then Miss Opal made her entrance.

She was the epitome of the seductress as she moved gracefully to center stage. She wore a red satin gown that, though demurely cut, clung enticingly to her perfect figure. The men shouted their approval as she stopped before them.

"Good evening, gentlemen," Crystal greeted them in a throaty voice, smiling warmly in welcome. She had taken to using the name Opal since she'd come to San Antonio some months before. No one knew her real name, and she intended to keep it that way.

"Evenin', Miss Opal!" they shouted back.

The piano player began the first melody, and she started to sing. Her voice rang out pure and sweet.

These men were a rough-and-tumble bunch, but they knew true talent when they heard it. Miss Opal had the voice of an angel, and they were enchanted. When she finished her first selection, they roared their approval and clamored for more. She obliged them.

"Hey, Bill! This new singer of yours is one pretty woman, and she's as good as everyone's been saying. Where'd you find her?" Joe Meyers asked as he shoved his empty glass toward the bartender for a refill. He had been drinking heavily all evening, and he didn't intend to stop.

"Opal found me," Bill answered as he poured Joe another drink. "She came in here about two months ago looking for a job. When I heard her sing, I hired her on the spot. It was one of the smartest things I ever did. Business has been booming."

"I can see why. What's she do besides sing?" Joe asked hopefully. A lecherous gleam lit his eyes as he imagined himself spending the rest of the evening with her, upstairs in one of the private rooms. He'd make her warble real good.

"Nothing." The bartender's answer was firm.

"Nothing?" Joe repeated, surprised. In his experience, the women who worked in saloons were willing to do just about anything to make money.

"That's right. Opal is a lady."

Irritated that he would have no chance to seek his pleasure with the beautiful singer, Joe turned his attention back to the stage to listen to the rest of her performance.

Crystal had learned long ago how to keep an audience entertained. She flirted openly with her admirers. She wanted each man to believe she was singing just for him.

Crystal didn't know what made her glance toward the front of the saloon, but as she did a tall, dark-haired stranger appeared through the swinging doors. She was sure she had never seen the man before, for she certainly would have remembered him. He was ruggedly handsome, and he had a compelling aura of power and command about him. There was also an element of danger—in the way he wore his gun low on his hip and the way he moved. Attractive though he was, Crystal made it a rule never to get involved with any of her customers. With that rule in mind, she started to force her attention away from him.

And then he looked her way.

Their gazes met across the crowded room, and a surge of sensual awareness shot through Crystal unlike anything she'd ever experienced before. Her reaction to him took her completely by surprise. Wanting to maintain her composure, she quickly looked away and continued to sing to her adoring fans. She couldn't afford to be distracted.

Brent Hunter had come to the Six Gun Saloon because he needed a drink, and that was saying something for him. He couldn't remember the last time he'd had one. He generally had no use for liquor, and, in fact, did not allow it at the Half-Moon. He had seen firsthand the tragedy drunkenness could cause, and he wanted no part of it.

But tonight was different.

After what he'd dealt with today, Brent needed not only a drink, but some peace and quiet, too. As he'd neared the saloon, he'd heard the loud cheering going on inside and realized he wasn't going to find much peace there. He'd almost decided to go on to another bar when he'd heard the woman singing inside.

Drawn into the saloon by her siren's song, Brent wasn't quite sure what to expect. Certainly he hadn't expected the entertainer to be anything like the vision gracing the stage at the back of the room.

The woman was beautiful. She had the voice of an angel, and she looked like one, too.

If she's working at the Six Gun, she's no angel, Brent reminded himself as he made his way over to the bar.

"Whiskey," he ordered, and he was glad when the barkeep quickly complied. He drained the glass. The whiskey burned all the way down, but he didn't care. He needed the relief it would give him tonight. He pushed the glass back for a refill.

"Thirsty tonight?" Bill asked, trying to be friendly.

"Yes," he answered in a curt tone he hoped would let the bartender know he didn't want to talk.

Brent picked up the tumbler and took another swallow of the powerful liquor. He hoped it worked fast. It had been a hell of a day, and what he faced tomorrow would be even worse.

"You new in town?"

"Just passing through."

"Well, enjoy your stay." Bill moved off to wait on another customer.

Brent was glad when the bartender had gone. The last thing he wanted was company. He had some serious thinking to do.

He frowned as he thought about the meeting he'd had at Fort Sam Houston. He'd made the trip there to work out the details of an arrangement to sell horses to the army.

He'd thought they had had a deal. He'd thought everything was settled. He'd been wrong.

When the officer negotiating with him demanded a "payment" to secure the transaction, Brent had been outraged and walked out.

He shook his head in disgust at the memory and downed another drink.

Money talked.

He knew that.

God knew, he'd just spent the past ten years working twelve- and eighteen-hour days to make enough money to get the ranch out of debt. He finally had paid off the last of his father's loans and had been counting on the army contract to put the Half-Moon in good financial shape. But they'd wanted a bribe—a big bribe—and he didn't have the cash to pay it.

Brent swore under his breath in frustration. He looked up and found himself staring at the singer's reflection in the mirror behind the bar. She'd finished her song and was leaving the stage to move about the room. The woman was mesmerizing, but he dropped his gaze away from her.

Beautiful though she was, Brent couldn't let himself relax and just enjoy watching her. There was no time in his life for fun. There hadn't been for a very long while.

Crystal slowly made her way toward the bar where the stranger stood with his back to her. She wasn't sure what it was about the man that intrigued her so, but she meant to find out.

Moving between the tables, she kept smiling and flirting outrageously with her audience of admirers. She spotted Andy Gaynor, a portly white-haired gentleman who was every bit of seventy years old but who came every Friday night just to hear her. She stopped to talk with him.

"Evening, Andy."

"Miss Opal, you were wonderful again tonight," the old man praised her.

"Why, thank you, Andy. You are so sweet." She leaned down and kissed his weathered cheek.

The other men at the table roared their approval. In all the weeks she'd worked there, they'd never seen Miss Opal kiss anybody.

Andy blushed bright red at her rare display of affection.

"No, ma'am, you're the sweet one," he said shyly, and grinned from ear to ear.

Crystal winked at the other men, then moved on.

Joe saw that she was coming toward the bar, and the heat he'd been feeling for her grew. The bartender had told him she wasn't an ordinary working saloon girl, but he figured there was no harm in trying.

"Hey, sugar, I'm looking for some company tonight." He took her arm as she tried to move past him.

Though she wanted to jerk her arm free of the cowboy's hold, Crystal managed to keep smiling as she turned to face him.

"I'd say you have lots of company here at the Six Gun," she told him easily.

"Yeah, but not the kind of company I'm looking for," Joe said as he drew her closer.

"You weren't looking for a good time?"

"That's exactly what I want." He pulled her tight against him. "And you're the one I want to give it to me."

Brent was standing farther down the bar, trying to lose himself in his liquor. The last thing he wanted was trouble. When he saw the man grab the woman, though, he turned, more than ready to go to her aid.

The bartender caught Brent's eye and gave him a quick look that stopped him from taking any further action. Brent could see that the bartender's hand was already resting on the shotgun he kept behind the bar just in case of trouble. Brent relaxed a little, but still stayed alert in case he was needed to help with the drunk.

"I'll be happy to sing a song just for you," Crystal told the cowboy, playing along. She didn't want to cause a scene, even though she was physically repulsed by the man. It was obvious he hadn't bathed in a very long time, and his rank, heated breath made her flesh crawl.

"I'm gonna make you sing, all right." Joe grinned lustfully, thinking of how he wanted to spend the rest of the night. He tried to kiss her.

Somehow Crystal managed to avoid his slobbering lips and slip free of him. Relief swept through her as she backed up a few steps and gave him her brightest smile. "I'm sorry, cowboy, but there's only one man for me tonight."

Joe looked irritated.

"And that's Andy," Crystal finished quickly before he could say or do anything else.

For a moment everyone in the saloon had gone quiet. They feared a fight was about to break out, but at her words the tension was broken. They started to laugh and cheer again.

Even Brent, who had been expecting trouble, found himself chuckling over the artful way she'd handled the drunk. He was impressed by her quick thinking.

Crystal blew a kiss to the older man, who immediately hurried to her side.

"That's right, Miss Opal, ain't nobody gonna treat you as good as me!" Andy understood what she was doing and wanted to play along to help her. "Give my lady a drink, Bill!"

Bill did just that, pouring her a tumbler of her preferred beverage—sarsaparilla. He handed her the glass. After Crystal accompanied Andy back to his table, Bill looked at the drunken cowboy, who remained standing by the bar. It was obvious he was still angry.

"Ain't no use in you getting all upset, Joe. I told you Miss Opal was a lady."

"And she's Andy's lady, at that," he muttered

sourly as he drained the last of his drink. Thorougly disgusted and humiliated, he left the saloon.

Crystal was glad when she saw the drunk leave. She didn't want any trouble. She wanted the customers to relax and have fun at the Six Gun.

"You are my hero tonight, Andy," Crystal told him.

"Anytime, darling."

She gave him another quick kiss on the cheek before returning to the bar—and the handsome stranger.

"Good evening, big guy," she said, smiling up at him.

"Evening, ma'am," Brent replied.

"I'm Opal. What's your name?"

"Brent Hunter." He gazed down at her, dazzled by her beauty. He realized she was even lovelier up close—if that were possible. There was an innocence about her, along with the innate sensuality he'd sensed from the first. Although he'd heard the bartender say she was a lady, he hadn't honestly believed it until now.

"Well, welcome to the Six Gun, Brent Hunter."

"It's my pleasure to be here. You did a good job handling that drunk."

"Why, thank you."

"Our Miss Opal is good at everything she does," the bartender put in as he stopped to refill Brent's glass again.

"I can tell," Brent said.

"Well, Brent, would you like to buy me a drink?" Crystal asked with a teasing smile.

"Another sarsaparilla?"

"That's right."

"Will it get me a kiss like Andy?" he found himself asking in a teasing manner.

"Oh, no. Andy's my hero. He's the only man I'm going to kiss tonight." She looked over to where the elderly man was sitting and waved flirtatiously at him.

Andy grinned and winked boldly in response.

A foreign emotion jarred Brent, and he actually found himself resenting the old man. He frowned, puzzled.

"You might as well drink up, friend," the bartender said with a chuckle when he saw the frown. "Opal's made an art out of playing hard to get."

She laughed at his statement. "Are you saying that I drive men to drink, Bill?"

"Yes, Opal, I am, and I'm mighty glad of it. Business has been booming since you started singing here."

They laughed together, and even Brent joined in.

"I would be honored to buy you a drink," Brent offered.

"Thank you." Crystal looked up at him, amazed by the transformation in him when he smiled. When she'd first seen him she'd thought he was handsome, but now, when he was smiling, she thought him the most attractive man she'd ever met. "You should smile more often."

Brent suddenly realized he was smiling, and stopped. His expression sobered.

"Why did you stop smiling?" she asked.

"Some days there's not much to be happy about."

"Well, you're at the Six Gun. Enjoy yourself." She wondered what was troubling him so deeply. A man like him should have the world at his feet.

"I am," he admitted to his own surprise. "You've been the highlight of my day."

"I'm glad I could make things better for you."

He gazed down at her and could see the earnestness in her expression. A part of him believed she really meant it.

"Are you sure your Andy won't be jealous of me buying you a drink?" Brent asked, evoking a mischievous smile from her.

"Andy is very understanding that way," Crystal quipped. "He won't mind."

"Good."

"So what brings you to San Antonio? Are you from around here?"

"No, I'm just passing through, but I'm glad I came into the Six Gun tonight."

"So am I," she answered.

For a moment, as their gazes met again, it seemed to both of them that time was standing still.

Only the raucous sound of the piano player as he began pounding out the tune that signaled her second performance was about to begin jarred Crystal back to reality. She gave herself a mental shake and took one last sip of her drink.

"I have to go."

Crystal hurried away to return to the stage, leaving him without a backward look. Applause erupted from the crowd again as she broke into song.

Even as she entertained them, though, Crystal's thoughts lingered on the man named Brent. She never flirted seriously with her customers. She always made it a point to be friendly, but nothing more. She couldn't risk getting involved with anyone, but she had to admit there was something about Brent Hunter that set him apart from all the others.

Crystal brought herself up short. She told herself she was being ridiculous. The man was just passing through town. After tonight she would never see him again. But all the logic in the world didn't change the fact that she was drawn to him in a very elemental way—and it was something she'd never experienced before.

Chapter Four

Brent had had too much to drink, and he smiled to himself as he realized it. It wasn't often that he indulged his need to escape reality, but tonight he had, and he had to admit it felt good.

Brent stayed on at the saloon until Opal had finished her last song and disappeared from the stage. Only then did he begin to think about heading back to his hotel room for a good night's sleep. There was no doubt in his mind that he needed the rest—especially considering what he was going to face over the next few days.

As Brent stepped into the street in front of the Six Gun, he was struck by how beautiful the evening was. A sliver of a moon glowed high overhead, and the stars were bright and twinkling in the cloudless night sky. The fact that he even noticed made Brent smile. He couldn't remember the last time he'd bothered to look.

The streets of San Antonio were deserted. All was quiet, and he was glad. The liquor had mellowed his dark mood. As angry as he'd been over his earlier failed business dealing, he was now confident he would find a way to keep the Half-Moon running. It wouldn't be easy, but that didn't surprise him. Nothing he'd done in the past ten years had been easy.

Brent's thoughts were untroubled as he crossed the street and walked toward his hotel. His sense of peace lasted for only a few moments, though, for he noticed a man lurking in the heavily shadowed alley behind the saloon. In the darkness he couldn't tell who the man was, but it puzzled Brent that he was moving so furtively.

Brent took a step back, closer to the buildings, so he wouldn't be noticed. He didn't know why anyone would be hiding out in the alley that way, and he feared it might mean trouble. He decided to keep watch for a little while—just in case.

Crystal had regretted the end of her second performance, for she'd known she would never see Brent Hunter again. Her thoughts had lingered on the handsome stranger even after she'd left the stage and gone to her dressing room to change. She had found Brent intriguing, but knew there was no point in dwelling on him. As he'd said, he was just passing through.

Crystal donned her ordinary day gown, then left the dressing room. She was more than ready to call it a night.

"Opal, before you go, here's your pay. Bill told me to give it to you." It was Belle Moran, one of the saloon girls.

"Thanks, Belle," Crystal said as she took the money and tucked it into her small purse. She wouldn't get rich on what she made at the Six Gun, but she could pay her bills and she was safe. That was all that mattered to her right now.

"You have a good night, Opal," Belle said as she left her there in the hallway. "I'm going back out front to see if I can get that handsome cowboy's attention."

"Which cowboy? Andy?" Crystal asked with a teasing smile.

Belle laughed at the thought. "I'm sure Andy was quite a man in his day, but I'm after the one you were talking to at the bar. I haven't seen him around here before, but I'd like to see more of him—if you take my meaning."

Belle was a ribald, lusty woman. She'd worked at the Six Gun for a long time, and she made no attempt to hide her inclinations. The men loved her for her honesty, and she loved them right back.

"Well, good luck, Belle. I'll see you tomorrow night."

Crystal slipped outside into the dark, deserted passageway. Because she wanted to maintain her aura of elusiveness, she always left the Six Gun this way so no one would see her.

As she started off down the night-shrouded alley toward her boardinghouse, Crystal found herself thinking of what Belle had said. She hoped the other woman had no success at all in enticing Brent Hunter to her bed.

Mick was waiting in the shadows. He had been in the saloon drinking for most of the night, but when Opal finished her act and disappeared offstage, he knew it was time to make his move. This was the night Bill paid his working girls, and tonight Mick needed money.

Mick had seen the way Opal always left the saloon through the alley, and tonight he was waiting for her. He figured she was going to be an easy mark. He doubted the singer would be able to identify him in the darkness. Besides, she didn't know him. He never talked to her. He only watched her from the back of the saloon. He planned to strike quickly, grab her purse, and make his getaway just as fast. He wanted cash, and robbing Opal was the easiest way to get it. One female was no match for him. He'd be gone before she could even react.

He saw the back door open and Opal came out. He drew his knife, but he didn't plan to use it. Smiling grimly to himself, he crept nearer to wait for the right moment to attack.

Crystal didn't pay much attention to her surroundings. She came this way every night and always felt safe. Just then, though, she heard the sound of footsteps coming up behind her. She paused, puzzled, and began to turn to see who it was. As she did, she started to open her purse so she could get the small derringer she'd started carrying with her just in case of trouble.

Crystal didn't react quickly enough. The big man loomed over her before she could get the gun. He roughly grabbed at her purse and tried to jerk it from her grasp. Crystal had the strap wrapped around her wrist, though, and she held on for dear life.

It was then that she saw his knife.

"No!" she cried out, fighting back.

Time had passed slowly for Brent as he'd kept watch. He eventually began to doubt the need for his continued vigilance. There was no one else around, and he was getting tired. It had been a long day. He had just made up his mind to continue on to his hotel room when he saw the man emerge from his hiding place and move off down the alley. He waited a moment longer, wondering what the man was up to, but all remained quiet.

Brent was convinced that he'd overreacted, that

there was nothing going on. He started on his way again, looking forward to a good night's sleep.

"No!" The distant, faint sound of a woman's cry of distress came from the alley.

A sudden chill of dread filled Brent as he realized his instincts had been right. The man he'd seen had been planning to cause trouble. Brent drew his sidearm and raced off in the direction of the woman's scream.

"Give me that!" Mick said with a snarl, yanking on her purse again. When he still couldn't tear it loose, he tried to slash the strap.

Brent charged into the alley to see the man attacking a woman with a knife. Brent couldn't tell who the woman was in the darkened passageway, and it didn't matter. He had to help her. He fired a warning shot in the air.

"Hold it right there!" Brent ordered.

Mick stopped, startled by the gunshot. When he saw Brent aiming his gun straight at him, Mick reacted instinctively, grabbing the singer and holding her before him.

Crystal continued to struggle against her assailant, but he held the knife up for her to see.

"Hold still, woman!"

She froze, uncertain what to do. The man's grip on her was brutal.

Brent closed in on them. As he drew nearer, he could see the woman clearly for the first time. "Opal! Are you all right?"

"Yes," she managed.

"Let her go," Brent demanded. "Get away from her now or my next shot won't just be a warning. The next shot will stop you permanently."

"Go to hell!" In one violent move, Mick cut through the strap and made a grab for the purse as he gave Crystal a savage shove.

Crystal tried to resist, but she was no match for his strength. She lost her balance and fell as he yanked the purse from her hands.

Mick had what he wanted, and he took off running in the opposite direction.

Brent would have taken a shot at him, but he didn't want to risk putting Opal in danger.

"Are you all right?" he asked her quickly as he holstered his gun.

"Yes, but he got my purse!"

Assured that she was uninjured, Brent charged after the robber and caught up with him before he could get out of the alley. He tackled him full-force, knocking him to the ground.

The purse flew from Mick's grip as they began to fight savagely.

Crystal scrambled to her feet, shaken and dazed. She looked around for something she could use as a weapon to help Brent, but there was nothing.

Brent was furious, and when Mick managed to slash his upper arm with his knife, Brent's anger only increased. A driven man, he continued to pummel the thief, and finally managed to knock the knife from his hand.

Brent barely heard the shouts coming from the entrance to the alley.

"This is Sheriff Watson! What's going on down there?" the lawman yelled as he ran toward the scene of the fight.

George, his deputy, was right behind him, ready to back him up. They'd heard the gunshot as they'd been out making their rounds and had come to investigate.

Some saloon patrons had heard the shot, too, and had come outside to see what was going on. When they saw the lawmen heading down the alley, they followed them.

Brent didn't give up the fight until he'd finally landed a powerful blow to Mick's jaw. Only then did he rise up over the would-be robber. He jerked Mick up by his shirtfront, ready to hit him again, but the man had gone limp. In disgust, Brent dropped him back to the ground and got up to stand over him in triumph.

"Don't make any moves," the sheriff ordered, bringing his gun to bear on Brent.

"Sheriff Watson, it's all right!" Crystal spoke up quickly in Brent's defense. "Mr. Hunter just saved me from the other man—he robbed me." Her voice trembled slightly.

"Is that so?" The sheriff took a look at the unconscious man and recognized him as the drunk named Mick. Mick had a reputation around town as an ugly troublemaker. This wouldn't be the first time he'd had him under arrest.

"I don't know what I would have done if Mr. Hunter hadn't shown up when he did." Her voice remained unsteady as she realized the seriousness of the threat she'd just faced.

Sheriff Watson looked over at the stranger she called Hunter, and nodded. "Good work. We'll take Mick on back to jail and lock him up. Were you hurt, Miss Opal? Do you need to see the doc?"

"No . . . I'm fine." She was shaken but uninjured.

"What about you, Hunter?" The lawman saw the blood on his arm.

"It's nothing. Just a scratch." Brent reached down and picked up Crystal's purse.

Sheriff Watson looked at her again. "Do you want to press charges against Mick?"

"Yes . . . No . . . I don't know. I just don't want him hurting anyone else." Crystal knew the thief deserved to be locked up, but she didn't want to involve herself with the law. The farther she stayed away from the sheriff and his deputies, the better.

Watson thought he understood her hesitancy. "I'll take care of him. Mick won't bother you again," the sheriff said with conviction. "I'll make sure of it."

"Thank you, Sheriff." She was relieved.

"If you want to come along with us now, one of us will walk you home after we get him locked up."

"I can see her home," Brent offered, glancing at Opal.

"Yes, thank you," she told him appreciatively. The sooner she got away from there, the better she would feel.

Brent went to her side and handed over her purse as Sheriff Watson and George each grabbed one of Mick's arms. George picked up the knife and then they dragged the unconscious man bodily from the alley.

The men who'd come out of the saloon to watch hurried back inside to tell everybody what had happened.

Only when everyone had gone did Brent finally speak.

"Are you sure you're all right?" He realized how terrifying the attack must have been for her.

"Yes—you showed up just in time." She swallowed tightly, suppressing a shiver.

"I'm glad I did," he told her earnestly.

"So am I."

"Is everything there?" Brent asked, gesturing toward her purse.

Crystal looked quickly through the contents, then smiled at him in relief. "Yes."

She did not show him the derringer. She didn't want to have to explain to him why she'd been carrying it. She closed her purse again.

"Come on, let's get out of here," Brent said.

"What about your arm? Are you sure it's not serious?" She could see the blood on his shirtsleeve now.

Brent flexed his arm. "It's not bad. I'll take care of it later, after I see you back home."

They didn't say much as they made their way to the boardinghouse where she rented a room. Crystal appreciated Brent's powerful presence by her side. She had thought having the derringer with her would keep her safe, but she hadn't been quick enough to save herself. She silently vowed that would never happen again.

"This is where I live," Crystal said, stopping before the house. "Thanks for walking with me."

"You're welcome," Brent said as he gazed down at her. He had thought she was beautiful before, but there in the moonlight she was even lovelier.

"I know I said earlier that I was only going to kiss one man tonight, and that was Andy, because he was my hero. But I have two heroes tonight," she said softly. Reaching up, she drew his head down and kissed him on the cheek.

The faint, heady scent of her perfume surrounded Brent. He was tempted to take Opal in his arms and kiss her full on the lips, but he controlled the urge. Instead he managed an easy smile as she stepped away from him. "I'm going to have a hard time living up to the example of a man like Andy."

"I don't think so." Crystal smiled at her tall, handsome hero. "I think it might be the other way around."

"Why, thank you, ma'am." He grinned down at her.

"Good night, Brent Hunter."

"Good night, Opal."

She turned and quickly went inside.

Brent waited until she'd closed the door. Only when he was sure she was safely in the house did he leave.

He was glad that he'd trusted his instincts, and hadn't gone on back to his hotel, as he'd considered doing. He didn't want to think about what might have happened to Opal if he hadn't been there to go to her aid.

Brent glanced back at the boardinghouse once, committing to memory this moment, for he knew he wouldn't see her again. He had responsibilities weighing heavily on him. He had a ranch to run and a family to take care of.

Once Crystal had gone inside, she hurried upstairs to the privacy of her small, rented room. She did not light a lamp, but went to stand at the window so she could watch Brent leave without being seen. She was surprised when he stopped once and looked back her way. She slipped behind the curtain, not wanting him to know she was watching him. Her gaze lingered longingly on his tall, manly form as he disappeared down the night-shrouded street.

Brent Hunter had truly been her hero tonight. There weren't many men who would have put themselves at risk the way he had to save a saloon girl from being robbed. Brent was a rare man, a very special man, indeed.

When Brent had gone from sight, Crystal turned away from the window. As she undressed and scrubbed herself clean of any trace of Mick's vile touch, she wouldn't let herself think that her hero had truly gone from her life forever.

As he made his way to his hotel, Brent realized that the effects of the liquor he'd drunk had worn off. His earlier easy mood was gone, and his dark, troubled thoughts were returning with a vengeance.

Brent was tempted to go back to the bar for another few rounds, but he denied himself that cowardly release.

He wasn't like his father. He couldn't hide from the reality that was his life any longer. Tomorrow he had to ride for Huntsville. Soon his father was going to be released from prison after serving his ten-year sentence.

He had to be there to meet him.

Chapter Five

Brent stood in front of the warden's office at the Huntsville prison, waiting for the moment he'd been dreading.

Today his father was being released from prison. At any minute he was going to be walking out of the office, a free man.

Brent girded himself for the confrontation to come. He was as ready as he would ever be.

He had arrived in Huntsville late the night before and had taken a room at a small, run-down hotel. He'd gotten little sleep overnight, though, for he was tense and troubled over the reunion to come.

How could he face his father again? This was the man who'd shot his mother. . . .

Brent's jaw locked as he fought to maintain the steely control he usually kept over his emotions.

He'd thought he'd gotten over the loss. He'd thought he'd learned how to handle life and all its troubles.

The feelings churning within him proved him wrong. The emotions tearing at him were almost as painful now as they had been all those years before.

Brent prided himself on being a man who was always in control, and it angered him to feel this way. He felt it was a weakness, and he couldn't afford to be weak. Too much depended on his being strong. He was the head of the family now—at least, he was until his father returned.

Brent knew the upcoming reunion was going to be difficult. As hard as he'd worked in the last ten years to save the ranch, he was not about to turn it back over to his father and risk having him run it into ruin again. His father had put him in charge that terrible, fateful day, and he intended to stay in charge. Even as he thought it, though, Brent knew his father's name was still on the ranch title. His father was the legal owner of the Half-Moon.

Brent remembered clearly the day when the letter had come from the prison informing him of their father's upcoming release date. It had stated that Jack requested his family meet him there at the prison. Brent hadn't understood his reasoning. He wanted them there that day, but he hadn't wanted any contact with them for the ten years he'd been locked up.

The request hadn't really mattered, though, for there had been no way to arrange such a reunion.

Both Quince and Matt were gone from the Half-Moon, and though Abby lived at the ranch with him, Brent wasn't about to subject her to such an ordeal. He knew she thought she was tough enough, but she wasn't. Sometimes he had to protect his sister from herself.

So Brent had come to meet him alone. He would take care of this, just as he had taken care of most everything else since their father had been locked up.

Brent had worked night and day for the past ten years to get the Half-Moon free and clear of debt, and he'd done it—his way, by saving every cent he could, by breeding and training the best horses in three counties. Quince had helped for a long time, and, to Brent's surprise, so had Matt, in his own way, whenever he'd shown up. But Brent was the one who had worked from sunup to sundown, day after day. He had always believed that hard work and smart dealing were the way to make the Half-Moon financially stable. And he'd proven himself right. He was proud of what he'd accomplished, but he wouldn't be satisfied until the ranch turned a regular profit.

The horses stirred behind him, and Brent went to tend to them, wondering how much longer it would be until his father came out. He had ridden his own black stallion, Storm, and had brought along a mount from the ranch. Brent had a little cash on him, too, and he was almost hoping his father would take the horse and the money and just disappear—go away. He doubted he would miss him, and he didn't think Abby and his brothers would either.

Brent heard the door to the warden's office open, and he looked up. He tensed, waiting, dreading the reunion to come.

For the first time in ten years, Jack Hunter stepped outside into the sunshine as a free man. There was no joy in his heart over being released, though. There was no happiness in his soul. The long years he'd spent toiling in the prison had taken their toll. He was a tired man, a broken man, and he knew what he was about to face.

Brent stared at the man walking toward him. It had been so long since he'd last seen him that he seemed almost a stranger now. He remembered his father as a tall, powerful, vital man. The man coming toward him looked old and bent. His dark hair had gone gray, and his shoulders were stooped.

Brent hadn't spoken to him since that day at the Diablo jail, when Jack Hunter had ordered his children to leave him alone and to stay away from him. Considering what he'd done, they hadn't found it too hard to put him from their lives. There had been only a few times over the years when he'd been missed, and then the memory of what he'd done would return and the gentler sentiment would vanish.

But now their father was a free man.

Jack Hunter recognized Brent immediately, though his oldest son had changed quite a bit in the time they'd been apart. When he'd last seen him, Brent had been only twenty years old. He was a full-grown man now—tall, confident, and serious, Jack judged from the look on his face.

Jack hadn't been certain how things were going to go upon his release today. He hadn't known if anyone would come to meet him or if he would be left on his own to get back home. He was glad Brent had shown up, but he wondered why Quince, Matt, and Abby hadn't come with him, too.

"Where is everybody?" Jack demanded.

"You haven't wanted to see us for ten years. Why should everyone come rushing at your beck and call?" Brent countered as he met his gaze straight-on. He saw no warmth in his father's regard, only condemnation.

"You're here."

"That's because we've got some things to settle between us before we go back to the ranch."

Jack's gaze hardened on him. "We don't have a damned thing to settle."

"Yes, we do." Brent was not about to back down. "But this isn't the place." He unhitched the horse he'd brought for his father and held out the reins. "Let's go."

Jack looked the stallion over and was impressed.

"Good bloodlines," he remarked as he took the reins.

"I know," Brent said.

Jack swung up in the saddle. "Let's go home."

He didn't wait for Brent. He turned the horse and rode off without looking back. He couldn't get away from the prison fast enough.

Brent mounted up and followed him. He could no longer deny reality. His father was coming home.

Brent spurred his horse and caught up with his father. They rode on in silence, leaving Huntsville and the prison behind them.

Edmund Montgomery sat alone in his office at the bank in Diablo. He knew what day it was: today was the day Jack Hunter was being released from prison.

An ugly smile twisted Edmund's mouth. It had been ten years since they'd locked Jack up, but in his opinion ten years wasn't nearly long enough—not for what Jack had done.

Rage filled Edmund.

Jack had been the cause of all the misery in his life. True, they had once been friends long ago, in their younger days in New Orleans, and everyone thought they were still friends. Edmund alone knew the truth.

Jack had always been a high roller, a wild, daring man who was never afraid to gamble—even when he should have been.

Edmund prided himself on being smarter than Jack. Certainly, he'd proven it over and over again by his ability to make money.

When he had met the beautiful Beth at a social occasion, she had been witty and bright, and he'd wanted her from the first. Beth had been attracted to him, too. Edmund knew he was handsome; he had money; he was certainly debonair and confident.

Then Jack came back to New Orleans, and Beth began seeing him, too.

To Edmund's fury, Beth had seemed to prefer Jack to him. When Jack had proposed to her, Edmund had been forced to propose, too. Edmund had expected her to accept his proposal immediately, but, even though her family preferred him because he had money, Beth had eloped with Jack.

At the time Edmund had appeared indifferent to their marriage, but inwardly he'd been furious. He'd pretended to remain friends with them, even though he'd always despised Jack for winning her.

Edmund had told himself Beth would eventually realize she'd made a mistake in her impetuous marriage. She hadn't realized that she would have had a far better life with him. He was rich enough to give her everything, while Jack could offer her nothing.

When Jack won some land outside of Diablo, Texas, in a poker game, Edmund had followed them west. He had wanted to stay close to Beth. He had wanted to be there when she finally came to her senses and turned to him; then he would make her pay for his years of frustration.

Eventually he had married a wealthy widow, Iona Sullivan, in the hope of making Beth jealous. Iona adored him and was easily led, which made it simple for him to control her. He had never loved her.

But Beth was dead now. And Jack was responsible.

Edmund was glad Jack had been sent to prison. He was glad that he had suffered all those years behind bars, but no matter how much Jack had suffered, it wasn't enough.

Nothing would ever bring Beth back.

Pain filled Edmund, and he got up to pace the room. Jack would be returning to the Half-Moon soon, and Edmund knew he was going to have to deal with him again. He would make Jack pay for all the pain he'd caused. He was going to make Jack's life a living hell.

Jack deserved no less for what he had done.

Edmund frowned thoughtfully, wondering how best to accomplish his goal without anyone discovering what he was doing. Early on after Beth's death, he had pressured Brent about his father's loans. He had claimed it was strictly business, but in truth he'd been determined to ruin Jack and his sons.

Edmund hadn't believed Brent was smart enough to be able to come up with the money to repay his father's debts, but the young man had surprised him. He had proven to be nothing like his father. Brent was intelligent, hardworking, serious, and tenacious, and he had managed to stay current on the payments. Brent had paid off the entire balance and had refused to borrow any more money when Edmund had extended the offer.

Damn Brent Hunter!

Edmund was going to have to find another way to get to Jack Hunter. And he would; he had no doubt about it.

Edmund went to stare out his office window. It appeared a calm, ordinary day on the streets of Diablo, but deep in his heart he knew there was nothing ordinary about it.

It was almost dark when Brent and Jack finally decided to stop and make camp for the night. Little had been said during the day, and the tension had worn on Brent. They were going to have to set things straight between them before they reached the Half-Moon, and as far as he was concerned, the sooner they did it, the better.

"We need to talk," Brent declared as he sat down across the campfire from his father.

"What about?" Jack returned.

"About what's going to happen once we get back to the ranch."

"We're going to go to work—that's what's going to happen," his father answered.

"What the hell do you think I've been doing while you've been gone?" Brent demanded, becoming angry. "I've done nothing but work—to keep from losing the ranch. Did you have any idea how deep in debt you were?"

"I had to build the bloodlines. It was the only way."

"No, it wasn't the only way, and I've proven that."

"You've proven what?"

"I got us out of debt by learning everything I could about horseflesh, by hard work, and by saving every penny I could. We don't owe anybody right now, and I intend to keep it that way."

"*You* intend to keep it that way?"

"That's right."

"My name is on the deed," Jack said coldly. "The Half-Moon is my ranch."

"Because I saved it." Brent glared at his father.

"*You?* What about your brothers?"

"Quince and I had a fight, and he left about five years ago."

"What did you fight about?"

"Quince didn't like the way I was running things. I told him if he didn't like it he could leave, and he did. Last we heard, he was out hunting renegades for the army."

"And Matt? Did he ever show up?"

"He started mustanging and training horses for ranches west of here. He brings us some mustangs and the money he's earned, but otherwise we don't see much of him. He did some betting on horse racing, but he used his own money. His gambling never cost the Half-Moon anything. Right now he's in England, looking to buy a thoroughbred with the money he's won."

"So what you really mean is, he's run off again."

"I told him that's what he was doing, but it didn't stop him from going." Brent shook his head, thinking of his youngest brother and the wild streak that hadn't faded with the years. He'd told Matt he was stupid to waste his time and money going to England, but his brother was not to be deterred. Racehorses were an obsession with him. They were his passion. Matt was very much like their father that way.

"I'm sure it didn't," Jack said, sneering. "And I'll bet that's the last you'll see of him. He won't be back."

Brent was shocked. "Sure he will. Matt thinks he can make us some big money with the horse he's after."

"We'll see." Jack did not want to hear another word about Matt. "How is Abby?"

"She's not the little girl you remember."

"No, I don't suppose she is."

"She works hard around the ranch. She can ride and rope with the best of the men."

"So she hasn't married yet?"

"Not yet." Brent didn't remark on the trouble he had trying to get Abby to start dressing and behaving like a female. Brent girded himself as he went on, finally broaching the subject he'd so far avoided. "You know, this isn't going to be easy, you coming back to the ranch."

"I didn't think it would be."

"I'm just telling you the truth. We're never going to be able to forget what happened that day, though God knows we've tried over the years."

"The Half-Moon is my home. That's where I'm going. If you don't like it, you can leave."

Brent looked him straight in the eye, his expression stony. "That isn't going to happen. You put me in charge ten years ago, and I intend to stay in charge."

Chapter Six

It had been five days of hard riding and little conversation, but Brent and his father had finally arrived. They were at the Half-Moon.

They were home.

Leaving the horses hitched in front of the house, they walked up the few porch steps to the door. Brent knew this would be his father's first time in the house since the day of the shooting, and he wondered how he was going to react. He waited as his father entered the house before him, then followed him in.

Jack stopped just inside the door and stood looking around.

"Nothing's changed." He sounded amazed.

"Everything has changed," Brent stated flatly, closing the door behind him.

Jack moved forward. When his gaze fell upon the portrait of Beth still gracing the wall over the fireplace, turbulent emotion was evident on his face.

"Your mother was a very beautiful woman."

"Yes, she was," Brent answered. He clenched his fists in an effort to control his anger. He wanted to rage at his father that it was only because of him that she was gone. "We buried her in the family plot."

Jack nodded, then looked around. "Where's Abby?"

"Hard to say."

"You don't keep track of your little sister?" he asked.

"Abby is not so 'little' anymore, and besides, I've been gone for almost two weeks. There's no way of knowing where she might be," Brent said coldly.

"Well, she should be here at the house."

Brent's mouth twisted in a sardonic smile. "Abby doesn't spend much time around the house. Usually she's out working with the horses or checking stock. I already told you she can ride and rope."

"That's no job for her."

"I'm sure she'll be interested to hear your opinion on that, since she's been doing it for years now."

"Oh, Brent, you're back." Frances Riley, the housekeeper who'd been hired while Jack was in prison, had been working in the kitchen when she'd heard the sound of voices.

"We just got here," Brent told her.

"You must be Frances," Jack said quietly. "Brent's told me about you."

She nodded in his direction, then quickly looked back at Brent. She didn't want anything to do with Jack.

"Is Abby around?"

"No. She went into town yesterday for a visit with Iona."

"Iona?" Jack repeated, surprised at the mention of her name. It had been so long since he'd seen any of his friends.

"She helped Abby a lot right after . . ." Brent paused, then went on, "They've stayed close ever since."

"And Edmund? How is he?"

"As successful as ever," Brent answered, hoping his silent resentment didn't show. He had never been able to forget Edmund's coldness the day he'd shown him the extent of the Half-Moon's debts. He looked at Frances. "When is Abby coming back?"

"Sometime tonight," Frances told them. "She just needed to get away for a little while."

Brent understood what Frances wasn't saying— that Abby was torn by the prospect of their father's return and needed time away to gather her thoughts and prepare herself to see him again.

"Are you two hungry?" she offered. "Would you like anything to eat?"

"No, not right now."

"Well, if you change your mind I'll be in the kitchen." She directed her comment to Brent.

"Thanks."

She hurried off, leaving the two men alone.

Jack was tense as he glanced up at his wife's portrait again. Nothing had changed, yet everything had changed. He realized painfully that Brent had been right.

"The front bedroom is still yours," Brent said.

"You didn't take it over, too?" His tone was sharp with resentment.

"No."

Jack turned away from Brent and stalked off to the master bedroom. He didn't pause before the closed door, but opened it and went on in, shutting it behind him.

Jack had thought seeing the house again had been painful, but nothing had prepared him for the sight of his and Beth's bedroom. The room was seemingly untouched even after all these years. He closed his eyes, fighting back the stabbing ache of emptiness that filled him. This room had been their haven. He and Beth had always found their bliss there—in the wide comfort of their marriage bed—holding each other, loving each other. But that comfort was lost to him now—forever.

Memories of Beth overwhelmed him suddenly—all the joy they'd shared and all the love. He sank down on the side of the bed, struggling for control.

This room might look the same, but it would never be the same. Nothing would. Life as he'd known it was over. There was no going back.

There had been times during his long years in prison when Jack had dreamed of this moment— of being free and back home. But he felt no elation, no thrill at being home. He felt only sorrow for all that had been lost.

Jack remembered his dreams for their future, and all that had been lost on that fateful day. . . .

It had been a long, long time since Jack had had a drink, but he desperately needed one. He got up and left the bedroom. He'd always kept his whiskey in the cabinet right by the dining room table, and he was glad to see the cabinet was still there. He was a driven man as he strode to it and opened the door. He stared inside in great frustration. There was no liquor of any kind. It was empty.

"Damn it!" In a frustrated fury, he slammed the door shut.

"What are you looking for?" Brent asked. He had been in the back of the house, but heard the commotion.

"Where's the whiskey?"

Brent went cold as he faced him down. "There isn't any."

"Why the hell not? I need a drink."

Brent's expression hardened even more. "I would think after what happened the last time you got drunk, you'd never want to touch another drop of liquor." His words had the desired effect. His father went pale. "Ma would still be alive if you hadn't been drunk that day. Since then, I don't allow liquor in this house—ever."

Jack glared at him, shaken and yet furious, too, over being denied what he needed. He turned away and stormed out of the house.

Brent watched him go. He didn't care how angry his father was.

"There's no way to avoid this, is there?" Abby looked at Iona as Edmund drove them back to the ranch late that afternoon.

She was seated between the couple, a place that should have made her feel secure. Instead she felt suffocated, as if all the open air in Texas wouldn't be enough to help her draw a deep, peaceful breath ever again.

Distracted as Iona often was lately, she didn't answer Abby right away. She appeared almost confused for a moment before finally responding, "No, dear, there's not. I wish I could make it easier for you, but I can't."

Iona's seeming confusion and the unsteadiness in her voice made Abby feel worse, for it reminded her of what she had learned in town earlier that day. Iona had been like a mother to her since her own mother had died. Abby loved her dearly. When she'd overheard Mrs. Spindle and Mrs. Herbert talking about her in the general store, saying that she had a problem with drinking spirits, Abby had been ready to defend Iona. She had wanted to confront them and make them apologize for their hatefulness, but in that moment she'd realized that what they were saying was the truth. It explained why Iona always drenched herself in rose water—she did it to cover the smell of the liquor.

Abby felt fiercely protective of Iona, and she wondered where her daughter, Juliana, was. Juliana had married young and then been widowed. The last Abby had heard, she was living back east somewhere. Abby believed Juliana should have come home to take care of her mother. If her own mother had been alive, she would never have abandoned her in such a way.

"I'm here for you, Abby," Iona told her with a reassuring smile, extending a shaking hand to her.

"I know," she answered, smiling weakly in return as the carriage turned up the road to the main house. "I guess it's time to get this over with. It's not going to get any easier, no matter how long I try to avoid it."

She felt Edmund's eyes on her, and an unexplained shiver went through her.

"You're certain they'll be here?" he asked.

"According to what Brent told me when he left, they were due back today."

He reached over and patted her hands, which

were clutched tightly in her lap. "I'm glad that we're with you."

She shifted free of his touch.

"I am, too," she said, and tried to mean it. Staring straight ahead, she steeled herself for the confrontation to come.

Jack had been furious when he'd left the house. Needing to get away, he'd headed for the stables to have a look around.

No liquor . . .

He had been ten long years without a drink, and he'd desperately needed one today. There might not be any whiskey on the Half-Moon right now, but he'd take care of that the next time he went into town.

"Jack? Is that you?" Curly had been working in the stable and was surprised to see his old boss standing in the doorway.

"It's me. I'm back," he answered, glad to see the longtime hired hand.

Curly stopped what he was doing and went to speak with him. "Brent said you'd be coming back. It's been a long time."

"Too long. How have you been?" he asked.

"Fine. We had some hard years here on the ranch, but everything's worked out now. Brent's done a good job."

Jack wasn't about to give Brent credit for anything. He was the one who had worked endlessly to establish the Half-Moon as a thoroughbred ranch. Raising racehorses was his dream. "What about the bloodlines?"

Curly shrugged. "Brent said there was more money in breeding and training working stock, and he was right. It's hard work, but we've gotten good at it."

Jack didn't want to hear him sing Brent's praises anymore. By taking up mustanging and concentrating on cow ponies and the like, his son had forsaken everything he'd planned for the ranch. The Half-Moon was his ranch, not Brent's! He had worked his whole life toward achieving his dream, and now he was going to have to start all over again.

Start over . . . The thought jarred Jack, for in the past he'd always had Beth's support.

Beth . . .

Jack suddenly needed to get away by himself for a while.

"Well, it's good to be here," Jack told Curly as he moved off.

The ranch hand nodded and watched him leave the stable. He thought Jack was a sad figure of a man now, nothing like the vital, commanding boss he used to be.

Jack left the stable. He knew where he had to go, and he was glad there was no one else around. He needed to be alone for what he had to do. He made his way to the family cemetery a distance away from the house.

Elizabeth Quincy Hunter

Jack stared down at Beth's name on the tombstone.

If only he could turn back time. If only he could change what had happened that day. If only . . .

Pain tore through him. Anger rose up within him. There could be no changing what had happened. There was no way to make things right again.

Beth was dead.

So deep was Jack's grief as he mourned at his wife's graveside, he didn't notice the carriage arriving at the house.

"Don't be nervous, dear; everything is going to be all right. We're here with you," Iona told Abby as Edmund brought the carriage to a stop before the house.

"Thank you." She gave the older woman a heartfelt look as she mentally prepared herself for what was to come. No matter what Iona's problems were, the older woman's presence would be welcome at her father's homecoming.

Abby took a deep breath and descended from the carriage. Iona had wanted her to wear a dress today, but she'd decided not to. She wore pants to work around the ranch, and the good Lord knew today was going to be work.

Just as Abby turned and started up the walk, the

front door opened. Abby actually found herself holding her breath as she waited to see who was going to come outside. Relief flooded through her when she saw it was Brent.

"So you're back," Abby said, her expression still wary as she glanced past him, expecting to see their father following him.

"We got back a few hours ago," Brent explained. Then he looked at the banker and his wife. "Hello, Iona, Edmund."

They returned his greeting as they, too, climbed down from the carriage.

"So Papa did come with you. He's really here?" Abby asked.

"Yes."

"Where is Jack?" Edmund inquired.

"I don't know for sure. He left the house a while ago, and I haven't seen him since."

"You don't sound too concerned," Edmund remarked.

"I'm not. He'll be back. Come on inside." Brent held the door for his sister as Edmund took Iona's arm to steady her as he helped her up the porch steps and into the house.

"How is Papa?" Abby asked once they'd settled in.

Brent shrugged. "The years in the Huntsville prison were hard on him. His return isn't going to be easy—for any of us."

"I know." She had adored her father as a young

girl, but all that had changed on that horrible, fateful day. "Why did he come back at all, Brent? Why?"

"He says the Half-Moon is his home, and he's staying."

"He always loved this ranch," Edmund agreed.

"And he almost lost it, too," Brent said, unable to disguise the note of bitterness in his voice. "Edmund." He looked the banker straight in the eye. "Before Pa gets back here, I want you to give me your word that you won't make any more loans to him if he comes to you."

"Do you think he might?" Edmund asked.

"Anything is possible with Pa, but we've worked too hard getting the Half-Moon out of debt. I don't want to put the whole place at risk again over any of his wild-eyed schemes."

The banker's eyes narrowed, but his voice was as silky as ever.

"I'll do what I can to support you, Brent, but your father is still the ranch's rightful owner, isn't he?"

"His name may be on the title," he admitted, "but when he left, he put me in charge."

"You know, Brent, if the situation did arise, you'd be far better off borrowing from me than anyone else."

"The situation is not going to arise. We won't be borrowing money from anyone ever again," Brent declared fiercely, remembering all too clearly how hard-pressed he had been to make their payments on time. Edmund had never been able to seize their property, but after their conversation ten years ago, he'd known the banker wouldn't have hesitated to take it if they'd fallen behind.

"That's right," Abby agreed with her brother. "The Half-Moon means too much to us."

Iona stirred and glanced nervously in her husband's direction. Her smile was shaky as she said, "Well, let's just hope you never have to worry about that. You've made the ranch a success now, Brent. There's no reason why that should change."

"Let's hope not," Brent said.

"Who's here?" Jack's voice boomed out in a commanding, harsh tone as he mounted the steps and crossed the porch.

They all looked up as he came through the front door.

Jack stopped as he saw Abby for the first time. He was shocked to see that she was wearing pants, and he was also shocked when he realized how very much she resembled her mother. He stood there silently as his gaze swept over her, taking in the dark mane of her hair, her green eyes, and the pale beauty of her complexion. She was lovely in spite of her choice of clothing. She was a vision. "Abby . . ."

"It's me, Papa." Her answer was almost a whisper, and her expression was guarded.

Jack wanted to go to Abby and sweep her into his arms in a desperate, loving embrace. He wanted to hold her to his heart, but he knew by the look in

her eyes that she wouldn't welcome any such over-
ture from him. The little girl he'd loved and left behind was gone. In her place was a woman now—
a beautiful woman—a woman who was the very
image of her mother.

He turned to Edmund and Iona, who were sitting
together on the sofa.

"Well, Edmund, I'd say seeing you again this way
deserves a celebration drink, but Brent doesn't allow
any liquor in the house." He cast an annoyed look
at his eldest son.

Edmund stood up and went to shake his hand.
"That doesn't matter. It's just good you're home,
Jack."

"Yes, it is," he said, but even as he said it to his
old friend, he wasn't sure his children agreed.

"Welcome back, Jack," Iona offered as she attempted unsteadily to rise.

"Hello, Iona." Jack was struck by how much
she'd changed over the past ten years. Edmund was
the same—tall, erect, with only a trace of gray in
his hair, but not Iona. It almost seemed as if she
had shrunk inside herself.

Iona's smile was wan as she went on, "It is a
shame we can't have a drink to celebrate your return. I know I'd certainly enjoy one."

Jack was shocked by her statement. He quickly
looked away from her as a hush fell across the
room, adding to the already heavy tension in the air.

"Come on, Iona," Edmund said, giving his wife a

harsh look, "we ought to head back to town. These people need their privacy." He glanced at Jack. "We'll be talking."

Edmund smiled patiently as he took his wife's arm to steady her on her feet.

"Thank you for bringing me home," Abby said as they started from the house.

"We wouldn't have it any other way," Edmund replied, looking back at her while he kept a firm hold on Iona.

Brent walked outside to see them off, leaving Abby alone with their father for the first time.

"You've been well, Abby?" Jack asked cautiously as he came to sit on the sofa near her.

She stared at him for a moment, feeling that he was almost a stranger to her. She wanted to tell him of all the nights she'd cried herself to sleep missing her mother, aching for her loving embrace, but she didn't. She kept her voice cool as she answered, "Yes, I have, Papa."

He was struck once more by how closely she resembled her mother. "I can see that. I worried about you while I was . . ."

Abby found that very hard to believe, since he hadn't had any contact with her in all the years he was in prison. "There was no need to worry. The boys took care of me."

"That's good."

Abby finally blurted out what she desperately needed to know, "Are you planning to stay on?"

"Yes. There's nowhere else I'd rather be than here on the ranch."

The last flicker of hope that he would leave died within her. He was going to stay. She would have to face him every day, knowing what he'd done.

"It's amazing," Jack said reflectively, his gaze upon Abby.

"What is?" She was puzzled by the change in his mood.

"How much you look like your mother. You've grown into a very beautiful young woman, Abby."

"Thank you," Abby replied uneasily. She wasn't sure how to take his comment. She'd never thought of herself as beautiful. The idea made her uncomfortable.

Jack sensed her coldness toward him and knew he should address it straight-on. "Abby, I understand how you must feel right now. It's not going to be easy for any of us—my coming back here after all that's happened."

"I don't think you have any idea how I feel, but you're right: it's not easy," she said bluntly.

He went on, "But the Half-Moon is my home, too. Somehow we'll find a way to make this work."

Abby had her doubts, but she said nothing. Just then Brent returned from seeing Edmund and Iona off. She was glad for the interruption and excused herself. She wanted to get away from the house and go to work. The farther she stayed away from her father, the better; and the busier she stayed the happier she would be.

Abby had heard the old adage that time healed all wounds, but she wondered if that were really true. Ten years had passed, yet the pain of losing her mother was still with her. In her heart she knew it always would be.

Abby realized now that she had lost her father ten years ago, too. The man she had loved and had thought wonderful was gone, and she wondered if he had ever really existed. The ugliness of what he had done had stripped her of her childhood innocence. She had been forced from the warmth of her mother's love into a cold, heartless world. Thanks to her brothers, she'd survived, but her scars ran deep.

Chapter Seven

Bill was in the back hallway of the Six Gun when he saw Opal come in.

"You're showing up awful early today," Bill said, surprised to see her. It was only midafternoon, and she wasn't due to perform until that evening.

"I needed to see Belle. Is she here?"

"No, not yet. I don't think she'll be here until closer to six tonight," he told her. Then he added, "I wish I'd known you were going to come by."

"Why?"

"A stranger was in looking for you. He was wanting to know what time you would be on tonight. He said he used to know you and wanted to see you again."

"Is the man still here?" she asked cautiously.

"No. He just left. From the way he was talking, though, he'll be back."

"Did he say who he was?"

"No. I asked him, but he said he wanted to surprise you."

"What did he look like?" Crystal tried to sound casual.

"Dark-haired, about six feet tall, I guess. Dressed nicer than most."

"Sounds like any number of men I've known," she said with a smile. "I'm sorry I missed him."

"He'll be here at showtime, I'm sure. See how you draw them in, Opal? We've got men riding into town from miles around just to see you perform. You've put the Six Gun Saloon on the map," Bill said as he headed back out to resume bartending.

Crystal smiled at Bill's praise, but the moment he had gone, her smile faded. A terrible sense of unease gripped her. She hoped everything was just as Bill thought—that word of how good she was had spread and that she really was drawing customers from far and wide. The fact that the stranger claimed to know her, though, worried Crystal. She had never told Bill the truth about her past. He knew her only as Opal.

Crystal grew tense as the fear that she might have been found haunted her.

It might be her brother—or it might be the law coming after her.

81

She tried to stay calm. She did not want to give in to her sense of panic. She still had time to get away before that evening's show. She knew she had to learn the identity of the man looking for her. She could take no chances.

Leaving the saloon by the back door again, Crystal made her way down the alley. Bill had said the man had left only a short time before, so she hoped she would be able to spot him on the street. She was glad she was wearing a demure day gown that would not draw attention to her. She wanted to blend in with the townspeople as she searched for him. She was glad, too, that it was a busy time of day. There were people on the streets, so she wouldn't be obvious as she searched faces looking for her mysterious "admirer."

It didn't take Crystal long to find him. She was only a block from the saloon when she saw him walking ahead of her—a dark-haired, nicely dressed man. Even from a distance there was no mistaking him: it was her brother Dan.

Fear and dread and anger surged through her. Dan had found her! And if Dan had found her, had he brought the law with him, too?

The desire to break into a dead run seized Crystal, but somehow she fought it down. Instead she calmly turned away and deliberately walked in the opposite direction. Turning at the first corner she came to, she hurried toward the boardinghouse. She had to pack and get out of town as quickly as she could. She had to get away. She'd managed to escape from her brother once, and she could do it again.

Crystal reached the boardinghouse and entered unnoticed. She was glad no one was around, for she didn't want anyone to know the exact time she left.

It didn't take Crystal long to pack her things. The only dress she didn't pack was the one she had bought some months ago in anticipation of a night like this one. It was a widow's black dress with a veil. She hoped the ugly gown would provide the perfect disguise.

Crystal quickly changed into the smothering, high-necked, long-sleeved garment and then donned the veil. She glanced at her reflection in the mirror and nodded in approval to herself. Her disguise was complete. No one would ever guess she was Miss Opal from the saloon, and that was just the way she wanted it.

Crystal left enough money out on the dresser to pay for the rest of the month's rent and then slipped away, carrying her bag with her.

It was still early afternoon as she made her way to the stage depot. She offered up a silent prayer that there would be a stagecoach leaving town very shortly. She had to get away fast.

As she started into the stage office, Crystal saw the schedule posted out front. According to the listing, there were two stagecoaches leaving within the next several hours, and she offered up her thanks. One was heading to San Miguel and then on to a town called Diablo; the other stage was destined for Houston. She knew Dan would expect her to go to Houston, so she chose the other route.

"Is the stage to Diablo on time?" Crystal asked the clerk behind the counter.

"Yes, ma'am. It'll be leaving in less than an hour."

"Good. I'd like a ticket to Diablo, please."

She paid him, then went to sit on the bench in the office. She felt the clerk's gaze upon her, but made sure to keep her face averted for fear that even with the veil, he might somehow recognize her.

The minutes that passed as she waited there were some of the longest in her young life, but finally the stagecoach was ready to depart. The clerk stowed her bag and then took her arm to help her climb on board.

"Have a safe trip, ma'am." He still stared at her, thinking she seemed somehow familiar, but he wasn't sure just why.

"Thank you," she responded, and quickly looked away from him.

There were two other passengers, a husband and wife, already on the stagecoach. They ignored her as she sat down across from them. She was glad. The less attention anyone paid to her, the better. She wanted to make this trip unnoticed. She didn't want anyone to remember her. She didn't doubt for a moment that Dan—or the law—would try to track her down again, and she wasn't going to leave them a trail.

Crystal didn't breathe a true sigh of relief until they had put San Antonio well behind them.

Dan Stewart smiled to himself in satisfaction as he returned to the Six Gun Saloon.

Tonight was the night. Tonight he honestly believed he was going to catch up with Crystal. It hadn't been easy tracking her down, and once he found her, he was going to make sure she never got away from him again.

It had been a long afternoon, but this moment was worth the wait. Dan smiled thinly to himself as he strode up to the bar.

"Evenin', friend. I figured you'd be back," Bill greeted him.

"I told you I would," Dan replied.

"What'll you have?"

"Give me a beer."

Bill set the drink before him.

"How much longer until Miss Opal goes on?"

"About fifteen minutes," Bill assured him.

"Good." Dan turned and positioned himself so he had, an unobstructed view of the stage. He wanted to make sure he could see her perform.

Bill turned to wait on other customers. The saloon was busy, and he was glad. Opal always played to a full house. He was pouring a whiskey for a man at the far end of the bar when Belle came up to the bar and signaled for his attention.

"What is it?" He noticed she looked worried.

"I have to talk to you," she said urgently, but kept her voice low.

"So talk. I got customers to wait on."

"Not here."

Bill finally understood something was really wrong. "Let's go in back for a minute."

Belle came around the bar, and they disappeared into the small storage room.

"It's Opal," she began.

"What about her?"

"She's not here, and she's due to go out onstage in a few minutes," Belle explained.

"Opal will be here," he said. "She came by earlier this afternoon looking for you, and she seemed fine."

"She may have been here a while ago, but she ain't here now," she insisted.

"You checked her dressing room?" He frowned.

"I've checked everywhere. There's no sign of her."

"This isn't like Opal," Bill said, growing concerned. "She's never missed a performance before."

"That's why I'm so worried. She would have told one of us if there was going to be a problem."

"Maybe she got sick and went back to her room at the boarding house. I'll send one of the boys over to check."

"Thanks, Bill." Belle was relieved that he was as concerned as she was. Any of the other working girls they wouldn't have been worried about. The other girls were known for their wild ways, but not Opal. Opal was far different from the rest.

Bill took Gus, one of the men who worked for him, aside and sent him off to the boardinghouse to see if Opal was there. He went back to tending bar, hoping that everything was all right, and that she would show up on time for her performance. He didn't need a bunch of drunk cowboys getting angry at him.

Just a short time before Opal was due to make her grand entrance, Gus returned. Bill was relieved when he saw him.

"Well? Is she on her way? What did you find out? Is she sick?" he asked when they'd gone in the back room to speak privately.

"I don't know what happened to her, but she wasn't there."

"What do you mean, Opal wasn't there?" he demanded. "Where is she?"

"Damned if I know," Gus answered. "The lady who runs the boardinghouse checked her room and said it looked like Opal packed up her things and took off. She didn't realize she'd left until then."

Bill was shocked and troubled by Opal's sudden and unexplained disappearance. It wasn't like her. She'd proven herself reliable the whole time she'd worked for him. He couldn't believe she'd go off without a word—especially since he'd just talked with her that afternoon.

Disgusted, he prepared himself for the fury to come as he went out into the crowded saloon to announce that the show had been canceled.

"I got bad news," Bill shouted out as he climbed up on the stage.

"What kind of bad news?" one cowboy yelled back as a rumble of discontent went through the crowd.

"Miss Opal won't be performing tonight."

The rumble turned to a roar.

"Quiet down, now! The poor woman's feeling sickly," he lied. "She'll be back performing tomorrow night. She sends her regards to you."

The roar didn't abate much.

"Tell you what—I'll buy everyone a drink, and you can toast Opal's health. How's that?" he offered, desperate to quiet them down.

Their anger abated at the offer of free liquor, but their disappointment was still obvious.

Bill managed to keep smiling as he served up the liquor, but he couldn't help wondering what had really happened to Opal.

"Does Opal do this often?" Dan asked as Bill set his free drink before him.

"No. As a matter of fact, this is the first time."

"If you'll tell me where she lives, I'd like to go pay her a visit. I'm not going to be in town for very long, and I don't want to miss seeing her."

Bill didn't know what it was, but something about this man bothered him. "Sorry. I don't give out that kind of information. Come back tomorrow night. She'll be here."

Dan was furious. He wanted to grab the bartender by the shirt and beat the information out of him, but he didn't. Instead he merely smiled.

"I'll do that. I'm looking forward to renewing my acquaintance with her."

"I'm sure she'll be glad to see you, too."

Dan didn't respond as he took a drink. He didn't want to wait until tomorrow, but what was one more day after all these months? He believed he'd finally caught up with her despite her efforts to hide, and that was all that mattered.

Dan got another drink and went to join in a poker game to pass the time. If he was going to be stuck at the Six Gun, he might as well enjoy himself.

"Damned shame Miss Opal ain't performing tonight," one of the men lamented as he anted up.

"It sure is. It ain't like her not to show up. She must be sick, like Bill said," another added.

"I'll bet you she ain't sick," the first man said with a knowing gleam in his eyes.

Dan listened attentively to their conversation, hoping he could learn more about her whereabouts.

"Why ain't she here, then?"

"I say she ran off with Andy!" He guffawed.

They all laughed except Dan.

"What's so funny?" Dan asked, suddenly fearing Crystal had gone away with some man, eluding him again.

"You ain't from around here, are you?" The first man looked at him.

"No. I'm just passing through, but the way you've all been talking about Miss Opal, she sounds real special." He pretended not to know anything about her to find out what these men knew. He hoped they might be able to tell him where she lived.

"Oh, she's special, all right. We all love her. She is a very talented lady."

"I see," Dan responded.

"No, you don't see," the man corrected him, understanding what he was implying and wanting to set him straight.

"But you just said she might have run off with some man named Andy."

"Miss Opal is a lady, and Andy . . . well, he's her biggest admirer in town, and he's also her oldest. How old do you boys think Andy is? Eighty? Ninety?"

The other men chuckled in good humor. "A hundred if he's a day," one replied.

He finally understood their joke. "Oh, well, the barkeep said she'd be back tomorrow. With all that I've heard about her, I was looking forward to seeing her performance tonight."

"We all were. I guess we'll just have to satisfy ourselves with playing poker instead."

It was late when Dan left the saloon and made

his way to the hotel where he'd taken a room for the night. Frustrated though he was by his sister's nonappearance, he had won handily at the poker table. He figured that was a sign his luck was finally changing. He needed some good luck for a change.

The next night Dan went to the saloon early, ready for the confrontation to come with his little sister. The Six Gun was crowded again with many of the same cowboys who'd been there the night before, and he eyed the poker tables with interest, trying to decide which game to join.

"So you did stay over to see Opal," Bill remarked as Dan came up to the bar. Bill had already made the announcement to his regular customers that Opal would not be performing that night, and he didn't look forward to telling this man about her absence.

"I had the time, and I wanted to see Opal," he explained simply.

"Well, I'm afraid I've got some bad news for you," Bill began.

Dan went still, and the look in his eyes turned cold. "What kind of bad news?"

"Miss Opal won't be performing tonight, either."

"Why not?" he ground out, barely in control.

"She's decided to take some time off," Bill said, stretching the truth.

"How much time?" Dan demanded.

Bill had known the stranger would be angry, but there was nothing he could do about it. He had checked back at the boardinghouse again that day to see if Opal had returned, only to learn that no one had seen her. She was really gone.

"I don't know."

"What do you mean, you don't know? Didn't you talk to her today?"

"No."

"Then how do you know? Where does she live? I'll go find her myself."

"I already told you, I don't give out that information. Besides, it doesn't matter. Opal is gone."

"She's gone?" Dan repeated. "What do you mean, she's gone?"

"Just that. She took off."

"Why, you son of a bitch!" Dan lost what little control he had. He lunged across the bar and grabbed the bartender by the shirtfront. "You told me she would be here tonight!"

"Take it easy!" Bill struggled to break free of his hold.

The customers around them started forward to come to the bartender's aid.

"Take it easy?" Dan raged back at him. "She's been gone for more than a day now, and you're telling me to take it easy?"

"Let him go," one of the customers demanded, ready to reach for his gun to protect Bill.

Dan gave the bartender a disgusted shove backward as he released him. He stepped away and gave him a look of pure hatred. "Where did she go?"

"She didn't tell me—but even if she had, I wouldn't tell you," Bill said, reaching under the bar for his shotgun. He brought it up for the stranger to see. "Get out of my saloon. Now. We don't want your kind around here. Right, boys?"

"That's right," his customers echoed.

Dan looked around at all the men ready to fight him, and knew there was no use protesting. He backed away from the bar and didn't say another word as he left the saloon.

"I need a drink," Bill announced with obvious relief in his voice.

His customers laughed and relaxed.

"What was that all about?" Belle asked nervously, coming to his side.

"He's out to find Opal for some reason."

"Then I'm glad she's gone."

"So am I. I never knew she was in trouble. If I'd known, I would have done more to help her," Bill said with regret.

"Don't go feeling bad. You and the boys treated Opal real good while she was here. And even though you didn't know it, you did help her. If she was trying to get away from that man, you managed to give her a full day's head start."

Bill felt a little better. "Let's just hope one day is enough of a lead for her. I don't want that bastard to find her."

Chapter Eight

"I don't know why you ever started concentrating on workhorses," Jack said critically as he and Brent studied the stock in their pasture.

Brent glared at his father as he answered, "I would think that's obvious. Without them, the Half-Moon would have gone under years ago."

Jack snorted in disgust. "My plan for the thoroughbreds would have paid off."

"Your plan for the thoroughbreds nearly cost us everything." Brent stated the plain truth harshly. He had known his father's return was going to be difficult, but he'd never thought it would be this hard. "If it wasn't for these workhorses, you'd be homeless right now."

"From the very beginning, my dream for the

Half-Moon was that it would be known for its thoroughbred racing stock."

Brent was disgusted. "That's a great dream, Pa, but a dream isn't reality. Reality is paying back what you owe people and keeping food on the table." Brent turned back to watch the horses, remembering those hard early years when he'd been trying to hold the family together and keep the ranch going.

Jack looked over at his son. It had been three weeks since he'd been released from prison—three long weeks. In all that time, it seemed they'd only been circling each other—talking at each other, but not to each other. He'd come to realize that Brent had grown into a fine man. He was smart with business and not afraid of hard work.

"Son . . ."

Brent warily glanced over at him, a bit surprised that he'd called him "son."

"It probably doesn't mean much to you, but I am proud of what you've done here," he said solemnly. "It couldn't have been easy for you."

Their gazes met and locked. For that one moment in time, all the ugliness of the past disappeared, and it was the way it used to be between them.

"It's been hard work, but this is our home."

"But with Quince leaving when he did, and Matt showing up only when he wanted to . . ." Jack shook his head in disgust. "We both know how much help Matt is."

The moment of understanding was shattered by his father's comment about Matt. Brent had never understood why Jack was always so hard on his youngest son. He'd been rough on him even before Matt had started getting into trouble. Brent defended his brother. "Matt's helped me a lot."

Jack didn't believe it for a moment. He said sarcastically, "And that's why he's here working right alongside you now."

"No, he's off chasing his dream, just like you did," Brent threw back at him, the tension between them returning. Then he added with certainty, "It may take Matt a while, but he'll be back."

"I wouldn't be so sure of that."

Brent heard the coldness in his tone and knew there was no point in discussing Matt any further. "Don't forget about Abby. She's been a lot of help around the ranch."

"She should be doing women's work, not riding with the hired hands."

It irritated Brent to realize he agreed with his father about Abby, but there was no changing her. He'd already tried. "We'd better be heading back. Tonight's the night for the social in town, and Abby won't be happy if we're late."

Brent wheeled his horse around, and Jack followed. Together they rode for the house.

Brent had been surprised when Abby had mentioned attending the social. She hadn't said why she wanted to go, but he had a feeling it had something to do with Iona. Pa had surprised him, too, by saying he wanted to go. This would be his first trip to town since he'd returned from prison.

Brent wondered how his pa's old friends were going to react to seeing him again. He knew Edmund and Iona would be there, and Edmund would welcome Pa, but Brent wasn't sure about the other folks. He didn't know how they would treat him. He could only hope that things would go smoothly.

"Since we're going into town," Jack began, "I'm going to need some cash."

"What for?" Brent cast him a sharp glance. He was very careful with the Half-Moon's money and didn't believe in wasting a cent.

"It's none of your business what I want the money for," his father answered, bristling. "I'm not going into town with empty pockets."

Brent didn't say any more. There was no point. When they got back to the ranch, he'd give Jack some cash. Brent tried not to be irritated by his request, but he had a feeling he knew where he was going to spend it, and he didn't want to think about his father buying liquor.

Abby came out on the porch to meet them when she saw them riding up.

"I was beginning to wonder if I'd be going into Diablo by myself. You two will have to hurry and change if we're going to get to town on time." Abby's expression was worried. "I don't want Iona to arrive at the social ahead of us."

"We're late because we've been working," Brent explained.

"That's what you always say," she replied, smiling. "Please hurry. I need to be there to meet her."

"All right," Brent agreed as he dismounted and tied up his horse. It wasn't often that he wanted to attend any social functions in town. He had little time for having fun. He had ranch work to do. But Abby was determined to go, and now Pa was, too, so he would go with them.

"How soon can you be ready?"

"Half hour."

"I'll be waiting for you."

"You planning on going to town looking like one of the hired hands?" Jack demanded.

Abby had had this same argument so many times with Brent that her father's criticism didn't trouble her at all. She gave him a proud look. "It doesn't matter what I wear. I'm not going to the social to *be* social, Papa. I'm only going because Iona asked me to." She turned her gaze to her brother. "Iona needs a friend right now, and I seem to be the only one who cares about her."

Brent and Jack hurried inside to pack what they needed to spend the night in town. They would stay at the hotel tonight and return home after church services the following morning.

Jack turned to Brent and said sarcastically, "I can see you raised her well."

"No," Brent said. "Abby raised herself. You saw to that."

Jack flushed at his remark and didn't say anything more.

"There were days when I thought I'd never see this town again," Jack remarked to Abby as he drove the buckboard down Main Street and Brent rode alongside. "It's changed."

"Yes, it has changed some," she agreed.

"Is the church still on First Street?"

"Yes, and there's a new hotel on the corner of First and Main," she pointed out, making small talk. The truth was, she was nervous. There was no telling what people would do when they saw her father.

As they passed the sheriff's office, Jack fell silent. Of all that was different in town, the sheriff's office had not changed—not one bit. He remembered every detail of the place far too clearly for his own peace of mind, and he deliberately looked away.

"Sheriff Miller's moved on," Brent offered. He'd noticed how uncomfortable his pa had looked and thought the news might help ease his mood a little.

"Who's the new man?"

"Mitch Dawson. He's a good sheriff."

Jack only nodded in response. He found himself wondering if the Lone Star Saloon was still in business. He hoped it was. He needed a drink badly. He planned to head over there the first chance he got, while Brent and Abby were at the social.

"So what kind of men have you got chasing after you, Abby?" Jack asked. "Are Brent and I going to have to fight them off tonight?"

"I never learned to dance," she admitted truthfully. Her gaze met Brent's. They both knew that it didn't matter if she knew how to dance or not, for none of the men in town would think of asking her.

Jack shook his head. "Your mother was a good dancer. If she were alive, she would have taught . . ." He fell silent when he realized what he'd been saying. He could feel the anger radiating from Brent and Abby.

"Yes, if she had lived," Abby said softly. "If she had lived."

"Well . . ." Jack wanted to change the subject. "You're pretty enough to need protecting, even if you can't dance."

Before Brent could say anything, Abby put in, "If anybody is going to need protection tonight, it's going to be Brent. I just bet Melinda is already counting the minutes until she gets to see you again."

"I hope not," Brent stated.

"Who's Melinda?" Jack asked.

"Her name is Melinda Barton, and she's very fond of Brent." Abby gave her brother a knowing look.

"Has her family been in town long?" Jack wondered, not recognizing the name.

"About four or five years, I guess," Brent offered. "Her father runs the stage office."

"And you're going to marry her?" he asked bluntly.

"No," Brent answered quickly, startled by his father's question. He hadn't even thought about marriage. It had been only in the last few months that he'd even allowed himself to pay attention to any of the girls in town. He was too caught up in taking care of things out at the Half-Moon to worry about women.

"Well, if Melinda has her way . . ." Abby began, then stopped when Brent glared at her.

They were silent until they reached the hotel and checked in.

"I'm going over to the town hall to meet Iona. Will you put my things in my room for me?" she asked her father and brother.

"You really are going to the social in those clothes?" Jack asked, frowning at her.

Abby did not reply as she headed for the door.

Edmund accompanied Iona to the town hall. She'd started drinking her sherry early that morning. She disgusted him. Her drinking was the talk of the town, while his own reputation as a patient, long-suffering husband was growing almost as quickly. Grateful to escape her, he went to supervise as the other men got things ready for the festive evening to come. Only the thought that Abby would be at the social made the prospect of spending the evening in his wife's company bearable. He knew he would have to be careful how he acted around Abby. He didn't want anyone to guess what he was really thinking about her, but at least setting eyes on her again would offer him some satisfaction.

Edmund headed over to join the men, casting one last glance back toward where the women were gathered. It was then that he saw Abby coming up the street. He stopped for a moment, just to watch her approach.

Abby was young—she was ripe. Just the way he liked them. Best of all, she was the image of her mother—even dressed as a ranch hand.

At once it both annoyed Edmund to see her wearing pants and excited him, too, for he could see her long, shapely legs, and imagine more easily what she would look like unclothed.

Edmund wanted her, but knew he couldn't have her. Heat filled him, and with the heat came frustration. Fighting it down, he turned away. He couldn't be too obvious about paying attention to Abby. He didn't want to cause any talk.

"I see little Abby's here," Cecil remarked as Edmund joined him. "I wonder if Jack is going to show up, too? I heard talk that he was out of prison and back living at the ranch."

"Yes, Jack is back," Edmund told him.

"You've seen him?" He was surprised.

"I was out at the Half-Moon a few weeks ago, right after he returned."

"I can't believe he's out already. Ten years behind

bars doesn't seem nearly long enough for what he did."

"Where's your Christian attitude, Cecil?" Edmund's smile was benevolent. "What about forgiveness?"

"Spoken like a true deacon of the church, Edmund, but the man is a cold-blooded killer. He isn't fit to be here at this social, mixing with good, clean-living folks."

"Well, if Jack does attend tonight, at least be civil to him." Edmund was playing his role perfectly, with quiet dignity.

"I'll try, but I'm not promising anything."

Glancing Abby's way one last time, Edmund saw that she was busy talking with Iona. He was glad they were close. The more Abby wanted to see his wife, the more chances he had to be around her. At least, he thought in disgust, Iona was finally good for something.

The ladies began serving the dinner at five o'clock. They had coldly but politely refused Iona's offer of help.

Abby remained with the older woman, knowing she would be on the receiving end of even more cruel barbs before the night was over. Abby was accustomed to being treated like an outsider, but Iona, as the banker's wife, had once been revered by the ladies in town, and her friendship had been cultivated. Abby saw the hurt and confusion in her eyes, and it wounded Abby deeply. Again Abby thought of Iona's daughter, Juliana, and wished that she had come home. Iona needed her help.

After they'd eaten, Brent went to talk with friends from town, while Edmund went off to work with the men, this time setting up for the coming dance.

Jack was left alone, so he sought out Leroy Jennings and some other men he'd considered friends in the past.

"Evening, Leroy—boys," Jack said as he joined them.

"I thought that was you sitting over there," Leroy responded, sounding less than enthusiastic.

"I got back to the ranch a while ago."

"We'll see you later, Leroy," the other men said abruptly, ignoring Jack. They started to walk away.

Jack had known it would be hard fitting in and being accepted again, but he'd never expected to be so completely ostracized.

"Where you boys going?" Jack challenged, anger growing within him.

They looked at him, their expressions condemning. "Away from here. We don't want to be around your kind."

"My kind? Why, you—" Jack took a step toward them, his hands clenched into fists at his sides.

"Pa—back off."

Brent's order jarred Jack and he stopped.

The men all looked toward Brent, then glanced

at each other and walked away. Even Leroy went with them this time, glad to avoid trouble.

Jack stood there glaring after them.

"What was the problem?" Brent asked. He had been watching what was going on, and had noticed how his pa's old friends were treating him.

Jack turned on Brent, not willing to admit how he'd been shunned. "There was no problem."

"That's not how it looked to me."

"Mind your own business," Jack said with a snarl.

Brent hadn't heard everything the men had said, but he could imagine the exchange. He started to say more, but his father turned his back on him and walked away. Brent didn't even consider going after him. He was just glad that there hadn't been any real trouble. Satisfied that things were quiet for now, he went back to his friends.

Jack sat down at one of the empty tables away from the dance floor. He realized how very alone he was as he watched the activities going on around him. Laughter and gaiety abounded as the dancing began, but none of it included him.

Jack's mood grew black.

He knew what he needed, and he knew where he wanted to go—where he had to go. He waited a few minutes longer, then got up and left the social.

It did not surprise him that no one noticed him leave, and he didn't care.

He was heading for the Lone Star Saloon.

He'd needed a drink for a long time now, and he was going to get one.

Chapter Nine

Brent was standing off to the side of the dance floor that had been set up outdoors for the evening's activities. He'd lost track of his father and was considering going to look for him when Melinda sought him out.

"There you are, Brent!" Melinda cooed as she came to stand at his side. Brent was the handsomest man in Diablo, and she was determined to make him her own. "I've been looking for you."

"You have?" he asked with a smile.

Melinda was a pretty enough girl with her dark hair and blue eyes, but as he looked down at her an image of Opal flashed in his mind. He'd thought of the lovely singer often at first, but as the weeks passed, the memory of their encounter faded. Opal was gone from his life. They wouldn't meet again.

Melinda gazed up at him adoringly, believing she had his undivided attention. "Yes. I was afraid you would be in a hurry to get back to the ranch after the dinner, and I wouldn't get the chance to see you."

"No, we're staying in town tonight."

"I am so glad."

"Would you like to dance?" Brent offered, trying to focus his thoughts on the present—on the pretty girl who wanted to be with him, and not on his father, or the beautiful blonde he would never see again.

"I was hoping you would ask," Melinda answered. She had never been accused of being shy, and she went straight into his arms.

Brent swept her out onto the dance floor. His mother had taught him how to dance at a young age, and the lessons had stayed with him. He smiled down at Melinda as he whirled her about.

Melinda knew Brent was watching her, and she batted her eyes at him flirtatiously. She was glad she'd worn her prettiest gown. She wanted to look her best for him. He didn't come to town that often, so she had to make good use of what little time they had together. Her secret plan for the evening was to get Brent alone, so she could steal a kiss. Of course, he had to think the kiss was his idea, but she would find a way to do it. She'd waited too long for this night to waste one minute of it.

Brent glanced away from Melinda for a moment

to scan the faces of those looking on. He was hoping to spot his father, but saw no sign of him standing in the crowd. He looked beyond the dance area, and he caught sight of him heading off down the street in the direction of the Lone Star Saloon. Brent frowned.

"Is something wrong?" Melinda asked, noticing the change in his expression.

"No, everything's fine," he lied. He had no intention of sharing his concerns with her. What went on between him and his father was going to stay within the family. He turned his attention back to her.

Melinda was pleased to have his undivided attention again. She gave him a coquettish smile and allowed herself to simply enjoy being in his arms, for that was right where she wanted to be. This was going to be a wonderful night. She was sure of it.

"We've got some new entertainment tonight, boys," Babe told the men standing at the bar in the Lone Star Saloon as she came to join them.

"What kind of entertainment?" a cowboy named Joe asked the pretty dance-hall girl. He was more than ready and very willing to be entertained by the beautiful Babe. He had heard tell that she knew all kinds of exciting ways to please a man.

"We've hired a new singer to perform for you, and I think you're going to enjoy her."

"I'd rather enjoy you," Joe told her.

She gave him a throaty laugh. "Thank you for the compliment, Joe, honey. Let's talk later. Right now I want you all to welcome Miss Ruby."

The piano player started a tune, and they all turned to the small stage.

"Good evening, gentlemen," Crystal said as she came out onstage, smiling.

The men in the Lone Star took one look at the beautiful redhead in the red dress, and they immediately fell in love.

"Evenin', Miss Ruby," one drunken cowhand called back.

Crystal smiled and winked outrageously at the man. As she began to sing, they all fell even more completely under her spell.

Crystal looked as beautiful as ever, but she was close to exhaustion. The weeks since she'd fled San Antonio had been long and tense. She had hoped to start a whole new life for herself in the small town of San Miguel. Liking the look of the place, she'd gotten off the stage there, and had tried to continue the ruse of being a widow looking for employment, but no one in San Miguel would hire her.

Night after lonely night, she'd lain in bed in her room at the hotel, unable to sleep. Her thoughts had been haunted by the fear that Dan or the law would find her. To calm herself, she'd thought of Brent Hunter. She'd remembered how the handsome stranger had rescued her during the robbery, and she'd wished he would show up again and save her from the terror her life had become.

But Crystal knew that was just a young girl's fantasy—being rescued by a handsome knight. Crystal knew the truth about life. That night with Brent had been an aberration. If she was going to be saved, she would have to save herself.

When her funds ran dangerously low, Crystal packed up again and moved on—this time all the way to Diablo. She resigned herself to returning to work in a saloon. She took a room at the small boardinghouse in town, registering under the name of Ruby Morgan, and then set about changing her looks once again. The widow disappeared, to be replaced by Miss Ruby, a flame-haired seductress.

Crystal had been worried about how Anne Pals, the owner of the boardinghouse, would react to the change in her appearance. The first time Anne saw her with red hair she'd been startled, but had not questioned her. Crystal had been glad to find out Anne respected her boarders' privacy. Perhaps she'd found a safe haven in Diablo after all.

When Crystal approached Ken Gilbert, the owner of the Lone Star Saloon, he hired her right away. She made certain he understood her job was for entertainment only, and he had eagerly agreed after hearing her sing.

Even though she was relieved that her concerns about money were over for now, Crystal could not completely dismiss the possibility that someone might find her. Dan didn't forget when someone double-crossed him—and she was sure her brother believed she'd betrayed him. But worse than her worry about Dan was the thought that the law was after her. She hadn't seen one yet, but she realized there might even be a wanted poster out for her.

It took a major effort on her part not to give in to pure panic, but Crystal managed. She kept smiling and concentrated on her performance.

Jack entered the saloon and went straight to the bar. He noticed there was a pretty woman singing, but paid her no attention. All he wanted was a drink. He had been ten years without one, and that was way too long.

Everyone in the bar was intent on watching the woman's performance, and Jack was glad. He didn't want anyone paying attention to him. He just wanted to drink in peace. The barkeep approached, and Jack was pleased that he did not recognize the man.

"Get you something?"

"Whiskey," Jack ordered.

"Coming right up." The bartender served him quickly.

Jack picked up the tumbler and studied the golden liquid for a long moment before taking a deep swallow. The whiskey was potent, and he relished its power. Soon, very soon, he would be feeling better.

*   *   *

"I could use a cool drink; what about you?" Melinda suggested to Brent when their dance ended.

Brent escorted her to the refreshment table and got them each a cup of punch.

"Thank you."

They enjoyed their drinks together.

"I wish I could see you more often," she said, gazing up at him adoringly.

"It's hard for me to get away from the ranch. Running the Half-Moon is a big responsibility."

"I know." She smiled. That big ranch was one of the reasons she wanted to marry him.

"Would you like to dance again?" he invited as another tune began.

"Of course. I love dancing with you."

Melinda went eagerly into his arms.

As they moved about the dance floor together, Brent saw Leroy again, and his thoughts were drawn back to his father. A part of Brent almost felt sorry for him, but he pushed that emotion away. It was going to be a while before he could deal with all the difficulties of having his father back home again after so many years away.

Brent wondered if Jack had gone to the saloon, as he suspected. If he had, there was no telling how drunk he'd get. He knew he would have to go check on him, but first he'd finish his dance with Melinda.

*   *   *

Edmund turned toward the table where Iona and Abby were sitting together, a slight distance away from the dance floor. He had left Iona there with a promise to return, but returning had been the farthest thing from his mind—until he saw Abby join her. He'd been trying to escape the company of his fellow deacons from the church ever since.

Edmund's gaze narrowed as he saw Dr. Gibbs approach Iona. He watched as the physician offered her his hand with a smile and then leaned toward her to study her with professional scrutiny. Edmund was ready when Dr. Gibbs looked his way, and he did not react to his angry, accusing gaze. When the doctor finally moved away and disappeared into the crowd after speaking with Iona and Abby for a few more moments, Edmund excused himself from his companions and went to join his wife.

"I'm glad you're back," Iona said when he sat down.

"I came as soon as I could." It wasn't a lie. He'd been trying ever since Abby had joined her.

Iona's smile was overly bright. "Abby has been keeping me company, but I missed you, you know. What have you been doing?"

"I'm sorry, dear. Some of the men asked my advice. I'm afraid the discussion lasted longer than I realized."

"It was good of you to help them, but . . ." Iona paused, then continued more softly, "I've been looking forward to dancing with you tonight."

Abby spoke for the first time, whispering, "Are you sure you want to dance, Iona?"

Attempting to stand with dignity, she replied, "Oh, yes, Abby. I'm sure."

Edmund managed a smile as he took Iona's hand and guided her out onto the dance floor. He couldn't remember the last time he'd enjoyed himself with his wife, and holding her up while she staggered through the dance was not his idea of a good time.

As they danced, Edmund realized disgustedly that Iona was beginning to sober up. At least when she was drunk it was easy to elude her. He would pay enough attention to her now to shut her up for a while, and then he was going to invite Abby to dance. He didn't know if she would accept, but just the thought of holding her close excited him.

"I think that's Jack Hunter at the bar," Seth Richards, one of the hands from the Bar W Ranch, told the other men sitting at the poker table as they listened to the new girl sing.

"Isn't he the one who—"

"That's him."

"They let him out already? Damn."

"Who's Jack Hunter?" another cowboy at the table asked.

Seth quickly explained about Jack's scandalous past. The other man eyed Jack suspiciously.

"I'm surprised he came back to Diablo."

"I imagine everybody in town is surprised by his return, but it ain't no surprise that he's here getting drunk. He was nothing but a drunk before, and it looks like he ain't changed any. If his coming home wasn't already the talk of the town, it will be after tonight."

The new singer began another song, and the men turned their attention back to her. Watching Miss Ruby was far more entertaining than watching the old drunk at the bar.

Jack drained his drink and signaled the bartender for another refill as he watched the pretty little entertainer. She was a talented girl, and he meant to tell her so once she was finished performing. He was very glad that he'd left the church dance. He was having a far better time here with his whiskey.

"Get me a bottle to take with me," Jack told the barkeep when he was filling his glass.

"How big?"

"Something I can carry in my coat pocket."

"Coming right up." The bartender brought him a good-sized flask of whiskey.

Jack smiled and put it in his pocket. So much for Brent's ordering him not to drink on the Half-Moon. It was his ranch, and he'd drink there if he wanted to.

Crystal finished her last song to rousing applause. In keeping with her usual friendly manner, she left the stage to greet everyone in the saloon. The cowboys gloried in her attention.

As she went from table to table talking to the men, Crystal noticed the older man standing at the bar. Something about him seemed vaguely familiar, although she was certain she'd never met him before.

"Good evening," Crystal said as she stopped before him.

"Miss Ruby, you sure have a pretty voice," Jack told her.

"Why, thank you, sir."

"I'm only speaking the truth," he assured her. "My name's Jack. Would you care to join me for a drink tonight?"

"I'd love to." Crystal looked at the bartender and ordered a sarsaparilla.

Jack was surprised. Usually the women who worked in saloons were heavy drinkers. "Why are you drinking that? Have some of the good stuff," he encouraged.

"Sarsaparilla is good stuff, for me," she answered. "I have to perform again a little later, and I don't want to risk not doing my best for my audience."

"You are a rare woman indeed, Miss Ruby," Jack said.

"I'll take that as a compliment, Jack." She beamed at him.

"That's what it was."

Crystal moved on to chat with the other customers. She wasn't sure why she'd felt drawn to the older man, but she had enjoyed talking with him.

Jack watched her go, and he was most impressed. She was pretty and talented, and she'd been kind to him, which was something that hadn't happened a lot since his return.

Edmund and Iona returned to the table where Abby was sitting alone.

"May I have the honor of the next dance, Abby?" he asked.

"I'm sorry. I don't dance."

"I could teach you."

"I'm perfectly happy sitting here with Iona."

Edmund studied her as boldly as he dared, keeping his expression carefully benign. He imagined himself touching her soft skin and running his hands through her dark hair. There were other things he wanted to do with her, too, but he put those lecherous thoughts from him—for now. Iona was already looking at him strangely, and he didn't want her to suspect the truth of what he was feeling for Abby.

Frustrated, Edmund silently cursed them both. He excused himself and left the two women, moving away from the crowd around the dance floor. He breathed deeply of the evening air as he struggled to control his anger. He was startled when Dr. Gibbs stepped out of the shadows before him.

"Iona is taking laudanum again, isn't she, Edmund?" he demanded accusingly. "I could see it in her eyes when I talked to her tonight. I warned you it was dangerous when I prescribed it for her. She was only supposed to use it temporarily, and now, with her present problem, there's a risk—"

"Her present problem?" Edmund countered coldly.

"Her drinking."

"Iona enjoys a glass of sherry now and then, but her drinking is controlled."

"Are you that naive?"

"Believe what you like," Edmund snapped back at him. "Iona asked me to find a way to get the medicine for her when you would no longer supply it. I found it was available through my contacts back east, so I complied with her request."

"But I told you—"

"I don't care what you told me. Iona is satisfied, and so am I."

"I'm warning you, Edmund—"

"Warning me?" A tight smile twisted his mouth. "What will you do? Report me to the sheriff?"

Dr. Gibbs went pale at his words.

Edmund gave a short, confident laugh. "No, I don't think you'll be doing that."

Edmund turned his back on the silent doctor and moved off to rejoin the crowd.

"Are you having a good time, dear?" Iona asked Abby.

Abby wasn't enjoying herself at all, but she couldn't admit that to Iona. It was painful to watch all the girls her age dancing and having fun while she sat on the sidelines feeling miserable. She had never been included in their merriment, and she never expected to be.

"The music has been lively," Abby said, hoping Iona would not notice that she'd sidestepped her question. "I believe Mr. Harding has improved his skills on the fiddle."

Iona nodded, and they sat in silence watching the festivities.

Chapter Ten

When Iona asked Edmund to dance again, Abby went to find Brent. She was aware that some of the people were staring at her and that some of the women were whispering to each other as she passed by, but she ignored them. She had more important things to worry about than what the folks in town thought about her.

"Where did Papa go?" Abby asked Brent.

"I have an idea, but I'm not sure," he responded.

"I don't understand. I thought he said he was going to stay here at the dance and visit with his old friends."

"That didn't work out, so I think he's renewing his acquaintance with some bottles of liquor down at the Lone Star. I'll go over there now to check on him. Will you be all right here by yourself for a little while?"

"Edmund and Iona are here. I'll be fine, but, Brent . . ."

He gave her a questioning look.

"I hope you're wrong about Papa. I hope he's not drinking."

"So do I, Abby." Brent steeled himself for what was to come. "If Melinda comes looking for me, tell her something came up, and I'll be back for you as soon as I can."

"I'll give her your message." Abby was tempted not to tell Melinda. If her brother was finally going to start courting, she didn't want it to be Melinda. Granted, the girl was pretty enough, but looks weren't everything.

Brent's mood was somber as he headed for the Lone Star. He remembered how his pa had reacted to the news that there was no liquor at the ranch. Brent was positive that he'd find Jack at the saloon drinking. He just hoped he hadn't gotten into any fights.

The Lone Star was the best saloon in town. Brent could hear the sounds of revelry coming from the bar as he drew near. The cowboys who were in town for a good time always found it at the Lone Star. He went into the crowded saloon and spotted his father immediately, standing at the bar with his back to the door. Even as Brent looked on, the bartender was refilling his glass.

Brent made his way to his father's side.

"I had a feeling you'd be here."

Jack had lost count of the number of drinks he'd had, and he didn't care. He glanced at Brent with annoyance.

"I'm a free man, and I can do whatever I want. Right now all I want to do is just relax a bit."

"You couldn't do that at the dance?"

"No," he answered harshly. "Folks are friendlier here at the Lone Star, and they got real good entertainment. I'm waiting for Miss Ruby to come back out again." Jack grinned as he thought of her. Ruby had smiled at him and treated him like a man. It had been quite a contrast to the way everyone else was treating him. Her acceptance had eased the pain in his soul.

"Who's Ruby?" Brent wondered if some dancehall girl were going after his father.

"She's the entertainment here. Stay with me. She's due back out in the next few minutes, right, Ken?" Jack looked at the man tending bar.

"That's right," Ken answered.

"I don't care about seeing Ruby."

"Go ahead and leave, then, but I'm staying."

Brent was frustrated, but he didn't want to pick a fight with his father.

"You want a drink?" the bartender asked Brent.

"Give me a beer," he said.

Ken served him and moved off.

"You're having a beer?" Jack looked at Brent in surprise.

"Shut up, Pa."

Jack changed the topic, his words starting to slur. "You're going to like Miss Ruby. Sings like an angel. She's damned sweet, too. She was real nice to me."

"Sure she was," Brent said cynically as he took one token drink of the beer, and then set the glass aside. "They're all nice to you—when they think you've got money."

"No, Ruby's different. Just wait—you'll see."

Brent took a look around and remembered the last time he'd been in a saloon. His mood had been dark then, too, but at least he'd had the girl named Opal to brighten that night up a little bit. He just hoped this Ruby was mildly entertaining, for he needed some distraction this evening.

The piano player began playing Ruby's introduction.

"Here she comes now," Jack told him, grinning as he looked eagerly toward the stage.

Brent frowned. The tune sounded vaguely familiar.

And then Ruby made her appearance.

Brent's expression turned from a frown to a look of surprise and disbelief.

It was Opal. . . .

The red hair gave her a very different look, but there was no mistaking her beauty or the sound of her voice.

Jack glanced at him and saw the look on his face. "She's damned pretty, isn't she?"

"You're right. She is," he agreed.

Brent gave his full attention to her performance, but he couldn't help wondering how and why Opal had ended up in Diablo disguised as Ruby.

Jack finished off his whiskey and motioned to the barkeep to refill his glass. He was glad Brent was so busy watching the singer that he didn't notice.

Crystal moved about the stage, singing her heart out to the men. They responded with genuine enthusiasm, cheering and clapping. As she finished her final song, she looked out across room to see if the older man was still at the bar. He was. She went completely still as she saw Brent Hunter standing at his side.

Crystal didn't know how it was that fate had brought them together again, but she was thrilled. Her gaze lingered on Brent. He was every bit as handsome and wonderful as she remembered.

"Ruby!"

The sound of one of the other customers calling out to her jarred her from her momentary reverie. She forced her attention back to doing her job. As she left the stage to mingle with the customers, though, she slowly and deliberately made her way toward Brent. She couldn't wait to talk to him again.

"Good evening," Brent said, his gaze meeting hers as she came to stand before him.

"Ruby, this is my son Brent," Jack put in, giving her a drunken smile.

"Hello, Brent," Crystal said softly, gazing up at him. She understood now why the older man had seemed vaguely familiar to her earlier. There was a definite family resemblance between the two. "It's good to see you again."

"You know each other?" Jack was shocked as he looked between the two of them.

"Yes, I met *Ruby* in San Antonio," Brent explained, giving a little extra emphasis to her name that only she noticed.

"Brent saved me from being attacked. He's a wonderful man," she quickly explained to Jack.

Jack glanced at Brent. "You saved Ruby? What happened?"

Brent wanted to ask her about her changed name and looks, but decided to wait until later, when he could speak with her privately. "Someone tried to rob her after she got off work. I was lucky enough to be close by so I could stop him." Brent turned to Ruby. "What brings you to Diablo?"

"It was time for me to move on, and Diablo seemed like a nice enough town." She had thought he was wonderful before, but the fact that he hadn't asked her about her disguise raised her opinion of him even higher.

"I'm glad you picked it."

"Isn't she beautiful?" Jack insisted drunkenly.

"Yes, Pa, she is," Brent agreed.

"And she's about the best singer I ever heard," Jack went on, draining the rest of the whiskey in his glass.

"Why, thank you," Crystal said.

"Have you been in town long?" Brent asked, for he hadn't heard any talk about her from the ranch hands.

"No, this is my first evening to perform."

"Gimme another whiskey, Ken," Jack called out as he turned clumsily toward the bar again.

"No. Hold that," Brent said, giving the barkeep a sharp look that stopped him from reaching for his glass. "It's about time for us to call it a night."

"You want to leave when we could stay here and visit with Ruby?" Jack argued.

She sensed what Brent was trying to do, and played along. "I'm going to have to put on another performance shortly, so I don't have much time to talk right now. I'm sure we'll be seeing each other again."

"That we will, little darling," Jack slurred.

"Come on, Pa." Brent started to usher him out of the saloon. He was aware that some of the other customers were watching them with condemning glares.

"Brent," she began.

He looked back as he kept a hand on his staggering father.

"It was good to see you again. Will you be back?"

Brent nodded slightly as their gazes met. If there

was one thing he could be certain of, it was that he would return to see her again.

Crystal gave him a small smile of understanding and went back to work. She hoped he returned quickly.

Brent got his pa back to the hotel and up to the room without too much trouble.

"So you liked Ruby, too," Jack remarked thoughtfully as he undressed. Even though he was drunk, he knew enough to keep his liquor bottle hidden among his clothes, where Brent wouldn't see it.

"In San Antonio she was going by the name of Opal."

"Opal? I wonder why she changed her name?" Jack repeated dully as he bedded down and slowly succumbed to his drunken stupor.

"I don't know. Maybe she's making a fresh start here."

"A fresh start," Jack mumbled, thinking the idea applied to him, too. "Maybe I should have gone somewhere else and . . ."

He passed out then, his liquor-blurred thoughts lost to sleep.

Brent stayed on a little while longer, wanting to make sure his father really was asleep. Only when he was sure Jack wouldn't be rousing anytime soon did Brent leave the room.

He wanted to go straight back to the Lone Star and Opal, but he knew he had to check on Abby.

He couldn't go off for the rest of the evening and leave his little sister to fend for herself. She was his responsibility. He would see her safely back to her room, and then return to the saloon.

Brent made his way back to the festivities and sought Abby out where she was sitting at a table with Iona and Edmund. She smiled at him when she saw him coming.

"Did everything go all right? I've been worrying about you," Abby told him.

"Yes, I got him back up to the hotel room."

"He was drunk?" Edmund asked quickly, sounding concerned.

Brent nodded.

"I'm sorry, Brent. I thought things might have changed." Secretly, Edmund was delighted Jack was still a drunk. It proved once again what a weak man he was.

"Some things never change." Brent's disgust was obvious.

"Melinda was looking for you earlier," Abby put in, wanting to talk about something besides their father, although Melinda wasn't exactly a favorite topic for her either. "I told her you'd see her again before the dance was over, so you'd better go find her."

"Wait here for me. I won't be long if I can help it."

Melinda had seen Brent return while she'd been dancing with another man. The minute the dance ended, she excused herself and went to find Brent.

"I missed you, Brent," she said sweetly. "I'm glad you're back."

"I had some business to take care of," Brent answered, deliberately not going into detail.

"Well, you're here now. That's all that matters. Let's dance," she said, taking his arm. She wasn't about to let him get away from her again.

Brent suddenly felt trapped. There was no way to escape from Melinda without causing a scene. Instead, forced to play the gentleman, he smiled down at her and took her out onto the dance floor.

The tension within Brent didn't ease as he danced with Melinda. If anything, it grew. He was glad when the music finally stopped.

"I have to get Abby back to the hotel now," he explained.

"I hope I get to see you again soon, Brent," Melinda said suggestively, forgetting all pretense of being coy.

Brent was just glad to make his escape. He immediately rounded up Abby, who was still sitting with Edmund and Iona. They bade the older couple good-night and left the dance.

"Did you have fun?" Brent asked, glancing down at her. He wondered if she would admit the truth to him—he'd seen her sitting all alone. He could only imagine how painful the social must have been for her.

"It's always pleasant to be with Iona. And . . . I think she needs me."

He nodded. "So do I. I can remember how good she was to you when Ma died."

Abby took a deep breath. "I'll be glad to get back to the ranch."

"We'll head back home right after church in the morning."

"I'll be ready."

Brent saw Abby safely to her room, then went to check on their father. He was still passed out in bed, and Brent was glad. He wanted to get away for a while, and didn't want any complications.

Certain that all was safe and quiet at the hotel, Brent strode briskly toward the Lone Star—and Opal.

Chapter Eleven

Crystal worked the room, talking with the customers and sipping her sarsaparilla. She kept watching and waiting for Brent's return.

"You sure you won't let me buy you a whiskey, sweetheart?" one of the drunken cowboys offered.

"No, but thank you for offering." She gave him a warm smile as she moved on to another table.

Time passed, and still Brent didn't return. Crystal was beginning to think he wouldn't be back, and she silently chided herself for caring. She'd always made it a point not to care about any of her customers on a personal basis. She'd remained aloof from everyone. But Brent was different. Even as she acknowledged that, Crystal tried to convince herself it didn't matter.

And then Brent walked back into the saloon.

Her heartbeat quickened. She smiled at him in welcome and went to greet him. She warned herself that it wasn't safe to get involved with anyone, but all the logic in the world couldn't change the way she felt.

"I'm glad you came back," Crystal said.

"I am, too," Brent said.

"Would you like to sit at a table? I have to perform again, but not for another half hour."

Brent nodded, and she led the way to an empty table near the back of the Lone Star.

The cowboys watched her with Brent, and they envied the rancher for having Ruby all to himself for a while.

"I can't believe you're actually here in Diablo," Crystal said as she sat down and faced Brent across the table. "I thought I'd never see you again."

"I thought I'd never see you, either," he agreed.

"How is your arm?" She remembered the wound he'd suffered saving her that night.

"It's fine," he said, dismissing her concern. "But what about you? Are you in some kind of trouble? Why are you using a different name, and why did you change your hair color?"

Crystal managed a smile to hide her nervousness. "After what happened in San Antonio that night, I thought it was time for a change. I wanted to start over in a new town, so I thought I'd alter my looks, too."

"So which name should I call you—Opal or Ruby?" he asked with a slight grin.

She looked up, her gaze meeting his, and she knew how to answer. She had to be as honest with him as she could.

"Those are just my stage names. My real name is Crystal Morgan," she told him. It wasn't a lie. Morgan was her middle name.

"Crystal," Brent repeated. "That's a beautiful name. It suits you."

"Thank you." She actually found herself blushing a bit at his compliment.

For a moment they only gazed at each other.

"So Diablo is home for you," Crystal asked, breaking the moment of silence.

"Yes, my family owns the Half-Moon. It's a horse ranch about an hour's ride out of town."

"Interesting name for a ranch."

"The first night Pa spent on the property, there was a half moon."

"I've met your father, but what's the rest of your family like?" she asked, curious about his life. "Do you like ranching?"

Brent told her about his two brothers and his sister, and then confided his plan to make sure the Half-Moon had the best stock in the area. He explained, too, how they rounded up the herds of wild mustangs, broke them, and then sold them.

"We raise some thoroughbreds, too," he went on. "Both Pa and my youngest brother, Matt, like racing. Matt's off in England right now, trying to buy another stallion to improve our bloodlines. I told him to save his money, that we make a better profit off mustanging, but he was determined to go. Matt's the kind that once he decides to do something . . ." He stopped.

"You didn't approve of his going?" She sensed the undercurrent behind his words.

"It's not for me to approve or disapprove what Matt does. He's a full-grown man. He can do whatever he wants. But I've got a ranch to run."

"You run the Half-Moon? What about your father?" Crystal was puzzled by the change in his tone.

Brent looked up at her cautiously. "What about him?"

"You said it was your family's ranch. Doesn't your father run it?"

He paused a minute, contemplating whether to tell her the truth or not. When he realized she would soon hear the gossip around town about his pa, he decided it was best she learn the whole truth from him. He hadn't spoken of it often; it was hard for him even after all this time. "I've been in charge of the Half-Moon for about ten years now."

She was surprised. "You must have been very young when you took over."

"I was old enough. I was twenty."

"Where was your father?"

"Away. He only got back here a few weeks ago."

"Where was he?"

Brent had known the question was coming. He answered her straightforwardly. "Prison."

Crystal was shocked by the news. "But your pa seems like such a nice man. What did he do?"

Brent looked up at her again. No matter how much time passed, the memory of the tragedy still hurt.

"He shot my mother." Brent went on to tell her all that had happened.

Crystal listened to his tragic tale. It was difficult for her to imagine that the man she'd spoken with earlier that night would shoot anyone, let alone his own wife. She couldn't stop herself from reaching out to touch Brent's hand where it rested on the table.

"That must have been a horrible time for you, and then you were left to take care of everything and everyone."

"Yes," he answered.

"But you did it," she said.

"The last ten years haven't been easy, but the Half-Moon is doing fine now."

"You should be proud of yourself, Brent. Not every man would respond to such difficult circumstances the way you did." She thought of her own brother.

"It was for my family. I had to take charge." He was deeply touched by her words.

Crystal couldn't help comparing Brent to Dan. Brent had been forced into a terrible situation, yet he had done the right thing. He had worked hard and had saved his family and their ranch. Dan, on the other hand, had never done an honest day's work in his life. He had always taken the easy way out. He had used her to help him with his gambling and then forsaken her at the very time he should have been protecting her.

When the terrible memory of that night and her reason for running away threatened to return full-force, she quickly put it from her. She wouldn't think about that. Not now.

"It hasn't been easy having Pa around again. Even though he served his time, it doesn't change the fact that he killed her," Brent said. "He almost got in a fight with some of his old friends over at the social tonight."

"Is that why he came in here and started drinking?"

"Drinking is nothing new for Pa. He always drank. I was hoping the years in prison had dried him out, but when he got home he started looking around the house for liquor again," he said bitterly, then decided he'd been morbid enough for one night. He managed to smile at her. "Thanks for listening. I don't talk about any of this very often."

"Sometimes it helps to get things out. You have to let yourself relax a little."

He gave a short, harsh laugh. "Relax? I can't tell you the last time I had the chance to take it easy."

"About ten years ago, maybe?" she teased.

"That's about right." He chuckled.

"What do you do for fun?"

"Fun? I don't know what fun is anymore." He looked over at her. "What about you? What do you do for fun?"

Crystal admitted, "I don't have time for fun, either. I enjoy my job, but I never really have any time off— any time for myself."

"How did you come to be singing in saloons?"

"I'd love to sing in a church choir. It might guarantee me a place in heaven, but it wouldn't pay my bills here on earth," she said, smiling derisively.

"What about your family? Can't they help you?"

"I don't have any family," she said, denying her brother's very existence. As far as she was concerned, Dan was no relation of hers anymore. "You're really blessed that way."

There were times when Brent had his doubts about his family being a blessing, but he didn't say so.

"My parents died some years back, and I had to learn how to support myself."

"I'm glad you were working at the Six Gun," he said honestly, remembering their first encounter.

For a moment their gazes met across the table.

Then the sound of the piano player starting up her introductory tune shattered the intimacy.

"I have to go—it's almost time for my last performance." Crystal tore herself away from Brent.

"I'll be watching," he promised.

She gave him a quick smile as she hurried backstage.

Brent settled in to enjoy her performance. Crystal was wonderful. He was mesmerized by her talent and vivacity, and was struck once more by what an extraordinary woman she was.

When she finished singing, he was in no hurry to leave the saloon. He remained at his table, watching her make the rounds of the room, flirting easily with all the men. He was amazed by her ability to charm the cowboys without blatantly arousing them like the regular dance-hall girls did. The fact that she was a lady showed through.

Crystal was very aware that Brent had stayed on, and she was delighted. She wanted to spend more time with him.

When she saw one of the saloon girls approach Brent, she actually felt the sting of jealousy. And when Brent quickly sent the girl on her way, Crystal's smile brightened even more. As the evening wound down, she made her way back to rejoin him.

"You're still here." There was a questioning note in her voice.

"I was wondering if you'd like me to walk you home tonight?"

"That would be wonderful," she answered quickly. "Just give me a few minutes to change."

"Are you going out through the back door?"

"It's best that way."

"I'll meet you there."

Crystal couldn't remember ever being so excited about seeing anyone before. Outwardly she appeared calm as she made her way to her dressing room, but as soon as the door was closed, she rushed to strip off her red satin gown and don her sedate street clothes. She didn't want to make Brent wait too long. Once she'd finished changing, she let herself out the saloon's back door to find Brent standing patiently outside.

"I hope I didn't take too long," she said apologetically.

"You're worth the wait."

"Why, thank you, sir." She grinned at him.

"I'm just speaking the truth, ma'am." He chuckled. "Where are you staying?"

She told him the address of the boardinghouse, and they started off in that direction.

The streets of Diablo were dark and deserted, and that was fine with Brent. He wanted to enjoy the pleasure of Crystal's company without worrying about interruptions. He was completely aware of her beside him as they made their way to the boardinghouse.

"Do you come into town often?" she asked, wondering when she might see him again.

"No, but now that you're here, I'll make a special effort."

She smiled and glanced up at him. "Oh—look at the moon," she said in a quietly awed voice.

Brent looked up. The night sky was clear and star-studded, and there high above them was a silvery half moon.

"It's beautiful," Crystal told him. "I can see why your father chose that name for the ranch."

"You'll have to come for a visit. We'll be riding out late in the morning. Would you like to go with us?"

"Tomorrow?"

"Yes. You don't work on Sunday, do you?"

"No. I'd love to go."

"Good. We'll plan on it, then. I'll come for you around noon."

They reached the boardinghouse, and Brent escorted Crystal up the porch steps. A low-burning lamp in the sitting room window cast the only light on the porch.

Crystal looked up at Brent as they stopped before the front door, her eyes aglow with the pleasure of seeing him again. He was every bit as wonderful as she'd remembered him to be.

"Thank you for bringing me home."

"My pleasure," he assured her, "but I didn't get to play the hero for you tonight."

She gave him a shy smile. "In my book, once a hero, always a hero."

Unable to resist the temptation, Crystal rose up on tiptoe and pressed her lips to his.

Brent responded immediately. He needed no further invitation to deepen the kiss. He took her in his arms and held her close as his mouth moved hungrily over hers.

Excitement coursed through Crystal. Instinctively she linked her arms around his neck and moved even closer to him. It felt so right to be kissing him and holding him.

It took a serious effort, but Brent managed to end the embrace and set her from him.

"I'd better go. I'll see you tomorrow," he said gruffly, and moved away.

Crystal had been caught up in the pleasure of his kiss. She looked up at him in confusion. She didn't understand why he was leaving so quickly. "Brent . . ."

"I'm being your hero again," he said, smiling gently. "Good night, Crystal." Brent leaned toward her and gave her one more quick, gentle kiss. He didn't trust himself to do more than that. "Sweet dreams."

With that he left her, disappearing into the night.

Crystal stood on the porch a moment longer, then turned and let herself into the house. She went to her room and got ready for bed. As she lay beneath the covers, the memory of Brent's passionate embrace stayed with her. She knew her dreams would be sweet indeed.

Brent took extra care to be quiet as he entered the hotel room and bedded down for the night. He didn't want to wake his father. He just wanted to enjoy the peace of the moment. He lay quietly staring up at the ceiling, thinking about all that had happened.

Opal . . . Ruby . . . Crystal . . .

Brent smiled into the night.

Whatever name she went by, Brent found her delightful. He didn't know how he'd been lucky enough to meet up with her again, but he was glad he had. Crystal was every bit as beautiful as he'd remembered, and her kiss . . . There had been an innocent sweetness about it, mixed with undeniable passion. He smiled into the darkness at the memory of holding her in his arms.

As he went over the evening just past in his mind, Melinda slipped into his thoughts. Holding her in his arms had been nice enough, but nothing like the excitement of Crystal's embrace.

Crystal . . .

Brent had been drawn to her in some elemental way from the first moment they'd seen each other. She was every man's fantasy, and she was proving to be his, too.

Brent was looking forward to spending the day with her tomorrow. He hoped morning came quickly.

Chapter Twelve

It was almost time for the morning service to begin, and the First Street Church was crowded.

Brent followed Abby and their father down the aisle. Because they were attending church, Abby was wearing a dress this morning. Brent thought she looked pretty, but he realized for the first time that the dress was a little snug on her. They would have to see about buying her some new clothes soon, now that they could afford them.

Brent saw Edmund and Iona sitting in the very front, but there were no seats available near them. Abby stopped at the first row they could find that had enough space for all three of them.

Brent was aware of the sidelong glances that were cast their way, but he ignored them. There was nothing he could do to change things. He just had to deal with everything the best he could.

As Brent took his seat, Melinda caught his eye. She was sitting across the aisle from them, with her mother and father. She gave him a brilliant smile. Brent managed a quick nod of acknowledgment in her direction, but respectfully turned his attention toward the front of the church to await the minister's entrance. He hadn't expected to see Melinda this morning and really didn't want to spend any time with her. There was only one woman he wanted to be with, and that was Crystal.

"I hope Reverend Crawford isn't too long-winded," Jack muttered to Brent. His head was pounding viciously from all his drinking the night before. He wanted nothing more than to get away from town and back to the Half-Moon.

Neither Brent nor Abby said anything in response, but each privately agreed with him. Abby wanted to change clothes and go home, and Brent was eager for the services to be over so he could see Crystal.

It grew quiet as the organist began to play a soft melody that signaled the beginning of the service.

"We'd better hurry, Ruby," said Anne Pals, the owner of the boardinghouse, as they came up the street, heading toward the church. "The music's already started."

Crystal quickened her pace to keep up. Anne had invited her to go along to the service this morning, and she had gladly accepted. Crystal glanced at the church, and she was impressed by the white wooden structure with its tall steeple. She followed Anne up the few steps that led to the double front doors.

As Crystal entered the church, a sense of peace filled her. Though the interior was starkly decorated, she found beauty in its simplicity. The walls were painted pristine white. Simple wooden benches provided seating for the worshipers. In front, off to the side, was the organ, and centered before the main aisle was the podium from which the minister would give his sermon, trying to save the souls entrusted to him. Crystal didn't envy the man his job. It had to be a most difficult calling.

It had been a long time since Crystal had attended church services, and she needed to pray. She realized some in the congregation might not approve of her being there, but she tried not to let that knowledge bother her. She had come to offer up her thanks to the Lord. It didn't matter what other people thought of her. It only mattered what God thought.

Anne led the way down the aisle, looking for a place where they could sit. Crystal followed. The older woman found two seats for them on a bench close to the front. Crystal gave Anne a warm smile as she settled in beside her. The peaceful atmosphere, coupled with the organ music, filled her with a quiet sense of serenity.

*   *   *

Brent sat silently, thinking about the day to come. He didn't pay a lot of attention to what was going on around him, until he caught sight of Crystal as she walked by on her way down the aisle with Anne Pals. A jolt of awareness shot through Brent as he watched Crystal take a seat just three rows ahead of him. She appeared every bit the lady this morning in her day gown, with her hair pinned back in a sedate bun. He let his gaze trace over her, studying the graceful line of her neck and the soft curve of her shoulders as she sat with her back to him.

"Is that Ruby?" Jack whispered to him, surprised to see the singer there.

"Yes."

They both fell silent and turned their attention to the front as the music stopped.

Reverend Crawford appeared before the congregation. The minister walked slowly to the pulpit. He had a reputation as a fire-and-brimstone preacher, and Brent wondered what the topic of his sermon would be today.

He found out quickly.

"Judge not, lest ye be judged!" the reverend roared, wanting to make sure everyone was awake and paying attention. He waited a moment in silence as he let his sharp-eyed gaze sweep over the congregation. He went on, "Who here has led a perfect life? Who here has never sinned? Stand up! I want to see you now!"

A low murmur went through the crowd, but no one dared to rise.

"You're still sitting," he said. "Are you telling me you're sinners?"

"Amen, Reverend," a man called out from the back.

Others echoed his sentiment.

Reverend Crawford smiled, and the smile transformed him. He no longer appeared cold and condemning. He was now warm and welcoming.

"So you have sinned. . . ."

"Amen, Reverend."

There was a long, quiet pause. Then he spoke again.

"You are forgiven," he said softly as he looked out over the congregation. "Jesus died for our sins, so that we might live. Think about the power of his love. How many of us would willingly sacrifice ourselves for another? How many of us love so deeply and so profoundly? Love is God's greatest gift to us. Always remember His words—'Love one another as I have loved you.' "

Melinda listened to the preacher's words and smiled to herself as she took a quick look in Brent's direction. He was sitting there looking so handsome that her heartbeat quickened.

She wanted to "love one another," all right. She wanted to love Brent.

Melinda wished the minister would hurry up and

end his sermon, so she could go practice what he'd been preaching.

Jack listened to the sermon, but doubted the truth of Reverend Crawford's words. Had his sins been forgiven? Considering how he'd been treated at the social the night before, he didn't think his "friends" in town had forgiven him. He scowled, thinking of the night before and trying to remember all that had happened. He remembered leaving the dance and drinking at the Lone Star, but not much else. The pain of his hangover pounded at him. He closed his eyes for a moment, wishing that the sermon were over so he could leave.

Crystal was deeply moved by the minister's profound remarks. She needed to believe that she could be forgiven for what she'd done. She had only been defending herself, but even so, she had taken a man's life. . . .

She suppressed a shudder and tried to forget that fateful night. She was in Diablo now, starting her life anew. There were many things to be thankful for—and having the opportunity to spend the rest of the day with Brent was one of them. Crystal wasn't going to let anything ruin these next hours. It had been so long since she'd had the chance to just relax and try to enjoy herself, she wondered if she even knew how anymore.

Reverend Crawford spoke a little longer, then dismissed the congregation with a blessing and the admonition to love as Jesus had loved.

Everyone filed from the church, greeting one another and making smalltalk.

"I thought we'd never get out of there," Jack complained as they started down the steps. "Let's go."

"No, not yet. There's someone I have to speak with first." Brent moved off to the side.

"Who? Melinda?" Jack asked.

Abby offered up a silent prayerful plea that it wasn't Melinda.

"No, Ruby." He used her working name to avoid confusion. He planned to tell his father her real name later.

"You want to talk to Ruby? Why?"

"Who's Ruby?" Abby interrupted.

"She's a friend," Brent answered. "I met her in San Antonio and then found out last night that she's working here in Diablo now. I invited her out to the ranch today for a visit."

Abby was astonished. Brent had never done anything like that before.

"When did you do that?" Jack asked. He didn't remember Brent having any conversation with Ruby about making a trip to the Half-Moon.

"After I put you to bed at the hotel, I went back to the Lone Star to see her."

Abby was staring at her brother as if he'd lost his mind. "And you're going to bring her to our home?"

"That's right."

"A woman who works at a place like the Lone

Star?" Abby was shocked. It wasn't like Brent to bring any woman home, and especially not one who worked in a saloon.

"It's not what you think," Brent admonished, seeing her reaction. "Ruby is a singer—that's all."

"And she's here at church? Where is she? I want to meet her." Abby was suddenly curious about this woman who so intrigued her brother. This Ruby couldn't be respectable, but then again, if Brent cared about her . . .

"You're just about to meet her. She should be coming out any minute now," Brent said, watching the folks leaving the church.

"You tell Ruby I'll see her in a little while. Right now I'm going on back to the hotel to get packed up so we can leave," Jack told them, eager to get away. The townsfolk he had known for years were walking past him without speaking to him, or even acknowledging him.

"We'll meet you back there."

Brent waited with Abby off to the side of the church entrance for Crystal to come out. Before Crystal could exit, though, Melinda appeared before them.

"I am so glad you had time to attend services this morning, Brent. I was hoping I'd get to see you again before you had to go back to the ranch," Melinda cooed, gazing up at him in open adoration and completely ignoring Abby. Even though the other girl had donned a dress this morning, Melinda wanted nothing to do with her. She was only after Brent. "I had a wonderful time with you at the dance last night."

"I'm glad." Brent peered past her, trying to catch sight of Crystal.

"Are you heading back home soon?" Melinda asked brazenly.

"Yes, it's time to go back to work." He gave her his attention for a moment, but then saw Crystal come out of the church. "Excuse me, Melinda."

Brent walked off without another word, leaving Abby to deal with Melinda.

"Where's he going?" Melinda asked, testy at being so easily dismissed.

"There's someone he wants me to meet," Abby said, as curious as Melinda was.

Melinda watched as Brent walked up to a pretty young woman with red hair.

"Who is that?" she asked Abby, annoyed.

"A friend of Brent's from San Antonio," Abby offered. She rose up on her tiptoes so she could see over the crowd and get a better look at the woman with Brent.

Melinda stiffened. Jealousy shot through her as she saw Brent greet the woman with warmth and familiarity. Melinda didn't know who the other woman was, but she planned to make it clear that Brent was hers.

* * *

"Brent!" Crystal was surprised to find him standing before her as she came down the church steps. "I didn't know you were here."

"We were sitting farther back than you were." He looked at her companion and smiled. "Good morning, Mrs. Pals."

"Morning, Brent," Anne replied. "So you two know each other, do you?"

"Yes, we're old friends," Brent answered her, and then turned back to Crystal. "My sister, Abby, is here. I'd like you to meet her, and then we can get ready to leave for the ranch."

"All right." She turned to Anne. "Thank you for inviting me to attend church with you. I'm going out to the Half-Moon for a visit, so I probably won't be back to town until later this evening."

"Have a good time," Anne said before going on her own way.

Brent escorted Crystal over to where Abby was waiting. He was irritated to see that Melinda was still standing there.

"I'll introduce you as Ruby for now, since Melinda is there."

"Who is Melinda?"

"Just a friend." They reached the two women, and Brent made the introductions. "Abby, this is Ruby. Ruby, my sister Abby."

"Hello," Abby said tentatively. She'd never met anyone who worked in a saloon before, and she found herself staring at the woman's red hair.

Though she was wearing it attractively styled, the color was too bright to be natural.

"And this is Melinda Barton," Brent added.

Melinda was seething that he was treating her so cavalierly—almost as an afterthought. She covered her fury with a polite smile. "Hello, Ruby."

"Melinda," she returned.

"You're new in town?" Melinda asked.

"Yes, and it's wonderful to see Brent again." Crystal gazed at him.

"You've met before?" she asked tersely.

"Oh, yes," she answered, but offered no details.

Melinda did not like the way the woman was looking at Brent. Brent was hers!

Abby sensed Melinda's mood and grew uncomfortable. They had already given the townsfolk enough to gossip about, with Papa being back. They didn't need any unpleasantness right there in front of the church.

"Brent, are you ready to go? We should leave now," Abby urged her brother.

"Leave?" Melinda butted in.

Abby handled her easily. "Ruby's going to spend the day with us at the ranch, so we need to get started back."

"I'm ready," Crystal told her.

"Good. Well, 'bye, Melinda," Abby said as she started to walk away.

Brent gave Melinda a quick, dismissive smile before following his sister and Crystal. "I'll see you later."

Melinda was glaring at Brent's back as she stood there, watching him leave. Outrage roiled within her at being so ignored. Melinda's jealousy was tinged with hurt, too. Brent had invited Ruby out to the ranch for the day, but he hadn't invited her.

Melinda didn't know who Ruby was or how she had come to know Brent, but she intended to find out.

"Where's your father?" Crystal asked. "Didn't he come to church with you?"

"Pa was here, but he went on back to the hotel right after the service. He'll be riding out with us," Brent explained.

"It'll be nice to see him again."

Since he had told her the truth about his father last night, Brent had expected her to react like everyone else in town did. Crystal had proven herself to be truly different.

"Abby?" Brent said. When his sister looked his way, he quickly explained, "Ruby's real name is Crystal."

"Crystal's a pretty name. Why do you use Ruby?"

"Because of working in the saloon. I thought it was better to have a stage name." Crystal told herself her answer wasn't really a lie, but she felt a twinge of conscience anyway. "Please call me Crystal."

"All right." Abby glanced at her brother. He seemed apprehensive about her reaction to this woman, and she realized it was important to him that she accept Crystal. She managed a small smile.

"Thanks."

Brent relaxed, glad that the two women seemed to be getting along.

"So how did you two meet?" Abby asked Crystal, still unsure of her opinion of her.

"I'll tell you all about it on the ride out to the ranch," she said with a grin.

Abby met Brent's gaze. "This should make the ride much more interesting."

Chapter Thirteen

They went to the hotel, and Crystal waited downstairs in the lobby while Abby and Brent went up to their rooms to get their belongings. Brent returned quickly with Jack.

"Good morning, Crystal," Jack greeted her with a big smile. Brent had already told him the truth about her name.

"Hello, Jack. It's good to see you again."

"Brent tells me that you're coming out to the Half-Moon for a visit today."

"He was kind enough to invite me," she answered, looking up at Brent with a smile.

"It's our pleasure, believe me," Jack said. "I hope you like our place."

"I'm sure I will," Crystal assured him.

"I'll go get Storm and the buckboard, Brent, and meet you out front," Jack told them.

"Where's Abby?" Crystal asked Brent once Jack had gone.

"She's changing clothes. She'll be along in a minute."

Brent paid the hotel bill, and Abby appeared by the time he was finished.

"I'm ready to go," Abby announced, coming down the steps carrying her bag.

Crystal's eyes widened in shock at the sight of her. "You're wearing pants!"

"Yeah, I only wear a dress to church," she answered, then changed the topic. "Where's Papa?"

"Outside waiting for us," Brent told her.

"Let's go." She was more than ready to go home.

Brent ushered them out of the lobby.

"Why don't you take Abby and Crystal in the buckboard?" Jack suggested to Brent. "And I'll ride Storm."

"Sure." Brent wasn't about to object. The thought of sitting next to Crystal all the way to the ranch definitely appealed to him. He helped the women up, then took the seat between them and grabbed the reins.

"We're on our way," he said, urging the team on. Jack rode alongside, keeping pace with them.

The miles passed quickly as Abby encouraged Crystal to tell them how she had met Brent in San Antonio. She was surprised to learn how her brother had saved the singer from being robbed that fateful night.

"It's wonderful that Brent showed up when he did," Abby said. "Were you hurt?"

"I was fine, except for a few bumps and bruises, but Brent was cut on his arm during the fight. I was worried that it was serious, but he said it was only a scratch."

Abby looked at her big brother and frowned. "You never told us you were hurt."

"It was nothing," he said, dismissing her concern. "I was just glad I was there to help Crystal."

"So was I," Crystal agreed. Then she asked, "How much longer until we reach the ranch?"

"You've been on Half-Moon land for the last twenty minutes," Brent told her, slanting her a grin.

It was a wicked, almost devilish smile, and it reminded her all too clearly of the heated kiss they'd shared the night before. She was suddenly very aware of him physically. Her heart skipped a beat. "Really? The Half-Moon must be a really big ranch."

"Not big enough," Jack said. "My dream has always been to make it the biggest and best horse ranch in Texas."

Brent knew all about his father's dreams of glory, but he said nothing. He didn't want to ruin a perfectly good day by starting an argument.

"It's good to have dreams, but you've already been blessed to have a home like this." She looked around the countryside. Live oaks grew in magnificent splendor, and the rolling hills were beautiful and lush.

"So what would you like to do when we get to the house, Crystal?" Brent asked.

"Anything you want," she answered easily, looking at Brent.

Her innocent answer sparked heat deep within Brent. The memory of her kiss the night before had kept him awake long into the night, and he was hoping to spend some time alone with her that day.

"Frances won't have dinner ready until five, so we'll have plenty of time to show you around," Brent told Crystal.

"I'm looking forward to it."

Abby remained quiet, wondering at their relationship as they talked.

When the main house, outbuildings, and corrals came within view, Crystal was even more impressed. The Half-Moon looked very prosperous.

Jack rode on to the stable, while Brent reined in before the house. Abby jumped down from the buckboard easily on her own; then Brent climbed down and turned to help Crystal descend.

"Crystal, let's go inside," Abby said.

Crystal looked at Brent to see what he planned to do.

He waved her on with Abby as he unloaded their bags and put them on the porch. "I'll take care of the horses and be back in a few minutes."

Abby grabbed her own bag and led the way into the house.

Frances heard them outside and was on her way out to help bring their things in from the porch when Abby and Crystal came inside. Abby quickly introduced them.

"If my brother's planning on showing you around the ranch, I think you'd better change into something a little more practical," Abby told her.

"But I didn't bring anything else to wear."

"Come with me." She started to usher her down the hallway toward the bedrooms.

"Abby—" Crystal stopped as she caught sight of the portrait hanging over the fireplace. There was no doubt about the family resemblance. "That's your mother?"

"Yes."

"She was lovely."

"I know," Abby answered; then she quickly changed the subject as she led the way down the hall. "There are some extra clothes in a trunk in Papa's bedroom. Why don't you wait in my room while I see if there's anything that'll fit you."

"Thanks." Crystal went into the bedroom Abby indicated to wait for her return.

Abby went into her father's room and opened the chest that had been her mother's. There wasn't a lot to choose from, but she did find her mother's split leather riding skirt. She hurried back to Crystal.

"Here," she said, handing her the skirt. "You can

wear this and one of my shirts. I've got a pair of boots that ought to fit you, too."

She quickly gave her the other things.

"I appreciate your help, Abby."

"You're welcome. I'll leave you here to change. Just come on out when you're ready."

"I will."

With that, Abby left her, closing the bedroom door behind her to give Crystal privacy.

Crystal grinned to herself as she quickly stripped off her day gown and shed her petticoats and slippers. She had been trapped for so long working in a saloon that it was a real adventure for her to don the riding wear. The skirt was not a bad fit, and the shirt was fine. The boots were a little tight, but Crystal figured that didn't matter, since they wouldn't be doing too much walking that afternoon.

Crystal went to stand before Abby's full-length mirror to study her own reflection. She was amazed at how different she looked. Any vestige of the sensual singer from the Lone Star was gone. In her place stood a true woman of the West.

For a moment she wished her hair were its natural blond color, but she pushed the thought away. She was Ruby now, and that was how she had to stay. Determined to put the ugliness of her own life out of her mind the rest of the day, Crystal left the room to find Abby.

"It looks like everything fits," Abby told her as they came face-to-face in the sitting room.

"I'd like to dress like this more often," Crystal agreed, "but I don't think the men in the Lone Star would appreciate the change."

Abby had always heard that only tarnished women worked in places like the Lone Star, but Crystal didn't seem tarnished.

"Let's go find Brent and see what he thinks."

They left the house and started down to the stable. Brent and Jack had just come out of the building when they saw Abby and Crystal approaching.

Brent's gaze skimmed approvingly over Crystal. "I see you got a change of clothes."

"Abby was kind enough to help."

"You look like you're ready to go to work." Jack said to her.

"Looks can be deceiving." Crystal laughed.

"Come on and take a look around the stable," Brent suggested.

They all went in, and Crystal admired the horses in the stalls there.

"These are three of our best thoroughbreds," Brent told her. "Moon Racer is Abby's stallion."

The stallion was a big roan with a blaze down his forehead. He was sleek and powerful, and she could see the intelligence in his eyes.

"He's gorgeous—if a horse can be gorgeous," she corrected herself.

"You're right, Crystal, he is," Abby agreed. "Brent traded for him a few years ago for me. He is one of Half-Moon's best, for sure."

"I can see why, but I thought you said you worked with mustangs, too?" She looked over at Brent. "What's the difference between a mustang and a thoroughbred? I know mustangs run wild, but they're all just horses, right?"

"Just horses?" Jack gave a snort of disgust. "Don't insult Moon Racer. Thoroughbreds are refined stock. They're long-legged, they're graceful, they're elegant, *and* they're fast. That's why I started this ranch. I wanted the Half-Moon to be known for its racing stock."

"Mustangs aren't fast?"

"Mustangs aren't—" Jack began, ready to tell her what he thought of the wild stock that roamed the Texas land.

But Brent interrupted him before he could go on with his tirade. "Mustangs may not be the most beautiful horses in the world, but they serve their purpose. They're smaller than thoroughbreds, but they're strong. They've got better stamina and endurance, and they're smart."

"Could you race a mustang against a thoroughbred?" Crystal asked.

"Why would you want to?" Jack said disparagingly.

"You could," Brent answered her with a grin, knowing she was just trying to understand the differences between the horses, "but the mustang probably wouldn't win—not unless it was a long race."

"There are some mustangs in the corral out back," Abby told her. "Just take a look at them, and you'll see."

They went outside to show her the mustangs so she would be able to understand the difference.

Crystal studied the smaller, more sturdily built horses and couldn't help admiring them. They didn't have the finest of bloodlines, but from what she was coming to understand about them, they were survivors. She found herself identifying with mustangs. She saw a palomino grazing among them.

"The palomino is pretty."

"That's Honey. Do you want to ride her?" Brent offered.

"I'm not the best rider," she admitted.

"That's all right. Honey's gentle. You'll be able to handle her," Brent assured her.

"Her name suits her."

"She can be yours whenever you come out to the ranch," he told her.

Brent went to get the mare, and Abby went along with him. Brent cast his sister a quick look.

"Don't you have some chores you have to take care of?"

"I do need to help Curly groom some horses this afternoon."

"Good."

Abby had never known Brent to be so interested in a woman before. He'd rarely had time for fun, and if Crystal could make him forget about work for a while, that was fine with her.

Abby helped Brent with the horses, and they led the mounts to where Crystal was waiting with their father.

"We'll just take a short ride today, so you can get used to being in the saddle again," Brent said, handing Crystal the reins to the palomino. "Do you need any help?"

"We'll be fine," Crystal said as she stroked the mare's neck. "Won't we, Honey?"

The mare was calm, just as Brent had said she would be, and Crystal took heart. She swung up into the saddle without any difficulty.

"You look like you were born to the saddle," Jack complimented her.

"Thank you, sir."

Brent mounted up, too, and they rode off at a leisurely pace, away from the house.

"We'll be back," Brent called to them.

"Why didn't you ride along with them?" Jack asked Abby.

"I've got some chores to do," Abby answered casually, casting one last quick look toward her brother and Crystal as they rode off. She was impressed by the way Crystal was handling the horse. The singer didn't seem as unschooled as she'd said.

Jack watched them ride off, too. Crystal had been the only good thing to come from his trip to Diablo.

Well, he amended, Crystal and the bottle of whiskey he'd hidden in his bag on the trip back.

Seeing that Abby was going stay at the stable, he started back up to the house. He needed to be alone for a while. His thoughts lingered on their time in town, on the social, and, worse, on how he'd been treated at church that morning. Those he'd once considered friends had shunned him even after the minister's sermon on loving one another. He'd expected it, but it still troubled him. Edmund was the only friend he had left, and Jack knew he was lucky to have him.

Feeling the need for a drink, Jack went up to his room when he reached the house, and got his whiskey. He didn't bother with a glass, but opened the bottle and took a drink. His thoughts were troubled, and he felt very alone.

Jack was glad Frances wasn't around as he walked through the house. She was a stranger to him. She couldn't understand what he was going through. No one could.

Memories of better times haunted him—times of loving and being loved. He stopped before the portrait of Beth and stood there staring up at her. She had been a beautiful woman and a wonderful mother. Even now his heart ached. He took another deep swallow of the potent liquor as tears burned his eyes.

He had loved her. Oh, how he had loved her.

Beth had been his whole world. Everything he'd ever done in his life had been for her.

"I'm sorry, Beth. So sorry," he whispered.

He sank down in a chair nearby and continued to drink as he gazed up at her image.

Chapter Fourteen

The sky was blue and cloudless. The sun was warm. Horses grazed in the pasture before them. In the distance a small cabin was nestled among a grove of trees, and a tree-bordered creek wound its way across the land.

"I'm glad you brought me here. I think this is as close to heaven as you can get," Crystal said to Brent with a sigh.

"It is peaceful here," he agreed. This was his favorite place on the ranch. He came whenever things got tough and he needed time alone to think.

"Who lives in the cabin?"

"Nobody right now. We use it whenever we're up this way, working a herd," Brent explained. "Do you want to ride down to the creek? Or are you ready to head back?"

They'd been gone from the house for almost an hour, and he wanted to make sure she wasn't getting too tired. Crystal had proven to be a better rider than she'd thought. She was having no trouble handling the mare.

"Let's go down to the creek," she answered, not ready to give up her time alone with Brent just yet. Then, suddenly feeling almost wild and carefree, she dared him, "And you know what? I don't care what anyone says about mustangs and thoroughbreds; I know Honey can take Storm any day! Let's race!"

Without waiting for a response from Brent, she urged the mare to a gallop and raced off.

Brent was caught off guard by her unexpected challenge, but he was up to the dare. He was laughing as he gave chase.

Crystal reached the creek first and reined Honey in triumphantly. "I won!"

"You cheated!" Brent declared when he reached her side.

"You and Storm are no match for us," she bragged, stroking the mare's neck. She dismounted and led the mare down to the water's edge for a drink.

Brent had deliberately held Storm back to let her win, but he wasn't about to tell her that. He let her enjoy her glory as he, too, dismounted. He walked Storm down to join her.

"There's a prize for the winner, you know," he told her.

Crystal was very aware of his lean, powerful presence beside her. She turned and lifted her gaze to his. "What kind of prize? Do you have a trophy for me? Or a big purse?"

"No, your prize is even better than that."

"It is?" she asked, delighting in his teasing.

"That's right. Your prize is a kiss."

"Oh. That is more valuable," she agreed breathlessly.

Brent took Crystal in his arms and bestowed her prize upon her, claiming her lips in a hungry caress.

She needed no urging to surrender to his embrace. She met him in the exchange, eager to be close to him, thrilling in his nearness. When she was with Brent she felt safe—and she was happy.

When he ended the kiss and stepped back, Crystal smiled up at him, her eyes twinkling with delight.

"Do you want to race again? I like the prize for winning."

"So do I." Brent laughed and drew her back into his arms. He couldn't remember the last time he'd laughed so much or felt so lighthearted. When he was with Crystal he was relaxed and at ease. Brent kissed her again, cherishing the moment.

Only the horses' stirring forced them regretfully apart. They were discovering heaven in each other's arms. Brent went to tie the horses' reins to a nearby low-hanging branch.

"Let's go look around the cabin," Crystal said, intrigued.

She led the way, and Brent followed her. The cabin was run-down. It hadn't been used in a while and was definitely in need of some repairs. She stepped carefully onto the porch, completely avoiding the broken steps, then opened the door.

"What do you think?" Brent asked as she went in.

Crystal took a quick look around the two small, sparsely furnished rooms and came back outside to where he was standing on the porch.

"I love it. The view is wonderful," she told him as she stood at his side and gazed out across the countryside.

"I love it here, too. One of these days, if I can figure out how to do it and still run things, I'd like to live up here."

"How far are we from the main house?"

"It's about a twenty-minute ride."

"That's not too bad. I can understand why you like it here." She looked down at the stream flowing by. An idea came to her as she watched the sparkling waters. "Come on. Let's go down to the creek."

Crystal led the way, and when she reached the creek she walked along the bank. Brent was slow to follow her down, for he was just enjoying watching her. He was surprised when she sat down on the bank and began to take off her boots and socks.

"What are you doing?"

"I thought it would be fun to go wading."

"Wading? Fun?"

"When was the last time you went wading?" she challenged him.

"I don't know—it's been years. I don't have time for playing in creeks."

"Today you do. Come on." Crystal stood up and walked daintily to the water's edge.

Brent stayed right where he was, watching her make her way. He found his gaze drawn admiringly to her shapely legs as she hiked up the riding skirt a little and stepped into the water.

"Oooh, that's cold!" She shivered as the flowing stream circled around her.

"Be careful; it might be slippery in there," he advised as she began to tiptoe around, exploring.

Crystal looked up at Brent, standing tall and proud on the bank before her. He looked like the man who ran this ranch—the boss. His arms were folded over his chest in a pose of authority, and his expression was serious, commanding and critical. She realized he was an intimidating man—but he didn't intimidate her.

Crystal smiled wickedly to herself and decided right then and there that she wanted to see Brent smile again. He was far too stern for his own good, and she was going to change that.

"How would you know it's slippery if you haven't been in here in years? Why don't you come in with me?"

"That's all right."

She'd known before she'd asked that he would refuse her invitation, and his refusal played right into her scheme.

"What are you afraid of, Brent Hunter?" she taunted. "Are you afraid to get wet?"

Unable to resist the temptation to break through his controlled demeanor, Crystal quickly bent down and, before he could react, splashed water at him with all the force she could muster. Her aim was excellent.

"Why, you . . . !" Brent was shocked—and soaked—by her unprovoked attack.

The change in his expression was so quick and so complete that Crystal started laughing out loud. Her glee was only momentary, though, for his shocked look quickly turned to one of fierce determination.

"So that's the way you like to play," Brent said ominously. He wasn't worried about getting any wetter. She'd already soaked him thoroughly. Revenge was all that was on his mind. He smiled a devilish smile and went after her.

Crystal had wanted to see him smile again, but she hadn't intended for it to be the one that was on his face now. She started giggling and let out a squeal of sudden fear as she tried to flee upstream from his coming assault.

She managed to elude Brent for a moment, but she discovered that he'd been right all along—the creekbed was slippery. A startled shriek escaped her as she lost her balance and started to tumble backward.

In an instant Brent was there to save her. He lifted her up in strong arms and kept her from being drenched. He held her childlike against his chest as he carried her out of the creek.

"You've rescued me again," Crystal said breathlessly.

"That seems to be my fate lately," he acknowledged with a half grin.

"You are always there when I need you most."

Once they were on solid ground, Brent stopped and gazed down at her. Gone were all thoughts of revenge for the soaking she'd given him. The only thing that mattered to him now was holding her close and kissing her again.

"Do you need me now?" he asked quietly.

"Oh, yes." Her answer was a passionate whisper.

His mouth found hers in a rapturous exchange that left them both breathless. Lowering her to the bank, he stretched out beside her on the lush grass. They lay in the sun-dappled shade, aware only of each other and the glory of each kiss they shared.

Crystal reached out to Brent, wanting him even closer. She touched his wet shirt and couldn't help giving a throaty giggle.

Brent drew back to look down at her, a smile curving his lips. "So you think playing in the water is fun, do you? I can take you back in the creek right now if you want to go."

"I think I like playing with you here on the bank better," she purred.

Crystal pulled him down to her and kissed him. She wanted him close to her. She *needed* him close to her. She had never been so intimate with a man before. Since her parents had died, she had been under Dan's control. She had never had any serious suitors—he wouldn't allow it.

But now there was Brent. She had never felt so close to anyone, and his kiss was proving to be heaven.

The invitation in Crystal's embrace stirred the fire of Brent's desire for her. He sought the sweet curve of her breast in a gentle caress. Crystal shivered at the intimacy of his touch and instinctively arched against him in an unspoken offering. His lips left hers to trace a path of excitement down the side of her neck. Pleasure radiated through her. When he parted her blouse and pressed heated kisses to the tops of her breasts, she gasped in delight.

Brent wanted Crystal more than he'd ever wanted any woman. She was beautiful and loving, and they were there alone.

He was tempted to take her right then and there, to lose himself in the glory of her lovemaking. He sensed no resistance in her, but he forced himself to stop.

He had to move away from the temptation that she was to him. He left her to sit a short distance away. He didn't trust himself any closer to her.

"Brent?" Crystal was surprised and disappointed that he'd stopped kissing her. "Is something wrong?"

"No, sweetheart, nothing's wrong."

Brent couldn't look her way. He took pride in being a man in control, but Crystal had tested him to his limit. He wasn't sure he'd be able to deny himself again if he did dare look at her. Brent decided to watch the stream flow by instead, and he realized he just might need to go wade in the water after all. It was cold, and he certainly needed to cool off a bit.

Crystal felt humiliated. She realized she'd all but thrown herself at Brent, and he'd rejected her. She quickly refastened her blouse as she sat up. He had his back to her, and she was glad that he couldn't see her shame.

She'd never acted so brazenly before. She'd never wanted any man the way she wanted Brent—his touch had been ecstasy.

She'd never cared so deeply for a man before— even now she wanted to go to him and wrap her arms around him and hold him to her heart.

Crystal froze as the knowledge came to her: She loved Brent.

The truth frightened her even as it thrilled her.

Crystal told herself she barely knew Brent. In her heart, though, it seemed she had known him forever. She had been drawn to him from the first moment she'd seen him at the Six Gun Saloon, but it seemed sadly obvious to her, as he sat there ignoring her, that he didn't share that tender emotion.

"Are you ready to go back?" she asked a bit stiffly as she got to her feet.

Brent was surprised by the coldness of her tone. He turned to see how uncomfortable she suddenly seemed, and he rose to go to her. He thought she was upset with him for being so forward with her, and he intended to apologize.

"Crystal, I'm sorry. I shouldn't have taken such liberties with you. I should have had Abby ride with us."

Suddenly Crystal realized what Brent was really saying—he had stopped kissing her not because he didn't want her, but because he did. She smiled.

"But if your sister had come along as our chaperon, I wouldn't have gotten to kiss you."

She reached out and rested a hand against his chest as he stood before her. That simple contact sent a jolt of sensual awareness through Brent.

"Don't tempt me, woman," he said in a growl.

"But I like tempting you," she teased.

"You do a fine job of it." Brent held her close and kissed her once more, this time with restrained tenderness.

She wanted to tell him of her love, but held back.

"We'd really better be getting back to the house," he said reluctantly.

They shared one last, sweet kiss before finally

moving apart. He brought her boots and socks to her.

"Are you sure you don't want to go wading in the creek again?" Crystal asked with a mischievous grin before she started to put them back on. "This is our last chance."

"I think I'm wet enough." His clothes were still damp from their earlier adventure. "I hope I dry off on the ride back."

He went to get their horses. Then they mounted up and started to ride away.

Crystal's gaze lingered on the cabin one last time. "It is a shame you can't live here."

"I know. I've had to stay at the main house to run things, and to take care of Abby."

"And you've done a wonderful job. I like your sister, and the more I see of the Half-Moon, the more impressed I am with what you've accomplished."

"Thanks." Her praise meant a lot to Brent. It was a rare day when anyone paid him a compliment.

It was almost time for dinner, and Abby had been watching for Brent and Crystal to return. She went out to greet them when she saw them riding in.

"It's about time you got back," she said. "Did you have a good time?" She eyed them speculatively, wondering why her brother's clothes looked slightly damp.

"Oh, yes," Crystal answered first, "it was great riding such a wonderful horse."

"Honey?" Abby had never thought of the mustang as anything special.

"Yes. She's not only pretty—she's fast, too. Honey and I beat Brent and Storm in a race down by the creek."

"You let her beat you?" Abby looked at Brent in shock.

"She cheated," he said defensively, knowing his little sister would use the news against him.

"No, you lost." Abby fought down a grin at the thought. "Come on inside. Frances has dinner just about ready to go on the table."

"Go on in," Brent told Crystal. "I'll see to the horses."

She dismounted and followed Abby inside.

"Abby, I think I'd better change before dinner, and I do have to apologize for something."

Abby looked her way.

Crystal went on. "When Brent and I were down at the creek, I got wet."

"And so did Brent, from the looks of things," Abby remarked with good humor.

"Well, I did splash him," she confessed with a grin.

"And you're still alive to talk about it?" Abby was amazed. She tried to picture the scene in her mind. "I wish I'd been there to see it. How did my big brother react?"

"The look on his face was priceless," Crystal told her, still smiling. "But he wasn't about to let me get away with it!"

"I understand. You don't mess with Brent Hunter."

"So I found out."

"Go on back in my room to change. All your things are still there."

"Thanks."

"And Crystal?" Abby found herself wanting to make her feel welcome.

Crystal looked up.

"Why don't you take these riding clothes with you so you'll be ready for another visit?"

Crystal liked the sound of that. *Another visit.* She wanted to spend as much time with Brent as she could.

Chapter Fifteen

A short time later Abby, Crystal, and Brent were gathered around the dining room table. Brent had taken the time to clean up and change clothes, and they were now ready for dinner.

"It's not over between us yet." Brent's tone held a mock threat as he looked at Crystal across the table. Their gazes met and locked. Tension flared between them.

"I know," Crystal said, her heartbeat quickening in response.

"Do I get to watch the next time?" Abby asked. "Providing, of course, that there is a next time."

"Oh, there will be a next time, all right," Brent said firmly.

"That's right," Crystal said with confidence. "And Honey and I will be ready for you. You just name the time and place for the race, and we'll be there."

"What race?"

Jack's question interrupted their conversation as he came into the room.

"Papa. We were wondering where you were," Abby said, surprised to see him.

"I had things to take care of." He deliberately didn't tell them what he'd been doing. It was none of their business. He went to sit with them at the table.

Brent knew immediately by the way he was acting what his father had been doing—he'd been drinking. Brent shared a knowing look with Abby, but said nothing. He didn't want to start an argument in front of Crystal. It enraged Brent to realize that his father must have brought back a bottle of liquor from town and kept it hidden among his things.

"Now, what's all this talk about a race?" Jack repeated as he dished himself up a plate of food.

Crystal proudly told him the story of her triumph over Brent.

Jack looked at his son, his expression condemning. "You lost a race to a mustang and you can still show your face at this table?"

Brent ignored his insult. He turned their conversation into a compliment for Crystal. "Crystal had me fooled. She turned out to be a better horsewoman than she said she was. With practice, one of these days she might be able to keep up with Abby."

"You'll have to come visit us real regular, Crystal, so you can get your riding in," Jack invited.

"I'd like that."

Brent was glad when Crystal finally finished eating, so they could leave. The less time he spent with his father in his present condition, the better. He had the buckboard brought up to the house for the trip back to town.

Abby and Jack walked Crystal outside. Crystal thanked them and said good-bye. Brent helped her into the buckboard, then climbed up next to her and took up the reins.

"I'll be back," he told them.

Crystal waved as they drove off. She knew each passing mile brought her closer to the time when she and Brent would have to part.

"Will you be back in town soon?" Crystal asked.

"I'll try to get in to see you as often as I can," he promised.

"Good." She knew she would be counting the days.

They reached Diablo far too quickly to suit Crystal.

"I had a wonderful time, Brent. Thank you for inviting me," she said when he reined in before the boardinghouse.

"I did, too."

So much had happened that day, he could hardly

believe it had just been that morning that they'd attended church.

"Would you like to come in for a minute?"

"Sure." He wasn't ready to say good-bye to her yet, and he did want to see her safely inside.

Brent followed Crystal indoors after tying up the team.

"Anne?" Crystal called out as she walked into the parlor. She saw a note on the table by the sofa and went to read it.

Crystal

I have a meeting tonight for the Ladies' Solidarity and will be gone until about ten. Hope you had fun today.

Anne

"Is she here?" Brent asked, coming up behind her.

"No. She's at a meeting." Crystal turned and looked up at him. She'd been hoping for the chance to kiss him before he had to leave.

"We're—"

"Alone," she provided with a soft, alluring smile. She was the only boarder in the house just then.

"Good." Brent needed no further invitation to gather Crystal to him and kiss her.

She linked her arms around his neck and held him close, treasuring their last few minutes together. Being with Brent was her joy. When she was with him, she could pretend that the world truly was a wonderful place and that heroes really did exist. It was a fantasy, but she didn't care. For a little while, with Brent, it was real.

Brent knew he should kiss Crystal only once and then leave. He knew what a temptation she was to him. He knew it was dangerous to hold her this way, to feel the softness of her against him. He'd learned earlier that day just how exciting her embrace could be, and he knew he should walk away from her while he still could. Brent fought for control. He broke off the kiss and looked down at her.

"I have to go," he told her, knowing that if he spent another minute in her arms he wouldn't be able to leave her.

Crystal gazed up at him and lifted one hand to caress his cheek. "But I don't want you to leave. Stay with me."

Brent was torn between doing the right thing and losing himself in the glory of her love.

And then she kissed him.

Brent found he couldn't deny himself the excitement of having Crystal in his arms. She was warm and willing, and they were by themselves in the privacy of the house.

He deepened the kiss.

Crystal responded instinctively, eagerly meeting him in that rapturous exchange. Excitement coursed through her. She wanted to be even closer to him.

Any trace of restraint was lost to them. Their passion was unleashed.

Brent brought Crystal fully against him. He began to caress her, loving her and arousing her.

Crystal drew away for a moment to whisper, "My room's upstairs."

He needed no further encouragement. He swept her up in his arms and cradled her to him. She wrapped her arms around his neck as he carried her up the staircase. She pointed out the room, and he went in, kicking the door shut behind them.

Brent laid her upon the wide softness of the bed, then went back to lock the door. He returned to the bedside, gazing down at her as she lay before him, her cheeks flushed and her eyes heavy-lidded with passion.

Crystal looked up at Brent as he stood over her. He looked so wonderful to her—so tall and broad-shouldered and powerful. She wanted to touch him, to be close to him, to love him—forever.

Brent was her hero.

Crystal lifted her arms to him in unspoken invitation.

Brent went to her. He lay down beside her and drew her to him, holding her close. Crystal responded eagerly. When he began to caress her, she gave free rein to her desire.

Their passion grew with each kiss and touch, until finally they could stand no barrier between them. With eager hands, Crystal worked at the buttons of his shirt and pushed the offending garment from Brent's shoulders. Her hands explored him, sculpting the hard muscles of his arms and chest. Then she traced an arousing line across his stomach at the waistline of his pants.

Brent shuddered at her intimate touch. He stood and drew her up from the bed. They shared one long, lingering kiss as he finished unfastening her gown. They had to move apart for her to step out of it, but it was worth the momentary separation. He went to her as she stood before him, clad only in her chemise, and kissed her softly.

Crystal felt shy and daring at the same time. She loosened the ties on her chemise and slipped it from her. She stood before him, her beauty fully bared to him for the first time.

"You're beautiful," he told her in a love-husky voice.

"So are you." Crystal reached for him.

They returned to the bed and came together in a firestorm of excitement. The moment was rapturous as they each sought to please the other with every kiss and touch. Crystal had never known such pleasure. The flame of their desire grew, searing them both, until there could be no denying their love.

Brent left Crystal only long enough to finish undressing. Then he went back into her arms, and they gave themselves over to the splendor of their need. Crystal thrilled to his every caress. When he moved over her, she accepted him eagerly, wanting to know the full glory of his love.

Caught up in the ecstasy of her embrace, Brent wanted only to make her his in all ways. His mouth sought hers in a passionate claim as he moved to make them one. But when he breached the proof of her innocence, he was jarred back to reality.

Crystal was a virgin. . . .

"Crystal . . ." He went still and drew back to gaze down at her.

She looked up at him and smiled softly. The momentary pain of his possession was quickly forgotten in the glory of this moment.

They were one.

She kissed him.

He began to move again, not wanting to stop, needing to know her completely. They sought the heights of passion, giving and taking, each wanting to please the other. In exquisite harmony they crested. Rapture burst upon them. They clung together in love's aftermath, aware only of each other and the glory of what had just passed between them.

Brent held Crystal close as the passion of the moment quieted.

She had been a virgin.

As surprised as Brent was by the discovery, he was also delighted. She played the part of seductress so well, yet she had been an innocent.

And she had given her innocence—her greatest gift—to him.

As the ecstasy of the moment faded, reality returned. Brent didn't know why she hadn't told him of her virginity, but he knew what he had to do. He had to protect Crystal and do the right thing.

"Crystal," Brent began as he moved away from her.

Caught up in the beauty and peace of the moment, she looked up at him dreamily.

"You should have told me. I didn't realize . . ." He hesitated, uncomfortably, trying to figure out what to do. "I'm sorry."

His apology jarred her from her fantasy world. Brent was sorry?

"We'll get married right away," Brent declared.

"Married?" Crystal repeated, still stunned by his apology.

Oh, she wanted to marry Brent. She wanted it with all her heart. Being Mrs. Brent Hunter would be pure ecstasy for her—a dream come true. And Brent was a true hero. His offering to marry her proved that yet again.

But as much as she wanted to spend the rest of her life loving him, Crystal knew it could never be. Not in the real world. In the real world, she was wanted for murder.

Her brother had almost caught up with her in San Antonio, and the law might just be waiting for her around the next corner. Her life was in turmoil—

she could not accept his proposal. She couldn't do that to him. She loved him too much.

"We can go to Reverend Crawford right now, tonight," Brent said, taking charge as he always did, and already planning how best to handle the situation.

"Brent—no."

He went still. "What?"

"I can't marry you."

Brent had never proposed to anyone before. He had never even thought seriously about marrying until now, until Crystal.

And she had just turned him down.

Proud man that he was, Brent wasn't about to take no for an answer.

"Crystal, we should get married. Now. Tonight. You were an innocent and I—"

"Brent, you don't have to marry me just because we made love. I wanted this to happen as much as you did."

"But—"

"It's all right." She moved closer and kissed him with great tenderness.

"No, it's not all right as far as I'm concerned."

"I know you're trying to do the right thing. You're being my hero again," she said wistfully as she gazed up into his eyes and gently touched his cheek. "But I don't belong in your world."

"Crystal, for God's sake, what kind of world do you think I live in? Do you think I'm some kind of knight in shining armor from some perfect king-dom?" He gave a harsh laugh. "I'm a man whose father just got out of prison after serving time for murder—I'm not living a fairy-tale life. I live in the real world, and sometimes the real world isn't a very pretty place. You can't change the way things are, but you can learn to live with reality."

It didn't matter to Brent that she worked in a saloon. He knew how special she really was.

"You are so wonderful, Brent Hunter." Crystal smiled gently at him. "We'll talk about this more later, but right now it's getting late. You'd better go."

She didn't want to risk the possibility that Anne might return early and find them together.

Brent knew she was right. He had to leave while he could. He got up from the bed and started to dress.

"We're not done discussing this yet," he told her in his most authoritative voice.

The tone he used with her was the one that always commanded instant obedience from the hands on the ranch and, most of the time, from Abby, but it didn't intimidate Crystal at all. She just smiled at him.

When he'd finished dressing, Crystal wrapped the sheet around herself and went to stand before him. She kissed him once more, a tender, heartfelt exchange.

"You are a very special man."

"And you are a very special woman." He held

Crystal close one last time, then put her from him. He knew he had to go, and her tantalizing nearness was too much of a temptation for him.

"I'll be back." It was a promise.

"I'll be waiting."

Darkness claimed the land as Brent made the trek back to the Half-Moon. His mood was as dark as the night. He kept trying to understand why Crystal had turned down his proposal. Nothing made sense to him. They had made love. He had taken her virginity. There had been no reason for them not to get married that very night.

Unless she didn't love him.

The thought surprised Brent, but as he thought back over their time together, he realized neither one of them had ever expressed their feelings.

Did he love her?

He wasn't sure. He'd never been in love before. He cared about Crystal. She was beautiful and gentle, and she had made him laugh more than he'd laughed in years. But love her? He didn't know.

Brent made up his mind then and there that he was going to find a way to spend as much time with her as he could. What they shared was to be treasured, and he couldn't risk letting it slip away.

As the house came into view, thoughts of his father returned. He hadn't confronted Jack about the liquor earlier that day, but now that Crystal was gone, he was going to have it out with him.

A short time later, after taking care of the horses

down at the stable, Brent went up to the house.

It wasn't very late, yet the place seemed awfully quiet as he let himself in. Only one lamp was burning, and he saw no sign of Abby. He hadn't thought she'd go to bed this early. Then he turned toward the study and stopped. There, seated at the desk, was his father, and it was obvious from the way he was sprawled in the chair that he had passed out. On the desk before him was a nearly empty whiskey bottle.

Rage filled Brent at the sight. It took all his self-control not to drag his father outside and throw him into one of the watering troughs to sober him up.

"Brent?" Abby said in a low voice, appearing from her room down the hall.

"I'm here. I was wondering why you'd gone to bed so early, and now I know. Has he been in the chair all night?"

"After you left, he got his bottle and kept drinking. I tried to talk to him, but there was no use. I gave up and went to my room. I wasn't sleepy, but I couldn't stand to be around him anymore." She looked over at their father. "Should we try to get him into his bed?"

"Hell, no," Brent ground out. "Let him sleep right there. If he falls out of the chair in the middle of the night, he's got no one to blame but himself."

She nodded in understanding as she stared sadly at her father. She looked at Brent and asked, "Everything went all right on your trip into town?"

"I stayed on at the boardinghouse talking to Crystal for a while," he told her casually, not revealing just how wonderful their visit had really been.

"You are going to see her again, aren't you? She's different from the other women in town."

"You're right. Crystal is different. I care about her, and I do plan to see more of her."

She glanced at their father once again. "Brent . . ."

"What?"

"I'm sorry about Papa. I know how upsetting it is for you to see him this way."

"There's nothing for you to be sorry about," Brent reassured her. "Pa's the one who made the decision to start drinking again."

"Are our troubles ever going to end?"

"Don't worry," Brent assured her. "I'll take care of things. I always have."

"What are you going to do about it?"

"I don't know yet, but I'm going to have a serious talk with him in the morning. We've got to get a few things settled between us."

He sat alone in his darkened hotel room. Fury ate at him. He had been close to catching Crystal in San Antonio—so close—and yet she had eluded him again.

Crystal was still out there somewhere. She hadn't just vanished. He would find her. And when he did, she would pay.

Chapter Sixteen

Brent went to bed hoping to dream of Crystal, but the visions that came to him in his sleep that night were tortured, not loving. In his nightmare he saw his father standing over his mother's dead body, holding the gun in his hand. The memory was powerful and painful, and Brent came awake with a violent start. He sat up in bed and stared around himself in the dark, trying to erase the vision of that hellish time from his mind.

After a while he lay back down, but peace did not come to him. He was beginning to wonder if it ever would, living in the same house with his father this way.

Brent was still awake and still tired when dawn finally began to brighten the eastern sky. His mood was tense as he got up and dressed. He wasn't looking forward to the confrontation with his father to come, but he had to do it. He had to speak his mind. He wouldn't be able to live with himself if he didn't.

Brent left his bedroom, ready for whatever the new day would bring.

When Jack awoke, his head was pounding, and the light pouring in through the window beside him only magnified the pain. He quickly closed his eyes again and groaned in pure torture. He reached out and groped around the desktop, trying to grab his bottle. If there was one thing he needed, it was another stiff drink to make the pain go away.

"We have to talk." Brent's voice alerted him to his son's presence.

Jack was in no mood for conversation. An image of Beth haunted him, and he had to make it go away.

"Where the hell is my . . ." He barely opened one eye as he tried to locate the whiskey.

"I said, we have to talk," Brent repeated as he stood facing his father, holding the bottle of whiskey out for him to see.

"About what?" Jack said in a snarl. The pounding pain in his head was so severe he could barely think, and Brent's arrogance infuriated him even more.

"I think you know," he answered.

"No, I don't know. Why don't you tell me?" Jack said with a sneer.

"I told you on your first day back here that I don't allow liquor on the ranch."

"So?"

"So look at yourself." Brent was disgusted with him.

Jack got to his feet and glared at him. "Give me that bottle!"

Brent's anger flared even hotter. Without a word he stalked to the front door, opened it, and threw the bottle out of the house.

Jack ran outside, desperate to get his bottle back. He picked it up, ready for a drink, but the bottle had cracked when it hit the ground and what whiskey was left had drained out.

"You arrogant bastard!" Jack snarled, throwing the bottle back down in disgust. "Who the hell do you think you are?"

"I know who I am," Brent answered seriously. "I'm the one who provided for the family and saved the Half-Moon while you were sitting in prison for the last ten years!"

"This ranch is mine," Jack declared, resentment filling him. "What I say goes on the Half-Moon!"

He turned and started to walk away from Brent.

"Don't you turn your back on me, you son of a bitch!" Brent ordered. He had had all he could stand. "Do you think you can come back here to the Half-Moon and just take over like nothing ever happened?"

"You're damned right I can!" Jack countered hotly. "And if you don't like it here, you can leave!"

"You know what? Maybe you're right!" he exclaimed. "Maybe I should go. Maybe I should just up and leave, and let you try to figure out how to run this place all by yourself!"

"Maybe you should!" Jack snapped, beyond fury.

"Well, Jack, if Brent goes"—it was Hank's voice, surprising them both—"I go." The ranch hands had seen the whiskey bottle come flying out the door and had heard the sound of their argument, and had come up to the house to see what was going on.

"Me, too," another one of the hands added. They were solidly behind Brent, whom they respected and trusted.

"Well, then, maybe I should be the one to go," Jack said sarcastically.

"Maybe you should," Brent said bluntly. He turned around and went back into the house, furious over the whole confrontation.

Jack looked around at the hands standing there staring at him. He was the one who had hired them years ago. Hell, he had hired Hank when he'd been barely more than a boy, and now he and the others were pledging their allegiance to Brent.

Jack's worst nightmares about returning home were coming true. Without another word he walked away. He went to the stable and looked for the fastest horse he could find. He needed to ride.

Crystal had lain awake long into the night, reliving in her mind the wonder of loving Brent. The fact that he'd proposed to her left her heart aching.

She had tossed and turned, trying to convince herself there was some way they could be married. Being his wife would be pure ecstasy for her.

But it wasn't possible.

The truth about her past was too ugly, and she loved him too much to involve him any more deeply in her troubled and dangerous life.

She would enjoy what time they could share together while she was in Diablo as Ruby, and then she would disappear when danger neared, just as she'd disappeared from San Antonio.

It had been long after midnight when Crystal finally managed to fall asleep. Her sleep wasn't restful, though, and she awoke early. She got cleaned up and went downstairs to join Anne for breakfast.

"Well, good morning," Anne said as she came into the kitchen. "It's nice to see you up and about so early. How was your visit with the Hunters?"

"I had a wonderful time. The ranch is beautiful. We went riding, and I got to see a lot of the countryside."

"Everyone in town thinks Brent has done a fine job of saving the place after all the ugliness that went on. You know about all the Hunter family trouble, don't you?"

"Yes, Brent told me."

"It was quite a scandal at the time. I mean, think about how horrible it would be to find out that your father had killed your mother! Your Brent's had a tough time of it on his own these past years, and now Jack is back."

"But Jack seemed nice enough," Crystal offered.

"Oh, he seemed nice enough back then, too. Which just goes to show you how good some people are at hiding the truth about themselves."

"I see," Crystal said noncommittally, but feeling guilty for the secrets she herself was trying to hide.

"I still feel sorry for Brent and Abby, even after all this time. It can't be easy for them, seeing their father every day now and knowing what he did."

"Brent told me he killed their mother, but he didn't say why."

"No one knows," Anne answered. "Jack confessed to the crime and went to prison. If you ask me, I don't think a ten-year sentence for murder is long enough. A murderer should have to stay in prison forever—if he doesn't hang!"

Crystal was sickened by her words. "He did his time. Maybe he's changed."

"We'll see. Time will tell."

Crystal was glad when Anne finally changed the subject. She ate her breakfast and returned to her room, needing some peace.

It was later that morning when Crystal decided to go to the Diablo General Store.

"Good morning, young lady," said Mr. Spindle, the owner. "What can I do for you today?"

"I'm looking for some dress material," she told him.

"It's right there in back. If you need any help, just let me know."

"Thank you. I will," Crystal said, making her way to the back of the shop.

It happened that Melinda Barton was also in the store, getting a few things for her mother. When she heard Mr. Spindle greet another customer, she glanced up to see who'd come in and was outraged at the sight of Ruby. Jealousy jarred her. She had made some inquiries about the other woman after Brent had gone off with her yesterday, and what she'd learned had shocked her.

Ruby was nothing more than a common dance-hall slut!

Melinda refused to give credence to the good things she'd been told about the singer. In Melinda's opinion, anyone who worked at the Lone Star Saloon was not worthy of a place in polite society.

And yet Brent had invited *her* to the ranch! And now here she was in the general store, acting as if she were normal folk.

Melinda knew better. Her jealousy and anger ate at her. Determined to put this Ruby in her place, she leisurely made her way to the back of the store, where the other woman was busy looking at material.

"Planning on making a new dress for your work at the Lone Star?" Melinda asked sarcastically as she came down the aisle.

Crystal looked up, surprised to see it was the girl she'd met at church. "Why, hello. You're Melinda, aren't you?"

"That's right. Did you have a good time out at the Half-Moon yesterday?"

Crystal was a little surprised by the question. "Yes. It was good to see the place, since Brent had told me so much about it."

"And since Brent told you about the Half-Moon, I suppose he also told you about us—didn't he?" Melinda asked with false-sweetness.

"No. Was he supposed to?"

"I thought he might have mentioned to you that we're almost engaged," she declared.

Crystal had dealt with enough conniving women in her life to recognize one of them on sight, and she knew Brent well enough to know that if he were engaged to any woman, he would be faithful.

"That's strange," Crystal answered. "He didn't say a word to me about being engaged to you. If that's true, I wonder why he wanted to spend the day with me?"

"I had other plans yesterday. I guess he was bored—and desperate," she remarked snidely.

Crystal smiled coldly at her. "Somehow I can't see

Brent Hunter ever being desperate for anything—least of all for female companionship."

"Well, sometimes a man has other needs, you know. The baser kind of needs that only a saloon girl can provide for."

Crystal was taken aback by Melinda's malice, but was a good enough actress not to reveal it. "You mean like making him laugh and enjoy life a little bit? We certainly did that. It's a pity you weren't able to go. Maybe the next time you will."

"Yes, maybe next time. Oh, and by the way, if you are looking for the black silk or the red satin, they're another aisle over." Melinda was seething as she turned and walked away. She thought Ruby nothing but a common slut, and she was furious that Brent had spent any time with her.

Crystal reacted coolly, but in truth, inwardly she was deeply shaken. Was what Melinda had said true? Did everyone consider her a slut just because she was a singer who performed in saloons? She'd always made it plain when she hired on that she was a lady and did not sell herself. But now her emotions were in turmoil.

Brent had made love to her. He had even asked her to marry him. Obviously he had never proposed to Melinda or she would have already had him at the altar.

That thought made Crystal smile, and eased the pain within her. But even as she felt a little better, she realized nothing had changed. She was not of

Brent's class. She did not belong in Brent's world.

No longer in the mood to think about shopping, Crystal left the store without buying a thing.

Dan finally admitted to himself that he'd made a mistake. Crystal had not gone to Houston. He'd been looking for her there for several weeks now, but had found no trace of her. He would have to return to San Antonio and then head out in the other direction. He had to check the towns where the other stage had been going the day she'd run away from him.

His hunt wasn't easy, but he wasn't going to give up. He had to find her. He knew Crystal could be a master of disguise, so he had to be careful.

He didn't want to risk missing her. He just hoped it didn't take him too much longer to locate her. Time was of the essence.

He knew her very life was in danger, and it was up to him to save her.

John Hall looked in the mirror of his hotel room in Houston and swore violently as he studied his own reflection.

Gone was the handsome, debonair gambler who'd gotten anything and everything he'd ever wanted.

In his place was a disfigured freak—a man so ugly that his scarred face caused revulsion in all.

Young children actually ran crying to their mothers at the sight of him.

John had always liked being the center of attention. He always liked people to stare at him and admire his good looks and slick ways. But he didn't want them watching him because he was hideous!

In one vicious, savage move, John hit the mirror with his fist. It shattered, destroying his mirror image.

His senseless attack left his knuckles cut and bleeding, but he didn't care. At least now he didn't have to look at himself anymore.

The pain and fury he was already feeling were far greater than any gash on his hand.

John just wished the mirror had been Crystal Stewart. He wanted to get his hands on her. He wanted to beat her and torture her. He wanted to see her dead for all the horror she'd caused him.

In frustration, he cursed out loud as he stared blankly around the hotel room. He'd been secretly trailing Dan Stewart, believing the man had had a part in his sister's disappearance and that Dan would eventually lead him back to her. But after endless days and useless miles, it seemed Dan was no closer to the elusive Crystal than he had been in the beginning.

The trek to Houston had been a complete waste of valuable time.

But Crystal was still out there somewhere, and John would not be deterred from finding her.

He would not give up. He would not let the woman who'd injured him so severely walk away unpunished. He would get his hands on her, and when he did, he would teach her a few lessons.

John was looking forward to their reunion. He planned to enjoy every minute of it.

Chapter Seventeen

Jack rode like the wind across the countryside. He thought if he rode long enough and hard enough he could escape the hell that his life had become. But when he finally reined in and sat there staring out across the endless miles of unspoiled Half-Moon land, he realized there was no escaping the misery. It was not those around him who caused it. The pain was deep within him. He could run from it, but he would never be able to escape.

Jack thought about his fight with Brent and remembered the last thing he'd shouted at his son: *Maybe I should be the one to go.*

In all the years he'd been in prison, the only thing that had mattered to him was coming home to the Half-Moon.

And now he was back, but nothing was working

out the way he'd hoped. His children despised him. Even the ranch hands, men who'd worked for him for years, didn't want anything to do with him.

Jack's mood turned even blacker as he thought of Beth, and with the pain that seized him, he knew he needed a drink. Silently he cursed Brent and the fact that he had destroyed his bottle of whiskey. His need to find forgetfulness drove him as he wheeled his mount around and rode for Diablo—and the Lone Star.

Ken would be more than happy to sell him another bottle.

And he knew no one would miss him on the ranch.

"Brent, what are you doing?" Abby asked when she glanced into his bedroom as she was passing by on her way down the hall. She could see him inside emptying out the drawers of his bureau.

"So you finally got up." He glanced over his shoulder at her, but didn't stop packing.

"I didn't expect to sleep this late. Why? Did something happen with Papa?"

"It's good you missed it."

"What happened?" She was worried as she came into the room. She looked from her brother's stern expression to the clothes he was packing away in a trunk. "Where are you going? Are you leaving on a trip?"

"I had it out with Pa this morning," Brent began,

wanting to explain his decision to her. "I'm leaving here, but I'm not going on any trip."

Abby stared at him as a deep, abiding sadness filled her. "Was it that bad?"

"Pa gave me no choice," he answered.

"But Brent, you can't leave!"

"The hell I can't, Abby," he said fiercely. "I confronted Pa about the liquor this morning, and he made it clear he has no intention of changing his ways. So I'm going to move out and go live at the cabin down by the creek."

"Why are you letting him push you out this way?" she asked, devastated by his news.

"He's not pushing me out. I'm walking out under my own power and of my own free will. You can stay here with him if you want, Abby, but I'm tired. I need some peace in my life, and I'm not going to find it living under the same roof with him."

"Brent, think about what you're doing!"

"I have thought about it, and I have to do this. You can come with me or you can stay here. The choice is yours."

Abby was shocked over everything that was happening. "But this is my home."

"Well, you know where I'll be if you need me." Brent picked up what he could and left the room.

As Abby watched him walk out, a great sadness filled her. It seemed she had lost everything.

Her mother was dead. Her brothers were gone. And now she was going to be left at the ranch house with only her father—the man who was the very cause of all her sorrow.

Brent knew he was going to have to do some work on the cabin to make it livable. He went out to the bunkhouse and got Hank and Curly to ride along with him and help him make the needed repairs. He hoped they could get most of it done in one day. They loaded up two wagons with Brent's personal things and the tools they'd need to get the work done.

As they rode away from the ranch house, Brent glanced back one last time. He was surprised to see Abby standing on the porch watching them leave. He lifted one hand to wave to her, but she didn't respond. She turned and went back inside.

Brent understood why she was upset, but he could not back down.

He was leaving.

It was time.

Jack took a deep drink from the tumbler of whiskey Ken had set before him. He enjoyed the power of the liquor as it burned its way down.

"So what brings you back into town today?" the bartender asked. He'd been surprised to see him so soon.

"I just needed a little relaxation," Jack answered, lifting his glass in a mock toast. He drained the rest of the whiskey and then shoved the glass back across the bar toward the barkeep for a refill.

Ken obliged.

"Looks like you've got company, Jack," Ken told him as Edmund walked in.

Jack glanced up as Edmund came to stand with him at the bar. Jack smiled at him. It was good to know he had one friend in the world. "What are you doing here?"

"I saw you ride in, so I came over to see what you were up to. I hadn't thought you'd be back in town so soon," Edmund replied. "Have you got something to celebrate?" He motioned toward his drink.

"No, I had a run-in with Brent this morning, so I went for a ride and ended up here."

"What's the problem with Brent?" Edmund sounded concerned.

"He's so damned high and mighty," Jack swore. "Just because he ran things while I was gone, he thinks he can order me around and tell me what to do on my own ranch."

Edmund was secretly pleased that the Hunters were fighting, but his expression betrayed nothing. "Brent did work hard while you were away, Jack. You should be proud of him."

"Proud of him? For what? Training a lot of nags?" Jack said with a sneer. "Brent's too damned arrogant. Quince would still be here helping out if it wasn't for him. He drove him off."

"Do you know what you want to do now? Have you made plans for the ranch?"

Jack's mood improved, for Edmund was talking to him as if he were in charge. "I have a lot of plans."

"I figured you did," Edmund said smoothly. "I know how much you love the Half-Moon."

"It's got to be the biggest and the best," he declared. He stopped to take another deep drink.

Edmund saw his opportunity and took advantage of it. "Why don't you come over to the bank with me? I've got an idea I think just might appeal to you."

"What kind of idea?"

"Well, there's some property for sale that you may want to add on to the Half-Moon."

"That sounds good." Jack smiled at the prospect of increasing the size of the ranch.

"Are you done here? Are you ready to go?" Edmund asked.

"Sure, but wait just one minute." Jack motioned to the bartender as he finished off the last of his drink. "I want a bottle to take with me."

Ken brought it to him. Edmund pushed Jack's coins aside and insisted on paying the bill; then they went to the bank.

An hour later, Edmund was ready to celebrate. He took out the decanter of whiskey and the two glasses he kept in the cabinet behind his desk in the office.

"Let's drink to this deal. It's a good one. I'll take care of finalizing all the negotiations for you," he assured Jack.

"I appreciate it." Jack trusted him implicitly. "And you did add in the extra hundred dollars cash for me, didn't you?"

"I sure did, just like you said. Just sign right here." Edmund indicated the place at the bottom of the loan papers where Jack was to sign his name. Jack proudly signed the document, and Edmund poured them each a drink. Edmund gave Jack considerably more than he took himself, but Jack didn't notice. He was just glad to have another drink.

"To the success of the Half-Moon," Edmund toasted their deal.

"Sounds good to me." Jack downed the whiskey, celebrating the heady feeling of knowing he was buying more property for the Half-Moon and getting some cash of his own to use as he saw fit.

He'd show Brent who was the boss.

Brent smiled in satisfaction as he looked around the cabin.

"Thanks," he told Curly and Hank. They'd worked hard all day to put the place in order.

"You're sure you want to do this?" Hank asked.

"It's time."

They shared a look. Hank understood his reasoning.

"Is there anything else you need?"

"Not that I can think of right now. You can head on back. I'll meet you tomorrow morning in the north pasture."

Curly and Hank left.

Brent took the time to look over the cabin once more. They'd repaired the roof and fixed the broken porch steps. Structurally it was sound. It still needed some serious cleaning, and he'd work on that as best he could. He'd brought his bed and bedding, and a chest from the main house, and Frances had given him a good stock of food.

This was now his home.

When he'd told Crystal he wanted to live there, he'd never imagined it would be so soon. He remembered Crystal's reaction to the place and wished she were with him now to see the improvements they'd made. The thought made him smile and motivated him. He set to work cleaning the inside. As soon as it was ready, he was going to go into town and bring Crystal out for a visit. He needed to see her again.

Jack's mood was confident when he returned to the Half-Moon late that afternoon. His deal with Edmund had made him feel powerful. For the first time since he'd returned, he felt like the man in charge, and it felt good.

Jack was drunk when he dismounted in front of the house. He stood there looking around for a moment, taking pride in what he owned. Bottle in hand, he went inside and stashed the whiskey in his room. Since it was so quiet in the house, he figured Abby and Brent were both out working. He was surprised when he returned to the living room and came face-to-face with Abby.

"I was worried about you," Abby told him.

"You shouldn't have been."

When he spoke, her expression darkened. "You've been drinking again."

"Whether I had a few drinks or not is none of your business, little girl," he said. "Where's your brother?"

"Gone." Her tone was flat, displaying little emotion.

"Well, go get him. I've got something I want to tell him," he said arrogantly.

"Brent moved out. If you want him, you'll have to go get him yourself. He's living down at the cabin." She started to walk away, but her father's next words stopped her.

"Don't walk away from me! I'm your father."

She turned and glared at him. She wished he had been the one who'd left. "Brent has been like a father to me for the last ten years, and now you've driven him away."

"Driven him away? What are you talking about?"

Abby went on, "After his fight with you this morning, he packed up his things and moved out. He's going to live in the cabin down at the creek."

"Let him move out. Who cares what he does?"

Jack couldn't decide if he was glad Brent was gone or angry because he'd dared to leave.

Abby looked at him coldly. "I care."

"You can think what you want, little girl," he replied snidely. "But I've got big plans. You'll see."

Abby had had enough. There were horses to groom and work to do. It wasn't going to get done if she stayed there listening to her father's boasting. She walked out of the house.

Crystal completed her final performance on Friday night and left the stage to mingle with the customers. Outwardly she was smiling and friendly, yet deep within, she was filled with disappointment.

Once again, Brent had not shown up. He hadn't come to see her all week.

Crystal greeted the men by name now as she circulated around the room, flirting outrageously with them, as was her trademark. They responded eagerly to her warmth.

"You're doing a good job, Ruby," Ken told her when she came to the bar for her sarsaparilla. "I'm glad I hired you."

"Thanks, Ken." Crystal managed to smile at him, but her heart wasn't in it.

She looked around the crowded saloon and wondered how she could be with so many people and still feel alone.

She wasn't sure she liked caring so much for Brent.

Chapter Eighteen

Late Saturday night Crystal spotted Brent entering the Lone Star during her performance. Her heart lightened and her spirits soared. Her fears of the night before disappeared. Brent had come back to her! That was all that mattered.

Brent went to stand at the bar, but he didn't take his eyes off Crystal as she sang for her audience. The Lone Star was as crowded as the Six Gun had been that first night they'd met, and he knew the men were there to hear her.

"What'll it be?" Ken asked as he came to wait on him. "You want a beer?"

"Sure," Brent answered. "And give me a sarsaparilla, too."

"Coming right up." He quickly brought the drinks

and Brent paid him. "Did your pa come with you tonight?"

"No. Why?"

"He was in the other day, and I was just wondering if he bought the property."

"What property?" Brent was suddenly wary.

"Looks like he didn't buy it if you don't know about it. Edmund Montgomery came in while your pa was here, and they started talking about improving your ranch. Edmund mentioned buying some land before they went off together. Your pa didn't come back, so I didn't hear any more. It probably was nothing. Your pa was drinking pretty heavily that day."

"We haven't bought any more property," Brent stated firmly, but he felt uneasy. The first chance he got, he was going to ask his father about it. For right now, though, he had only one thing on his mind— and that was enjoying an evening with Crystal.

"I guess they were just talking then." Ken looked back up at the stage and Ruby. "Well, enjoy the show."

"There's no doubt about that. She sure puts on a good show."

"Yes, she does," the bartender agreed.

Crystal was singing even more enthusiastically now that Brent was there, watching her from where he stood at the bar. The rest of her performance seemed to take forever, but finally she finished her last song and left the stage. It took her a few minutes to work her way through the crowd of admirers to where Brent awaited her.

"You came," Crystal said breathlessly. She wanted to kiss him right there in front of everybody, but she knew she couldn't. Any kiss she gave Brent would not be an "Andy" kiss.

"You knew I would." He handed her the sarsaparilla he had ordered for her.

"Thank you. I missed you." She looked up at Brent, feasting her eyes upon him, ashamed, now, that she'd ever doubted him.

"A lot happened this week—there was no time to leave the Half-Moon. But what about tomorrow? Can you get away? I'd like to take you out to the ranch again. There's something I want to show you," Brent said as they went to sit at a table where they could talk for a while.

"I'd love to. Are your father and Abby with you? Did they come into town, too?" Crystal was looking forward to seeing them again.

"No. I made the trip alone. You're the only reason I'm here."

Their gazes met and locked, and they shared a look of longing and remembrance.

Brent wanted to tell Crystal about moving into the cabin, but he decided to just wait and show her. He stayed on at the Lone Star until she got off work and then escorted her to the boardinghouse. They made arrangements to leave bright and early for the ranch, for they wanted to have as much time together as they could manage.

Anne was home this evening, so Brent did not go inside. He stole only one quick kiss before bidding Crystal a reluctant good-night.

Crystal's mood was light as she quietly went up to her room and got ready for bed. Any doubts she'd had were gone.

Brent had come to her.

She slept deeply that night, her dreams sweet.

Brent returned to his hotel room and bedded down. He was eager for the new day to come. He wanted only to spend time with Crystal. Morning couldn't arrive fast enough to suit him.

Brent awoke at dawn as he usually did, but he knew it was too early to pick Crystal up. He lay in bed and tried to relax and bide his time, but his overactive imagination would not rest. He pictured himself arriving at the boardinghouse early, only to discover that Crystal was still asleep and he would have to go up to her bedroom and awaken her. Memories of the last time he had been in her bedroom returned, and Brent was driven from his own bed. He busied himself packing up and getting ready for the trek back to the ranch.

Crystal woke early and dressed in the clothes Abby had given her. She was ready for her excursion to the Half-Moon. When Brent drove up in the buckboard, she had been watching from the parlor window and hurried out to meet him.

"Good morning," Crystal said with a smile as he helped her up to sit beside him.

"Yes, it is a good morning—now that you're here with me."

"You are a charmer, Brent Hunter."

"I only tell the truth, ma'am," he drawled.

Brent urged the team on, and they rode for the ranch. The miles passed quickly as they enjoyed each other's company.

"Where are we going?" Crystal asked when he didn't follow the main road that led to the house.

"There's something I want to show you."

"What?" She was curious.

"You'll see."

Brent said no more until they reached the stream and she could see the cabin in the distance.

"I've been working on it all week. What do you think?" he asked as they drove up and stopped out front.

"It looks wonderful, but why did you fix it up?" She jumped down by herself and went to take a look around.

"This is my new home."

"You're living here now? But why?"

"I decided it was time I moved out on my own."

Crystal went up the newly repaired steps and crossed the porch to let herself in. She was delightfully surprised when she stepped inside.

"So this is why you were so busy all week," Crystal said as he joined her there.

"It took some work, that's for sure."

"You did a good job. I wouldn't have guessed that it would turn out so well."

The main room was spotlessly clean. It was dominated by a kitchen table and two chairs. She cast a quick glance into the bedroom and saw his bed and a trunk in there. He had even hung some plain sheets at the windows for curtains.

"It is clean—and the roof had better not leak." Brent grinned. "It wasn't easy getting it ready. Hank and Curly worked with me the first day on the major repairs, and I've done the rest. I know it could still use a woman's touch, though."

Crystal would have loved nothing more than to be the woman giving him the "woman's touch" he wanted, but that was a dream she knew would never come true for her. The lightness of her mood fled as she mentally struggled to suppress thoughts of her past.

Brent saw the change in her and was sorry he'd even mentioned it. He hadn't wanted to put any pressure on her. He wanted to enjoy their time together.

"What about Abby? She could help you, couldn't she?" Crystal asked.

"The 'woman's touch' I was wanting isn't the kind my sister could give me," he said in a lower, seductive voice.

"It isn't?" She looked up at him and saw the glimmer of intent in his eyes. When Brent looked at her that way, her heartbeat quickened, and it was easy for her to forget everything but the joy she would ultimately find in his arms. She smiled invitingly in return. "Then what kind of 'woman's touch' were you hoping for?"

He needed no further invitation to take her in his arms. He'd been thinking about this moment all week as he'd worked on the cabin. He didn't want to wait any longer.

"Any kind of touch you want to give me," Brent said in a low voice just as his lips claimed hers.

The past seven days had seemed an eternity to Crystal as she'd waited in vain each night for Brent to come to her. But now they were finally together again.

It didn't matter that it was broad daylight outside. Being in his embrace was heaven.

With eager hands they stripped away their clothes and came together in a blaze of glory. Fiery kisses and searing caresses flamed the heat of their passion. A fever burned within him at her womanly touch.

They found their way to the bed and lay together on its feather mattress.

Crystal held Brent close and thrilled to the touch of his hard body against her. She caressed him daringly, sliding her hands over his broad shoulders and down his back. She found she loved to touch him—he was so solid, so strong.

Brent responded to her caress, his need for her growing more and more powerful. His mouth claimed hers in a demanding kiss that left them both breathless and hungry for more. He pressed hungry kisses to her throat and then lower. . . .

Crystal gasped at his intimate touch and arched beneath him. She was desperate to be even closer to him.

Brent moved over her and made her his.

They came together, two becoming one. A rapturous blending of male and female. A perfect union.

And then he began his rhythm.

It was a sensuous waltz that took them higher and higher. Passion lifted them. Ecstasy awaited them.

And they reached it together—the peak of bliss.

Heart-stopping excitement coursed through them. They held tightly to each other, finding the perfection that is love.

Brent shifted onto his side, keeping Crystal cradled against him. He wanted to stay as they were forever—their bodies joined, their limbs entwined, their hearts beating as one.

He kissed her, gently this time, adoringly. She gave a soft sigh of contentment.

"Was that the 'womanly touch' you had in mind?" Crystal teased easily.

"That was exactly what I had in mind," he answered with a low chuckle.

His lips sought hers in a tender exchange.

"I think I need a 'manly touch.' What do you think?" Crystal asked with a slow, enticing smile.

Brent didn't bother to answer; he just obliged.

Melinda was pouting. She didn't know why she'd been hoping Brent would be in town for church again this Sunday, but she was. She'd worn her best Sunday dress and taken extra care with her hair, just for him. And he hadn't come to church, and neither had any of his family. She was frustrated as she returned home with her parents.

Melinda was pretending to be fine, but deep inside she was upset. How was she ever going to get Brent to marry her if she never got to see him?

Melinda decided it was time she took matters into her own hands. If Brent Hunter didn't come to her, she would go to Brent Hunter.

It was a bold and daring move, and more than a little outrageous, but Melinda didn't care. When she made up her mind to get something, she got it. And she had made up her mind that she wanted Brent.

Melinda knew her parents had been invited out that afternoon, so it was the perfect opportunity for her to sneak off and find Brent. She saddled her horse and rode for the Half-Moon, excited about seeing him again. Though it was true that he had spent last Sunday with the slut from the saloon, this week it was her turn to see him.

Mrs. Brent Hunter. Melinda sighed to herself. She liked the sound of that. Now if she could only convince him.

Had she been less determined, she might have felt a bit nervous about making such a long ride on her own, but she had no time to waste worrying. She was after Brent. Nothing else mattered.

Jack saw the lone rider coming toward the house.

"Abby? You expecting some company?" he called out to her.

"No, Papa. Why?"

"There's someone riding in," Jack told her.

Abby had been in her room, at his call she came out. "Who is it?"

"It looks like that girl from town—that Melinda—and she's all by herself."

Abby went outside with him to welcome her.

"Melinda," Abby said as the other woman reined in and dismounted.

"Hello, Abby, Mr. Hunter."

"This is a surprise," Abby said.

"I know; I planned it that way. I wanted to surprise Brent. Can you get him for me?"

"Brent's not here," Jack offered.

"Oh." Melinda's disappointment was obvious. "Well, I can wait. Will he be back soon?"

"Brent doesn't live here with us anymore," he said bluntly.

"I didn't know," she said, shocked and suddenly worried that the man of her dreams was gone. "Where is he? He hasn't left the area, has he?"

"No," Jack answered, although there were times when he wished Brent *were* gone. "He just moved down to the old cabin by the creek. You can find him there."

"Could one of you show me how to get there?" Melinda asked. She had no idea where the cabin was and wasn't about to return home after riding all this way without seeing Brent.

"Abby, take her out to the cabin," Jack ordered.

Abby didn't really want to see Brent. She was still angry with him for moving out, but Papa had put her on the spot.

"Give me a minute to get my horse," she told Melinda. Her thoughts were not pretty as she went out to the stable to saddle up Moon Racer. The only thing that made her smile was the prospect of surprising Brent with Melinda. It was going to be interesting to see his reaction to her unexpected visit.

Chapter Nineteen

The day was passing blissfully for Brent and Crystal. In their own way, they had each chosen to live for the moment, and each moment they had together was paradise.

When Brent was with Crystal, he allowed himself no worries about his father or the work around the ranch. He allowed himself to relax and enjoy her company. Crystal, too, put from her any thoughts that might ruin her time with Brent. She took what pleasure she could, while she could.

With their passion for each other momentarily sated, they dressed and left the haven that was Brent's bedroom.

"Want to go for a ride? I brought Honey here for you."

"Oh, good, I'd like that." She was fond of the horse and eager to ride her again.

They left the house to saddle their horses and rode off to enjoy the peace and beauty of the countryside. They followed the stream for a few miles to a place where it formed a small pool. Crystal convinced Brent to go wading with her. She didn't splash him this time, but he still started to chase her.

This time Crystal did not run from him. This time Crystal ran *to* him.

Brent swept her up and carried her to the bank and laid her upon the soft grass.

"I told you wading was fun," she said, drawing him down for a provocative kiss.

Brent was tempted to take her again, right then and there. The heat of her kiss told him without words that she was ready and willing, but he held himself under restraint.

"We'd better go," he told her, standing up and moving away from her.

"Why?" Crystal asked softly. "I thought this was our day to do whatever we wanted to do."

"It is," he answered, trying to deny the passion he was feeling.

"Well, there's something I want to do." Her words were an enticement.

"What?" he asked, his voice gruff as he struggled to control his desires.

"I want to make love to you again," Crystal told

him as she smiled up at him invitingly. She was feeling terribly brazen, but right then it didn't matter. All that mattered was being back in Brent's arms.

Brent had always considered himself a man of iron self-control. During the years he'd spent building up the Half-Moon and paying off its debts, he hadn't given a thought to his own pleasures. He'd cared only about providing for his family and taking care of business. And right now he knew he should deny his need to make love to Crystal, but his desire for her overruled all logic.

There on the soft bed of grass they came together in a passionate blending that left them both exhausted.

They finally moved apart and got dressed again.

"I think I like spending Sundays with you," Crystal told him. "And I especially like going wading with you." She added the last with a grin.

"I like wading with you, too."

He kissed her one final time, and then they rode back toward the cabin.

"I wonder where Brent is?" Melinda said as she and Abby looked around the deserted cabin.

"Knowing my brother, he's out working somewhere. That's about all he does." To herself, she had to admit that he'd done a good job of fixing up the old cabin. It actually looked nice.

Melinda intended to change his devotion to work just as soon as she could get her hands on him. But where was he? "It's Sunday. He should be enjoying himself."

"I don't think we're talking about the same man," Abby said.

Melinda wasn't going to give up easily. "I'm going to wait here for a little while. He's bound to show up eventually. You can go on, if you want to."

Abby thought it was a little strange that Melinda wanted to stay there at the empty cabin to wait for Brent.

"I'll stick around for a while," she told her. "I haven't seen much of him this week."

Inwardly, Melinda was angry. She didn't want Abby anywhere around when Brent returned, but there was no way to get rid of her. Melinda managed a sickeningly sweet smile as they settled in together to await Brent's return.

"There are horses tied up at the cabin," Brent pointed out as they came within view. "One of them is Moon Racer—I wonder what Abby's doing here. I hope there's no trouble."

He urged Storm to a quicker pace, and Crystal followed after him as he rode in.

"Abby?" Brent called out as he reined in before the house and quickly dismounted.

He had just started up the porch steps when the door opened and Melinda walked out.

"Hello, Brent," Melinda purred, meeting him on the porch. "I've been waiting for you."

"Melinda?" He was caught completely off guard by her presence. "What are you doing here?"

"Why, I came to see you. Your sister was kind enough to bring me out here."

"Abby?" He looked past Melinda to where Abby was only just now coming out of the cabin.

"She came out to the house looking for you, so I brought her over here to see you," Abby explained quickly.

Melinda gazed at him adoringly. Obviously she was expecting a warm welcome from him. And then Melinda heard the other horse coming.

"What is she doing here?" Melinda demanded, her dreamy expression changing to an ugly sneer when she caught sight of Crystal.

"Crystal is here as my guest today," Brent said sharply, irritated by Melinda's audacity. He hadn't invited her to the Half-Moon, and he had no idea why she'd come so boldly on her own.

"But I came all this way just to visit with you," Melinda said, gazing up at Brent.

"Was there something that you needed?" he asked.

Melinda blushed with humiliation. "No. No, there's nothing I need."

She started down the steps, completely outraged over how things had turned out. No wonder Brent hadn't come to town this weekend! He'd been out here—with that slut!

Melinda realized miserably that she'd ridden all

233

the way to the ranch just to be with him, and he was sending her away. He was ignoring her!

"I'll be going."

"Can you find your way back to town from here?" Abby asked.

"Yes. I'll be fine." Melinda held her head high as she left them. She wanted nothing more to do with any of the Hunters. She knew the way to the main road, and she would go straight back to town. Her hope of winning Brent had been dashed. She tried to think of another man in town as desirable as Brent, but there wasn't one. No one measured up to him. Bitterness filled her as she mounted up.

Crystal had been surprised to see Melinda come out of the cabin when she rode up—and she'd been a bit jealous. For a moment she'd wondered what the other woman was doing there. But the abrupt way Brent had sent her off eased her anxiety.

Abby said nothing for a moment as she watched Melinda ride away. Then she looked at Brent. "Woman trouble, big brother?"

"You have no idea."

"Never mind," Crystal said smoothly, dismounting and going to stand at Brent's side. "I can see why any woman would want to have your attention."

Brent looked down at Crystal, his expression changing to one of affection.

"Honestly, if I'd known you were here, Crystal, I would never have brought Melinda out to see Brent."

Brent shot Abby another look of disapproval.

"All right. I'll leave." She started to go to her horse.

"If you'll wait a few minutes, we'll ride over to the house with you. I thought we'd come for dinner tonight," Brent told her. "There's something I need to talk to Pa about, and Crystal wanted to see both of you again."

"All right, I'll wait."

"What did you think about Brent's moving here to the cabin?" Crystal asked her. "He did a fine job of fixing the place up, didn't he?"

"Yes, he did," Abby agreed. She said nothing more, though, for she didn't want to share her true feelings about Brent's moving out.

Brent saw the hurt in his sister's gaze. "Abby, I told you that you can move in with me anytime."

Abby looked him straight in the eye. "I know you did, but I'm staying at the house. Papa can't make me leave, like he did you."

Brother and sister stared at each other for a long moment.

"Well, if you want to eat, we'd better head back now. Are you going to ride or drive the buckboard?"

"We'll take the buckboard," Brent answered, knowing he would have to take Crystal back to town after dinner.

They rode for the main house. Crystal glanced back once toward the peaceful setting of the cabin, and she smiled as she remembered their hours there.

Jack appeared to be glad to see Crystal again, and dinner was pleasant. Brent wasn't looking forward to talking to his father about what he'd heard in the saloon the night before, but he knew he had to ask him about it before he left to take Crystal back to town.

"I need to talk to Pa for a minute. I'll meet you outside," he told Crystal.

She went on outside with Abby to give them privacy.

"What's bothering you now?" Jack challenged, immediately taking the offensive.

"When I was at the Lone Star last night, the bartender told me you were there drinking last week."

"Yeah, so?"

"He also told me that Edmund was with you and that you were talking about buying more property for the Half-Moon."

"Talk is cheap."

"What did you and Edmund talk about?"

"He said there was some property for sale that adjoined the Half-Moon."

"You didn't do anything stupid, did you?"

Jack glared at him. "Remember who you're talking to!"

"I know exactly who I'm talking to! Don't forget I know how you are when you're drunk!"

"You think you're so smart, but you don't know anything!"

"What did you do?" Brent suddenly went cold.

Jack gave him a sly look. "Remember the Sullivan ranch?"

"Iona Montgomery's place—the one that belonged to her late husband? Edmund sold it right after he married her. Why? What about it?" A sense of dread filled him.

"The place has gone through several owners. The last one had some trouble with rustlers."

"So I heard," Brent said.

"It drove him under, so he needed to sell. Thanks to Edmund, I got the place for a good price."

"What did you use for money?" Brent demanded.

"Edmund took care of that, too. I took out a loan, but that's no problem."

"You didn't." Brent's jaw locked in anger as his hands clenched into fists at his sides.

"I did. I'm going to make the Half-Moon the most successful ranch in Texas," he said with pride.

Brent was beyond fury.

Ten years . . . For ten years he'd worked from dawn to dusk—and sometimes longer—to get the ranch out of debt.

And all for nothing. Pa was at it again.

"How could you do this? Didn't any of what I've done over these last ten years mean anything to you?" He was holding himself under rigid control.

"You did what I would have done," Jack said dismissing his argument. "You worked hard and held on to the ranch. Now it's time to start thinking about the future. It's time to make it grow again."

"How much did Edmund loan you?" he ground out, needing to know the full truth.

"I don't know."

"You don't know?" Brent was appalled.

"I signed the papers, and Edmund said he'd take care of it like he's always taken care of the banking end of things for me."

"Don't you think it's time you put your trust in me and *my* judgment about the ranch—instead of Edmund's?" Brent asked in a cold, harsh voice. "He could have repossessed the ranch while you were locked up serving your time!"

"But he didn't," Jack countered.

"Because I made the payments on time!"

They faced off, glaring at each other.

"It's my ranch," Jack answered, refusing to admit to Brent that he might be right.

"That I saved," Brent stated, then turned his back and walked out.

He was glad that Crystal was already in the buckboard. He climbed up beside her and drove off.

"See you later," Abby called as they left.

Crystal waved good-bye to her, but Brent didn't respond. He concentrated solely on his driving.

Abby wondered what had happened between him and Papa to so darken his mood. Whatever it was, it must have been ugly. She went back inside to see if she could find out what had occurred.

"Is something wrong?" Crystal, too, realized Brent's mood was drastically different.

"Nothing that I shouldn't have been expecting," he said, a note of bitterness in his voice.

"Do you want to talk about it?"

"Talking about it won't change anything."

"No, but I'm a real good listener."

He managed to smile at her then, knowing she truly cared and was just trying to help. He explained what his father had done. "After I take you back to the boardinghouse, I'm going to see Edmund."

"Will it do any good? Will he listen to you?"

"I think maybe I wasn't forceful enough when I talked to him before. This time I'll make sure he listens. Maybe there's still some way to stop the purchase."

Brent saw her safely home. Anne was there to meet her, so they had no opportunity for another kiss. Crystal was very sorry, but she had her memories of the early afternoon to last her through the week. As she watched Brent leave, she hoped he would be able to work things out with the banker.

Chapter Twenty

Brent left her and went straight to Edmund's house. Iona answered his knock and he was a bit stunned by how drawn and haggard she looked.

"Brent, what are you doing here?" Iona asked.

"I need to talk to Edmund, if he's around."

"Come on in. He's in the study," she said, holding the door wide for him to enter. "Go on in and see him."

"Thanks."

Brent had been in their house before and knew the way. He knocked only once on the door, and at Edmund's call, he entered. Edmund was sitting behind his desk looking very confident and secure.

"Why, Brent. This is an unexpected pleasure."

"I hardly think my visit here is unexpected, Edmund," Brent said tersely. "And I know it's no pleasure under these circumstances."

"What's wrong?" Edmund asked innocently.

"You know damn well what's wrong!" Brent approached his desk and stood before him, his rage evident in his expression. "I asked you not to make any new loans to my father! I told you that I wanted to keep the Half-Moon out of debt!"

"Ah, so Jack told you about the deal we got on the Sullivan property."

"Pa didn't tell me anything until after I found out from talk down at the Lone Star!"

Edmund shrugged as if it were of little importance where he'd learned of the sale.

"Jack wanted to expand the ranch, and I knew that property was for sale. It seemed a good arrangement for all involved," he explained easily, but, sensing Brent's fury, he slipped his hand into the desk drawer where he kept his gun.

"That property has been for sale for quite a while, and it's worthless to us! The Half-Moon doesn't need that land. We're already big enough."

"Well, the ranch is even bigger now."

"Cancel the deal."

"The sale was finalized. It's done."

"Why, you . . . !" Brent was ready to throttle him.

Edmund drew out his gun and aimed it straight at him. "Get out of here now, Brent. You come any closer and I'll be forced to use this on you."

Brent stopped. "So that's the way it is?"

"Yes," Edmund replied smoothly.

Brent stared at the man who was supposedly a family friend and then looked down at the gun in his hand. "Thanks for being such a good friend. I'll remember this."

"So will I," Edmund responded.

Without another word, Brent turned around and left.

Edmund followed him to make sure he was gone. Only when Brent had ridden off did Edmund return to the desk and put the gun away. He sat back down and thought about what had just happened.

And he smiled.

Edmund's smile faded when he heard Iona in the hallway. Fortunately she had gone back to her room when Brent arrived. Edmund hadn't wanted her to hear any of what had transpired between them.

"I just wanted to say good-night, Edmund," Iona offered as she stood in the study doorway.

Edmund could see that she was unsteady on her feet and knew she'd been drinking while she was in her room. He stood up and walked around the desk. "It's early, dear. I thought you'd keep me company for a little longer tonight."

Iona's expression brightened at his words.

Edmund was filled with disgust by her drunken state, but forced a smile as he went on, "I was thinking about the letter you received from Juliana a few days ago."

"Oh, yes. Juliana is doing so well. She's in Saratoga, New York, visiting her late husband's family, you know." Iona smiled as she thought of her daughter. "Who would have thought that my Juliana would be so well traveled at such a young age?" She gave a shaky laugh. "I was worried when she married Harlan Rains. He was so much older than she was, and so sophisticated. I thought . . ." She shrugged. "Well, it doesn't matter what I thought, does it? It all turned out well in the end."

Iona gasped and her eyes widened as she realized what she'd just said. "Oh, my—I didn't mean it was good that Harlan died. He was a fine man, and he left Juliana a rich woman. Of course, money isn't everything, and I'm sure she wishes he were still alive. I just meant—"

"I know what you meant." Edmund cut her off impatiently, tired of her endless ramblings. "I was thinking you could answer her letter tonight, and I could post it tomorrow for you."

"That's so kind of you, Edmund." She paused, then continued in a softer voice, "I know your relationship with Juliana was difficult. Juliana can be a very stubborn girl, and I know she tried your patience sometimes. I want you to know I appreciate your forbearance."

"She's your daughter, so of course I love her."

"Oh, Edmund."

The charade sickened him, but he continued.

"About the letter . . . We can write it now at my desk, if you feel up to it?"

"Oh, yes," she responded, brightening at the thought. "I'd like that."

Moments later Iona was seated at Edmund's desk, pen in hand, writing the letter as he dictated it.

My dear Juliana,

I was so pleased to hear you're doing well. I'm proud of your accomplishments. I enjoy hearing about the interesting people you have met and the places you have visited while staying with Harlan's family.

I am well and so is Edmund. We live a busy life. Our work at church is very satisfying.

Everyone in Diablo asks about you and sends you their regards. They enjoy hearing about your adventures almost as much as I do. Edmund and I look forward to your next letter, and we send our love.

Sincerely,
Mother

Edmund waited until she'd finished writing before asking, "Is there anything I left out that you want to add?"

"No, the letter is fine the way it is."

"Go ahead and address the envelope," he encouraged.

He sealed the envelope moments later and set it aside. Iona got up and went to him.

"You can go on to bed now, dear. I have an appointment to keep. I'll see you in the morning."

The disappointment in her expression was so obvious, Edmund almost laughed out loud. His lips twisted into a sneer as he watched her move unsteadily back down the hall toward the bedroom. He knew she had wanted him to make love to her tonight, and he shuddered at the thought of touching her.

Edmund watched Iona until she had disappeared into the bedroom and closed the door behind her. He'd mail the letter tomorrow, and when Juliana received it, she would read her mother's glowing report of her happy life. Juliana would stay in Saratoga, where she belonged.

Chapter Twenty-one

The weeks that followed passed in a blur for Brent. He was beyond anger, and he was almost beyond caring about the ranch. As his father had told him numerous times, Jack owned the place and he could do what he wanted.

Brent kept himself busy breaking stock. He tried to come to grips with what he'd learned, but there was no way he could reason his way out of this.

His father had done the unthinkable—he had put the ranch back in debt. And he'd done it without even asking him. Brent felt doubly betrayed, for Edmund had made the loan to his father after he'd specifically asked him not to.

Brent knew he was the driving force behind the Half-Moon. He had been for ten years. The men looked to him for leadership. Yet he had been helpless to stop his father from putting the ranch in jeopardy again.

He was tempted to leave—to just pack up and ride away. Night after night as he paced alone in the cabin, he thought of making a new life of his own away from the Half-Moon. But each morning as dawn cast its golden glow over the land, Brent knew he couldn't leave. He loved the ranch too much. The Half-Moon had been his life for too long. He couldn't forsake it now.

If he stayed, at least he would be there to fight to keep it going. He had saved the Half-Moon from his father's stupidity once. He could do it again.

Brent thought of Edmund and knew he could never look at him the same way again. It seemed his uneasiness about the man had been justified. Edmund was no friend of the family—not after making that loan to his father and then pulling a gun on Brent.

Only the time he spent with Crystal kept Brent from even darker despair. The memory of her smile and her kiss left him counting the days each week until he could get back into town to see her.

Tomorrow was Saturday, and he couldn't leave for Diablo soon enough.

"That's the first time you've smiled in quite a while," Hank said, as he watched Brent ride a newly broken mount around the corral.

"It's the first time I've felt like smiling," Brent responded.

"What are you thinking about?"

"I'm thinking about going to town tomorrow and visiting a pretty little lady."

"You seeing Crystal again? Or are you going to see Melinda this week?" Hank asked with a grin. "It sure must be tough having two of the best-looking women in town after you."

The other ranch hands chuckled at his humor. They had all heard the story from Abby about what had happened with Melinda out at the cabin a few weeks back.

Brent scowled at them, but it was a good-natured scowl. They laughed at him again.

"Crystal's the only woman for me," he answered.

"I can understand why," Hank agreed.

The following day Brent made his getaway. He took a room at the hotel in town again and got ready to go to the Lone Star to watch Crystal perform.

Tonight was his to enjoy himself, and Brent intended to do just that.

Crystal stood before the mirror in her dressing room, staring at her reflection. It was almost time to go onstage. It was almost time to see Brent again.

Crystal's mood was frantic as she tried to come to grips with all that was tormenting her.

She turned sideways and studied the fit of her dress. She breathed a sigh of relief. She looked the same. No one would be able to tell—yet.

Pregnant.

Crystal finally allowed herself to face the truth. She'd tried to deny it for days but her cycle was as regular as clockwork. There could be only one reason she'd missed her monthly flux.

She was going to have Brent's child.

The knowledge frightened her. She wasn't sure what to do. How could she care for the child by herself when she was on the run from the law?

During the time she'd worked with Dan, Crystal had known a saloon girl who'd found herself in the same situation. She had been horrified when the girl had gone to an old woman who had aborted the baby.

Crystal rested a hand protectively on her still-flat stomach. Growing within her was Brent's child—and her child. She would never cause her son or daughter harm. She was going to do everything in her power to protect her baby.

Her baby.

Crystal drew a calming breath and told herself there was no need to panic. She still had time to figure out the best thing to do.

There were moments when Crystal considered running away—just disappearing again, as she had in San Antonio, but in her heart she knew she couldn't—not this time. She had to tell Brent the truth about the baby.

Love him though she did, Crystal hadn't been able to justify marrying him when he had proposed before; she hadn't wanted to involve him in the danger surrounding her. She knew how he felt about his father, and she was terrified he'd feel the same way toward her when he learned of her past.

Now, though, Crystal realized that marrying Brent was her only hope. If she tried to continue on alone and the law caught up with her, their baby would suffer. If she and Brent were married, at least their child would have a home and be loved, no matter what happened to her.

All Crystal needed to do now was find the inner strength to tell Brent about her pregnancy. She only prayed that he still wanted to marry her.

As ready as she would ever be, Crystal looked up at her own mirror image once more and forced herself to smile. It was time to go to work. She had to transform herself into Ruby now and go entertain the customers.

Then Crystal remembered that Brent would be there in the saloon waiting for her when she went out, and her smile was no longer forced. It lit up her face with joy.

The Lone Star was already crowded and more than a little rowdy when Brent arrived.

"Ruby's sure drawing them in tonight," Ken said with a big grin as Brent came to stand at the bar.

"She's the reason I'm here," Brent agreed as the bartender set his usual beer before him. He relaxed at the bar, waiting for her first performance to begin.

"I just hope the rest of these boys behave themselves," Ken told him.

"It's payday," Brent said easily, looking around.

"Yeah, it's payday, all right," Ken answered, always glad when the ranch hands had money to spend. "But they just seem wilder than usual tonight. Some fellas are new here in town. I haven't seen them before."

"Maybe they heard that the Lone Star is the best place to come to have a good time."

"They'd be right then, wouldn't they?" Ken laughed as the piano player began the song to introduce Ruby.

The men in the saloon cheered, knowing Ruby was about to come out. All attention was riveted on the beautiful, mesmerizing redhead who appeared before them. The audience watched in drunken delight as she moved about the stage, singing with the voice of an angel. Some of her songs were ballads and some were fun and fast-paced, but no matter what she sang, the men applauded enthusiastically.

Brent enjoyed her performance, too, but he was eager for the evening to end so they could be together. He would have to bide his time, though, for she still had several performances that night.

Crystal had seen Brent standing at the bar the moment she'd first come out. Just knowing he was there inspired her. When she finally finished her last song, she left the stage to mix and mingle with the men in the audience. She made her way slowly and deliberately toward Brent.

"Evening, Ted. Good evening, Rick," Crystal said, flirting with some of the regular patrons as she passed by.

Crystal regretted there were no older men at the Lone Star like Andy. She'd always had a soft spot in her heart for the old man in San Antonio and found herself missing him on occasion. Andy had been a gentleman, and that was rare. She made her way over to a group of cowboys she didn't recognize.

"Evening, fellas," she said. "Welcome to the Lone Star. Are you having a good time tonight?"

"We are now that you're here!" Tex Bradley told her with a lascivious grin as he openly ogled her.

"Well, that's good to hear," she managed, but something about the man repulsed her.

"You can help me have a better time—if you want to, little lady," Tex said, giving the other men at the table a knowing look as he reached out to grab her hand.

Crystal avoided his touch and stepped away. "I'll try to do just that—in my next performance."

"That ain't what I had in mind," he said in a growl, turning red-faced and feeling humiliated as his buddies laughed at him.

"Take it easy, cowboy," one of the men at the next table said. He'd been watching and sensed trouble might be brewing. "Ruby ain't no saloon girl. She's a lady."

Tex glared at the man for interfering and then looked back at Ruby. He didn't say anything, but the lust he felt for her was still evident in his expression.

"I hope you have a pleasant evening," Crystal said, moving off. She couldn't get away from their table fast enough.

"Everything all right?" Brent asked in a low voice when she finally made it to his side. He'd been keeping an eye on her and had noticed the men at the poker table giving her some trouble. He knew how good she was at handling rowdy men, but he was always ready to go to her aid if she needed him.

"Yes, I'm with you now," she told him as relief flooded through her. "I missed you all week."

"I missed you, too."

Brent looked down at her, and their gazes met. For a moment it was as if the whole world disappeared and it was just the two of them—alone. The moment of peace didn't last long, though.

"Hey, Ruby! Come on back over here for a while!" one of the men at Tex's table yelled at her. "We got a poker game going, and I need you here with me to bring me some good luck!"

"I'd better go." Crystal did not want to leave Brent, but she was working.

"I'll be right here waiting for you," he promised.

Crystal made her rounds again, finally stopping by the cowboy who'd called out to her. She didn't like being around the card playing. It reminded her too much of the time she'd spent with Dan. Even so, she stayed on, knowing Ken counted on her to keep the customers happy.

"All right, let's see you win this big hand, cowboy," she said encouragingly.

"My name's Wes, sweetheart."

"Good evening, Wes."

"My luck's bound to change now that you're here." Wes was confident and more than a little arrogant.

Crystal was surprised by the tense mood at the poker table. She'd assumed these men were friends, but she realized now that they weren't.

The stakes in the game were very high, and each man was guarding his hand carefully.

When the play came around to Wes again, he matched their bets, raised them another hundred dollars, and called.

"Let's see what you got, Wes," Tex challenged, after throwing his money in.

"Three of a kind," Wes announced proudly, casting a triumphant glance up at Ruby as he spread three jacks out for them to see.

Two of the other three men threw down their hands in disgust, but Tex was smiling broadly.

"I hate to tell you this, but I don't think the little lady brought you any luck at all. I think she brought me all the luck," Tex said as he laid his hand down on the table for all to see. "My full house beats your three of a kind."

The other players were shocked. They'd thought for sure that Wes was the winner.

Wes was furious.

"You cheated!" Wes declared hotly, staring down at Tex's hand in disbelief. He'd just lost all his money, and he was furious.

"I don't have to cheat to beat you," Tex sneered, raking in the big pile of cash.

"Why, you . . . !"

Drunk and beyond reason, Wes surged to his feet in one violent move. He shoved the table so hard that he knocked it over. The cards and money went flying as he went for his gun, determined to put an end to what he believed were Tex's cheating ways.

Wes drew his gun, swaying unsteadily on his feet as he got off a shot at Tex.

Crystal gasped and rushed to try to get out of the way. She'd seen these kinds of fights before and knew they could be deadly.

Tex wasn't about to go down without a fight. He dove for cover as he drew his sidearm, too, and began firing.

When things had first begun to get ugly, Brent had started in Crystal's direction. He hadn't wanted her anywhere near the two drunks in case real trouble broke out.

And now it had. Everyone in the saloon was running for safety as Tex and Wes fired wildly. Brent drew his own gun, ready to do whatever was necessary to protect Crystal.

Behind the bar Ken grabbed his shotgun. All evening he'd been feeling like there was going to be trouble tonight, but he hadn't thought it would be anything this serious. He wanted to put an end to the shooting, but he couldn't get a clear shot at either one of the troublemakers.

"I can't get 'em, Brent! Can you?" Ken shouted to him.

"I'll try!" Brent struggled toward Crystal, frantic to keep her from being hurt. He prayed he could reach her in time.

Chaos reigned as Crystal sought safety behind a fallen table. She huddled down as more shots rang out. Screams and terrible, pain-filled shrieks echoed in the room.

Brent crouched low as he moved forward, trying to get off a shot at either one of the drunks to stop the bloody violence. He cast a quick look around for Crystal, but saw no sign of her anywhere. Terror unlike anything he'd ever known before filled him.

Had Crystal been shot? Was she lying hurt and bleeding somewhere?

A protective rage pounded within Brent as he realized just how deeply he cared for her—just how much he loved her. He had to put a stop to this now!

When Wes rose up to get another shot off at Tex, Brent saw his chance. He fired and hit Wes squarely in the shoulder. The force of the shot spun him backward, knocking him to the floor. Brent turned, ready to take on Tex.

"Hold it!" Ken shouted, his shotgun pointed straight at the other gunman.

Tex dropped his own sidearm as he looked down the barrel of the bartender's shotgun.

"Somebody get the sheriff—and the doc!" Ken ordered as he kept his gun trained on the drunken troublemaker who was still standing.

Two other customers lay on the floor, bleeding from gunshot wounds. Brent checked to make sure they were still breathing, then began his frantic search for Crystal.

She had to be safe! He couldn't bear it if something had happened to her.

He loved her.

Chapter Twenty-two

He loved her. . . .

The knowledge jolted Brent to the depths of his soul, but he finally accepted the truth of it. What else could explain the power of his feelings for her?

He loved Crystal. The thought of living without her was unbearable.

He offered up a fervent prayer that she was all right as he turned toward the place where he'd seen her last. Crystal was standing there watching him. She was pale and shaken, but he could tell she was uninjured.

Without a word, Brent rushed to take her in his arms and hold her close.

"You're all right?" he asked in a husky voice.

Crystal only nodded and clung to him, trembling. She was still too frightened to speak. She had seen

Brent going for his gun and had feared he would be shot down.

Brent felt her trembling and scooped her up in his arms. "We're getting out of here right now."

"But Ken—"

"Ken can handle this," he said tersely, and strode from the Lone Star without looking back. The sheriff and the town doctor were coming toward the saloon at a run, but he didn't pause. A crowd of townsfolk were gathering.

"What happened?" they shouted to him.

"A couple of drunks shot it out," he called back to them, and kept on going. Brent wasn't stopping for anyone or anything until he had Crystal alone back in his room. He knew what he was going to do. He had made up his mind that they were going to get married, and he wasn't going to take no for an answer. He would never allow Crystal to put herself in this kind of danger again. Never. She meant too much to him.

"Where are you taking me?" she asked.

"First, to my room at the hotel," he answered, his expression serious.

"Don't you think I should change clothes first?"

"No. We have to talk—now—and I want it to be somewhere private."

"I can walk now," Crystal said.

He looked so grim she thought he was angry with her, but at her words, his mouth lifted in a half grin, surprising her.

Brent looked down at her, his gaze warm upon her. "I like carrying you this way."

"Oh . . ." Her eyes were luminous as she gazed up at him.

Brent would have kissed her right then and there, but they were out in public. Granted, it was dark, but if he allowed himself to kiss her one time, he wasn't sure he would be able to stop.

He entered the hotel and was glad there was no one in the lobby. He strode straight upstairs and took her into his room. He set her on her feet, then lit a lamp and closed the door firmly behind them, insuring they wouldn't be interrupted.

"We're going to have a little talk," Brent announced as he faced Crystal.

"About what?"

"We're getting married," he said bluntly, offering her little opportunity to argue with him.

"Oh." She was shocked. It was what she'd hoped for. It was what she'd dreamed of, yet he sounded so . . . serious.

"And there's no point in arguing with me," Brent went on in his dictatorial manner.

"I wasn't going to," Crystal said in a soft voice.

Brent had been ready for trouble from her. He stopped in surprise. "You weren't?"

"No. I love you, Brent," she said simply. "I love you very much. When all the trouble started in the saloon and I thought you might get shot, I was frantic. I couldn't bear the thought that anything might happen to you."

Brent stood perfectly still, as if not quite sure that he'd heard her right. Only when Crystal went to him and reached up to kiss him sweetly on the lips did he accept her words as reality.

Brent looked down at her. "And I love you, too."

"You do?"

He could only nod in response as his gaze went over her in a loving caress.

"But Brent, there is something I have to tell you. Something you have to know," Crystal began as she drew physically away from him.

He sensed her withdrawing emotionally as well, and he worried about it. Brent put his hands on her shoulders and gently pulled her closer to him. Whatever she had to tell him couldn't be that bad. They loved each other.

"What is it?" he asked, concerned.

"Brent . . ." Crystal looked up at him anxiously. "I'm pregnant."

"You're pregnant?" he repeated, lost for a moment in the magnitude of what she'd just announced.

"Yes," she answered quietly, then awaited his reaction.

Brent didn't speak. He showed her instead what he thought by gathering her even closer and kissing her.

"We'll go to Reverend Crawford tonight. There's

no reason to wait any longer. You won't be going back to the Lone Star ever again. I want you with me always. That way I'll know you're safe," Brent told her, taking charge of her life.

Crystal gave him a gentle smile.

"You saved me again tonight, you know," she said softly, reaching up with one hand to tenderly caress his cheek.

"And I want that to be the last time you're in any danger," Brent said as he looked down at her. He couldn't bear the thought that any harm might come to her, and now that he knew she was carrying his child, his protective instincts were even greater.

Crystal wanted it to be the last time, too, but the horror that was her past still haunted her. She wrapped her arms around Brent and clung to him.

Brent was her power and her strength. He loved her. He was going to marry her.

And she wanted that. Oh, how she wanted that.

But could she marry him without telling him the complete and awful truth about her life?

Crystal knew the answer. She loved Brent too much to try to deceive him. She had to be honest with him. She knew how he felt about what his father had done and how that tragedy had torn apart his family. For that very reason, she couldn't put her child's future at risk. She had to be sure their baby would have a secure, loving home.

But what if she told him, and he wanted nothing more to do with her?

The uncertainty of her future brought tears to Crystal's eyes. She struggled for control as she prepared herself to speak.

"You're crying?" Brent asked, worried when he drew away from her and saw her tears.

Crystal nodded and drew a ragged breath. "There's something more I have to tell you."

He stared down at her, studying her tortured expression and trying to imagine what could upset her so badly. He wanted to reassure her. "I love you, Crystal. Whatever it is, it doesn't matter."

"Yes, it does matter!" she choked out. "You have to hear me out. I won't marry you until I've told you. . . ."

Crystal moved away from him, needing to put some distance between them as she made her confession.

Brent remained standing where he was, watching her and waiting for her to go on.

"Told me what?" he asked quietly, knowing from the way she was acting that what was troubling her was serious.

"You have to know that I haven't always been just a singer when I worked in saloons," Crystal began slowly.

"I know you're no saloon girl." Brent frowned slightly, confused by her distress. She had given him her innocence, after all.

"Please . . ." She paused, then began again. "My real name is Crystal Stewart—Morgan is my middle name. I didn't tell you the truth when I said I had no family. My parents are dead—they died when I was young—but I do have an older brother named Dan."

Brent was surprised that she hadn't acknowledged her brother, but he believed it didn't really matter.

"Dan's a gambler, and I used to work with him as his shill, helping him cheat people at cards," Crystal admitted.

"You cheated people? Why?"

"Dan made me do it. He said it was the only way we could make money and support ourselves. It was all I knew. But I know that's no excuse. It was wrong, and I told Dan the last night we were together that I was quitting—that I couldn't do it anymore."

"I'm proud of you," Brent assured her.

"But Brent . . ." She started to say more, to tell him everything, but she hesitated, afraid. Brent was being so kind and so understanding. She wondered if he would feel the same way after she told him the rest.

"What is it, Crystal?" Brent urged.

"Brent, I killed a man," Crystal finally blurted out the horrible truth. "That's why I've been using different names. That's why I keep moving on—the law is after me."

Brent went still as he tried to come to grips with what she'd just told him. He couldn't believe this was happening to him again. First his father, and now the woman he loved.

Could Crystal really have killed someone?

It didn't seem possible.

She had gone silent and was watching him closely, trying to judge his reaction to what she'd revealed.

"Crystal," Brent began slowly, seeing the torment in her expression. "Tell me what happened. I know you. I love you. I don't believe you could kill anyone."

"I did—it was horrible! Dan and I had been working a saloon in Long Horn one night, and he lost a lot of money in a poker game to a man named John Hall. I was worried because Dan didn't have any money to pay him. I went on up to my room, thinking Dan would figure out a way to take care of the problem. Later that night, I woke up to find Hall in my room. He told me Dan had sent him to me and said I was supposed to work off what he owed him. He wanted me to . . ." Crystal went pale as the memory of that terrible night returned full force. She swallowed tightly as her gaze met Brent's. "I couldn't let him touch me." She shuddered visibly at the memory of Hall's hands upon her. "I fought him off as best I could. He hit me, but I kept struggling. I managed to grab a lamp from the bedside table and I hit him over the head with it. That was what killed him."

If her brother had been there with them at that moment, Brent would have beaten the man within an inch of his life. He thought of Abby, of her youth and innocence, and he couldn't imagine treating a little sister the way Dan had treated Crystal. As a big brother and a guardian, it had been Dan's responsibility to protect Crystal and make life good for her—not use her in gambling schemes and then turn her into a whore to pay back his debts. Brent put his arms around Crystal. He could feel her trembling and wanted only to calm her and let her know she was safe with him.

"I'm proud of you, Crystal."

"You're proud of me?"

"I'm glad you defended yourself. You had the right to fight that man off," Brent said. "That was self-defense—not murder."

"But Hall was dead."

"Are you sure?"

"Yes. The lamp shattered when I hit him. He collapsed and didn't move. There was blood and glass everywhere." She shuddered violently at the memory.

"What did you do?"

"What could I do? I couldn't go to Dan—he'd betrayed me. I ran away that night, and I've been running ever since."

"You should have gone to the law."

"It wouldn't have mattered. Hall was one of the town's 'upstanding' citizens. I worked in the saloon. No one would have believed me."

Brent held Crystal away from him and looked down at her. When he spoke, he spoke quietly but with no hesitation. "I believe you."

Crystal's breath caught in her throat as she gazed up at him in wonder. "You do?"

"Yes, I do."

She went into the safe harbor of his arms, clinging to his strength. She had been on her own for so long, alone and frightened, but now she had Brent.

She had feared he would reject her. She had been terrified that he would walk away from her, that he would despise her for what she'd done. But he believed her.

"Thank you," she whispered, her tears dampening his shirt. It felt so good to have told him the truth. She had kept her terrible secret locked deep within her for so long, it was a relief to have shared it with him.

Brent stood there, holding Crystal in his arms for a moment longer; then he lifted her chin with one hand to look in her eyes. "Are you ready?"

"For what?" she asked in a whisper.

"To go see Reverend Crawford."

"You still want to marry me?"

"Yes, I still want to marry you. I love you, Crystal.

Somehow we'll find a way to work this out—together."

Without another word, Crystal drew Brent down to her for a cherishing kiss. There was no greater joy in her life than loving Brent.

Chapter Twenty-three

Brent kissed Crystal one last time and then they left the hotel room. As Brent locked the door behind them, he realized that when they came back he would be carrying her over the threshold again—as his bride.

They stopped at the boardinghouse so Crystal could change clothes. He had told her he would marry her no matter what she was wearing, but she wanted to look her best for him. Since it was after dark, Brent waited outside while she went in.

Anne was surprised to hear Ruby returning so much earlier than usual. Usually the young woman didn't return until long after midnight.

"Ruby? Is everything all right?" she asked as she knocked lightly at her bedroom door.

The knock at the door startled Crystal, but she quickly answered it.

"Anne! Yes, everything is fine," Crystal told her. "In fact, everything is wonderful!"

"I don't understand." Anne had never seen her so happy before.

"Brent and I are getting married—now, tonight!"

"Oh, darling, I am so happy for you! Brent is a wonderful man! You'll be so happy together."

"Yes, we will," she agreed.

"Can I help you? Is there anything I can do?"

"No, I'm just going to change my clothes. He's waiting outside for me."

"Well, if you need anything, you just let me know."

"I will."

Anne couldn't resist giving her a warm hug. "I'm so glad you've found your happiness."

"Thank you."

Crystal closed the bedroom door and went back to the armoire to look through her dresses. Her choices weren't many. She still had her widow's dress, and the thought of wearing it made her smile. Though it was demure and it did have a veil, the heavy black gown certainly wasn't appropriate for this joyous occasion. Crystal took out a day gown and set about changing.

When she'd finished dressing, Crystal went to check her appearance in the mirror.

Her heart swelled with joyous emotion. Soon she

would be married to the man she loved. Soon she would be Mrs. Brent Hunter.

Crystal was ready to begin her new life. She would no longer be alone in the world. She had Brent now—Brent, who knew everything about her and still loved her.

She left her room and descended the stairs. She found Anne waiting for her in the parlor with Brent.

"There was no point in letting your handsome fiancé wait for you outside," Anne told her when she appeared in the doorway.

Brent looked up at her. She was wearing the same dress she'd worn to church, but he knew he wouldn't have thought her lovelier if she had been wearing a bridal gown. To him, she was the most beautiful woman in the world. He stood up to go to her.

"Are you ready?" he asked.

"Yes." There was no hesitation. This was her dream come true.

"Do you have a ring?" Anne asked, wanting to make sure everything was perfect for them. She thought their elopement was so romantic.

Brent hadn't thought about a ring. "No. I don't."

"It doesn't matter," Crystal said.

"Yes, it does. Wait just a minute." Anne went into her own bedroom. She came back out a few moments later with a simple gold band. "Here. See if this will fit you."

Crystal slipped the ring easily on her finger. "It's perfect."

"Then it's yours."

"Oh, no, I couldn't take it," Crystal said.

"Let me pay you for it," Brent offered.

"No. It's my wedding gift to you. It was left to me by an aunt years ago. I want you to have it."

"You're sure?" Crystal looked up at her, amazed by her generosity.

"Oh, yes. I'm sure." She smiled.

"Thanks, Anne," Brent said, eager to be on their way.

"Oh! Wait! You can't go just yet. You need one more thing." Anne hurried out of the room, but returned quickly carrying a small bouquet of flowers from her garden. She offered them to Crystal. "No bride should be without her bouquet."

"Oh, Anne, you are so dear. Thank you." Crystal was touched by her thoughtfulness as she gazed down at the fragrant blossoms. She hugged the other woman.

"It's the least I can do for you. God bless you both. And Brent?"

Brent looked at her.

"You take good care of Ruby, you hear?"

"I will," he promised.

"I'll see you tomorrow, Anne," Crystal told her. She gave Brent the ring for safekeeping, and they left the house.

Anne watched them until they were out of sight,

then closed the door and sighed romantically over the happiness she knew they would find together. If ever she had seen a couple in love, it was Brent and Ruby. She wanted them to be happy forever.

"Will Reverend Crawford mind our coming to him this late?" Crystal asked as they made their way through town.

"I'll make it worth his while. You don't have to worry," Brent reassured her.

She smiled brightly up at him as they hurried on.

Roused from a sound sleep, Reverend Crawford looked suitably unkempt as he lit a lamp in the front hall of the parsonage. He had thrown on pants, a shirt, and shoes to be presentable, but he wasn't fully awake yet as he unlocked and opened the front door.

"What is it, Brent? Has there been trouble?" he asked. He wondered why the pretty singer from the saloon was standing at his door.

"No trouble, Reverend," Brent said. "We're just in need of your professional services tonight, that's all."

Reverend Crawford frowned for a moment in confusion, then noticed the bouquet she was carrying.

Brent spoke up, answering his unspoken question. "Yes, we want to get married."

"Brent, this is wonderful. I thought I'd never see the day."

"Neither did I, but Crystal changed my mind."

"Crystal?" He had heard her name was Ruby.

"Ruby's just my stage name," she explained quickly.

He smiled warmly at her. "Well, Crystal, you're getting yourself a fine young man."

"I know," she responded with a smile.

"Come on in and close the door. I'll go get my wife so she can be your witness."

The reverend went back into his private quarters, leaving them alone for a moment, and Brent took advantage of his absence by stealing a quick kiss.

"I love you," Brent told her again, wanting to calm any fears or uncertainties she might be feeling.

Crystal only smiled back up at him. Her spirits were soaring. For the first time in as long as she could remember, she was happy—honestly and truly happy. She was going to be Mrs. Brent Hunter.

Reverend Crawford returned with his wife, Mary, who had been wakened from a sound sleep, but was nonetheless thrilled to be witnessing Brent's wedding. They all went into the small room the reverend used as his office. After lighting the lamps there, he got his Bible.

"Do you have a ring?" Reverend Crawford asked.

"Yes."

"Now, let us begin," he intoned.

Brent and Crystal stood enraptured as they pledged their love to each other before God.

"Do you, Crystal, take this man to be your lawfully

wedded husband, to have and to hold, for better or worse, for richer or poorer, in sickness and in health, forsaking all others, till death do you part?" Reverend Crawford asked.

"I do," she answered clearly.

"And you, Brent—do you take this woman to be your lawfully wedded wife, to have and to hold, for better or worse, for richer or poorer, in sickness and in health, forsaking all others, till death do you part?"

"I do," Brent vowed.

"The ring . . ."

Brent slipped the band on Crystal's finger.

"I now pronounce you man and wife. What God has joined together, let no man put asunder," he said, concluding the ceremony. "You may kiss your bride."

Brent did just that, as the reverend and his wife looked on.

"Thank you, Reverend Crawford," Brent told him when he and Crystal moved apart.

"It's our pleasure, Brent. Congratulations, Mr. and Mrs. Hunter," he said.

Mrs. Hunter . . . For a moment, thoughts of his mother came to Brent. He remembered her love and her kindness, her warmth and her devotion to family. It saddened him that she would never know Crystal, but he knew she would have loved her, just as he did.

Crystal noticed a subtle change in his expression. "Is something wrong?"

He looked down at her. "No. Everything is fine."

Brent gave the reverend a generous stipend for performing the ceremony. After bidding the reverend and his wife good night, he and Crystal left the parsonage.

They moved off down the street, not speaking, simply enjoying the wonder of what had just passed.

"Look," Crystal said, pointing up to the sky.

There high above them in the star-studded night sky was a silver half moon.

"Isn't it beautiful?" She sighed.

"Yes, it is, but it's not as beautiful as you."

There on the dark, deserted street, Brent took his wife in his arms and kissed her.

"I love you, Mrs. Hunter."

They hurried on, eager to return to the hotel room, eager to be alone. When they reached the room, he unlocked the door and scooped her up in his arms.

"I have to carry my bride over the doorstep."

Brent carried her inside and laid her gently on the bed. He went back to close and lock the door.

As Brent returned to Crystal's side, neither gave any thought to all that had passed earlier in the evening. There was only the pure beauty of their love. They were man and wife.

Crystal welcomed him to her with open arms.

She had never known a man like Brent before—a man who was strong, yet kind; powerful, yet gentle; fierce, yet loving. Brent was her dream. He was her love.

They came together in a heated rush of desire. With eager kisses and caresses, they sought to arouse each other, to pleasure each other. They took little time stripping away their clothes. They wanted only to be one. When at last Brent moved over Crystal and made her his in all ways, their bliss was complete. The rapture of their rhythm quickly took them to heights of passion, and they crested together as ecstasy swept over them. They clung together, awed by the power of what had passed between them.

"Now that we're married," Crystal began in a whisper as she pressed a soft kiss to Brent's throat, "does that mean we can stay right here forever?" She felt a shiver go through him at the touch of her lips and smiled. It pleased her to know she could arouse him so easily.

"That sounds good to me," Brent said in a growl, rising up to claim her lips in a hungry kiss.

The kiss was all it took to ignite the fire of their passion again. His hands traced paths of excitement over her silken flesh, exploring her soft, lush curves. Crystal responded to his touch with abandon. She willingly gave herself over to his ministrations, glorying in his possession. Again they came together, uniting their bodies and spirits. They were one being, one love, and would be—forever.

The night passed far too quickly as they loved endlessly, celebrating the beauty of their union. Sleep finally claimed them just before dawn. They fell into an exhausted slumber, wrapped in each other's arms.

Brent awoke first, but didn't stir. He lay quietly, watching Crystal sleep beside him. His gaze caressed her perfect features and then dropped lower to the sweet line of her throat and the soft curve of her shoulder. She had pulled the sheet up over her, so the rest was left to his imagination.

As if sensing his gaze upon her, Crystal stirred in her sleep, and the cover fell partially away, leaving one slender leg uncovered. Brent remembered just how it had felt to have her legs wrapped around his waist as they'd made love.

The sudden heat that filled him was overwhelming, and he willingly surrendered to its power.

Crystal came awake slowly, rapturously, as Brent pressed a soft kiss to her lips.

"Good morning," he said huskily.

"Yes, it is," she agreed, and then she went on to show him just how wonderful a morning it really was.

Brent had never known loving anyone could be so beautiful. Crystal was everything he'd ever dreamed of in a woman—and more. As they lay together in the aftermath of their passion, he faced their future and knew that although it wouldn't be easy, somehow, some way, he would protect her and keep her safe.

It was late morning when they finally, reluctantly decided to forsake the privacy and comfort of the hotel room and return to the real world. Brent went to get the buckboard, while Crystal returned to the boardinghouse to pack her things.

Anne welcomed her with a warm hug. She was delighted to hear that everything had turned out perfectly for them. When Brent arrived with the buckboard, Anne offered them a late breakfast, and they gratefully accepted. Over breakfast Crystal confided in Anne about her real name and explained how she'd used Ruby as a stage name. They settled up on what Crystal owed for the room and left a note with Anne for Ken Gilbert at the Lone Star, telling him of his singer's marriage and explaining that she wouldn't be returning to work. Anne promised to see it delivered to Ken at home that very day. After thanking Anne again for her kindness, they rode out of town for the Half-Moon, ready to begin their new life together.

As they drove past the saloon, Crystal knew she wouldn't miss working there. She wanted only to be with Brent and to spend the rest of her life loving him.

Even as Crystal rejoiced in her marriage, though, she realized her future still wasn't certain. Brent had not deserted her when he'd learned the truth about her past, but the danger was still there. He had told her that they would face it together. Crystal could only hope that Brent's strength would see her through.

Chapter Twenty-four

"We'd better stop and see Abby and Pa before we head home," Brent said when they reached Half-Moon land.

"Home—I like the sound of that," Crystal said. It had been years since she'd had a home.

"We'll be living at the cabin."

"I know."

"You don't mind?" He wanted to please her and would even have considered returning to the main house if she had wanted it that way.

Crystal was surprised that he even asked. "I'm going to love living at the cabin with you. There are all kinds of wonderful things we can do there."

"I know," Brent said, a hungry glow shining in his eyes.

"Like wading in the stream," she said with a

laugh to deter his more sensual thoughts.

"I enjoy wading with you, but there are other things I like to do even better."

"Like racing horses?"

He laughed now, too. "That wasn't quite what I had in mind."

"Oh." Crystal played the innocent. "I guess you'll have to show me what you like to do best when we get there."

"I guess I will," he promised. "Are you ready to see Pa and Abby?"

"Are you?" she countered.

"The sooner we tell them, the sooner we can get on our way."

They shared a look of understanding as he reined the team in before the house.

Abby had seen the buckboard approaching and went out to greet them.

"Crystal! What a surprise to see you again," Abby said politely.

"Hello, Abby," she returned.

Abby watched her brother as he jumped down and tied up the horses, then went to help Crystal descend. Something seemed different about him today, but she wasn't quite sure what.

"What are you smiling about? You look like you've been up to something," Abby said astutely.

"You always did know me too well," he told her with a grin. "I've been up to something, all right."

"What?" She was instantly curious. It wasn't like Brent to act so mysterious.

Brent drew Crystal with him as he went to stand before Abby.

"Abby, Crystal and I got married last night."

"You're married?" Abby looked from Brent to Crystal and back again. She had known Brent cared more for Crystal than he had for any other woman, but he wasn't the impulsive sort. She'd never thought he would marry so quickly—or so unexpectedly.

"That's right. You've finally got a sister."

For a moment Crystal was uneasy. She wasn't quite sure how Abby was going to react to the news.

"My brother must love you very much," Abby said finally. One look at Brent's face revealed that. She hugged Crystal. "Papa's down at the stable if you want to go tell him."

Brent was grinning as he watched the two women he loved go inside. If ever he had set himself up for trouble, it was now, with those two. He had a feeling there would never be a dull moment at the ranch with Abby and Crystal together on a regular basis.

Feeling more lighthearted than he had in a long time, Brent went in search of his father. Brent had spent as little time as possible with Jack since he'd learned about the Half-Moon being in debt again.

He knew it was best to avoid him, but this news was too important to keep to himself.

"Pa!" Brent called out as he entered the stable.

"Back here."

Brent found his father in a stall, checking on one of the thoroughbreds.

"To what do I owe this honor?" Jack asked cynically.

"I've got some news for you."

"Yeah?"

"Crystal and I got married last night."

"Crystal married you?"

Brent ignored the sharp bite of his father's sarcasm. "That's right. She's up at the house with Abby. We just stopped by to tell you on our way out to the cabin."

"I can't say much for your taste in horseflesh," Jack began.

Brent tensed at his insult.

"But at least I know now that you've got good taste in women," Jack finished. After a pause, he added, "I guess you weren't all that worried about the ranch being in debt if you took on another mouth to feed."

"I'm worried, all right, but not about Crystal. Marrying her is the smartest thing I've ever done."

Before Jack could come back with any sarcastic remarks, Brent walked away.

Brent's good mood returned when he went inside the house and heard Abby and Crystal talking with

Frances in the kitchen. The sound of Crystal's light-hearted laughter did him good. No one had laughed that way in the house since his mother had died. He went to join them.

"There he is now," Frances said in delight. "Congratulations on your marriage, Brent."

"Thanks, Frances."

"I'm surprised a girl as sweet as Crystal would have you," she teased him.

"So am I. I'm one lucky man, that's for sure," he agreed. Then looking at Crystal, he asked, "Are you about ready to go?"

"Whenever you are."

"If you can give me just a minute or two, I'll pack up some extra food to take with you," Frances offered.

"Thanks."

"Crystal, I hope you will be very happy," Abby said.

"Thanks, Abby. You're sweet." It had been so long since Crystal had had anyone try to help her or take care of her that she felt a bit awkward.

Abby hadn't been called "sweet" by anybody in a long time, and she wasn't quite sure what to make of it. So she frowned. "You're family now," she offered.

Crystal looked over at Brent and smiled. "I know."

"Here's the food for you," Frances said as she came out of the kitchen with a full basket. "If you need anything else, you just tell Brent, and I'll take care of it for you."

Brent and Crystal thanked Frances for her help, and they all started outside. Brent was surprised to find his father coming up to the house.

"Hello, Jack," Crystal said brightly.

"I understand you went and married my son?" he demanded.

"I did, and I'm glad of it," she answered.

"I told him he had good taste in women."

"Thank you."

"No need to thank me, Crystal. It's just the truth. Welcome to the family."

"It's my pleasure, Jack. Believe me," she said, and on a sudden impulse she went to her father-in-law and kissed him on the cheek.

Jack was startled and deeply touched by her kind gesture, but he covered his emotions by being gruff and curt. "Brent, you take care of this girl."

"You don't have to worry, Pa. I plan to do just that," he said.

Brent stowed the basket in back, then helped Crystal climb up to the seat. He untied the team, then joined her there, and they were ready to ride out.

"We'll see you later," Brent said as he urged the team on.

Abby stood with her father, watching them ride away.

"I can't believe Brent's married," Abby said in amazement.

"It's about time," Jack said in a growl.

"I guess he just had to wait until the right woman came along," she said in defense of her brother. "And I think Crystal is the right woman for him."

"He could have done worse, that's for sure," Jack remarked.

"Yes, he could have," she agreed as she thought of Melinda in town.

Jack left Abby and returned to his work in the stable.

Crystal was filled with delight when the cabin came into view.

Home! She was home . . .

A deep, abiding warmth filled her, and she looked over at Brent to find his gaze upon her.

"What were you thinking?" he asked.

"We're home, Brent," she said softly.

"Yes, we are."

He stopped the buckboard before the cabin and helped her down.

"Wait one moment, Mrs. Hunter," he said, taking her into his arms again to carry her over this threshold, too.

"But you've already done it once!" Crystal laughed.

"Darling, I'll use any excuse I can to hold you."

"Well, Mr. Hunter, you don't need an excuse," she told him in a seductive voice.

Her tone ignited the carefully banked heat of his passion. He didn't pause in the main room, but carried her straight to the bed. He was glad the front door had closed behind them, for he had no intention of going back to shut it.

"What about the horses?" She gasped in delight as he lay upon the soft mattress with her.

"What about them?"

And then he silenced any more questions she might have had with his kiss.

"I love you, Crystal."

Caught up in the frenzy of their tumultuous desire, they made passionate love. Ecstasy swept over them as they came together in a blinding rush. They reached the heights together and gloried in the rapture that was theirs.

Crystal lay nestled against Brent's side, her head resting on his shoulder.

"I never knew I could be this happy." She sighed.

"Neither did I," he agreed.

Brent had not realized how empty his existence had been until now. The love he had found with her made his whole life worthwhile. Somehow he would find a way to protect her and keep her safe.

"I've been thinking about what you told me," Brent began slowly.

Crystal would have loved to have lived on in the dream world of Brent's embrace, but she'd known there could be no hiding from reality forever.

"And I think the best thing would be for us to talk to Sam Larkin in town."

"Who's Sam Larkin?" she asked cautiously.

"He's a lawyer. He could help us."

Brent's use of the term "us" filled Crystal with warmth, but even with his support she was fearful of telling anyone else the truth about her past.

"Brent, I don't know . . ." she began. "What if we told him and there was nothing he could do?"

Would her worst fears be realized? Would she end up in prison?

At the thought of going to prison, a chill went through her soul. She couldn't go to prison! Not pregnant, as she was! She couldn't have their child in prison.

Brent sensed her turmoil and drew her close. He cradled her to him. "I'll protect you with my life, Crystal. You're my wife. I'll keep you safe. I promise."

"I have to think about it," she whispered.

He kissed her gently, wanting to calm her fears. "We'll do whatever you want to do."

"Oh, Brent." Crystal's voice was choked with emotion as she hugged him close. "I love you so much, and I'm so afraid we might lose what we have."

Brent rose up over her and looked down at her, his expression fiercely protective. "I love you, Crystal. Nothing is going to separate us—nothing."

He made love to her again, this time tenderly and sweetly. He showed her with his every caress and kiss, just how much he cherished her. Crystal was his world. He wanted only her happiness.

Chapter Twenty-five

Diablo, at last.

Dan rode slowly down the main street of town, looking for the Lone Star Saloon. It had been a long search, but he believed he had finally caught up with Crystal this time. He'd heard some talk at the last town he'd stopped in about a pretty little lady named Ruby who was singing at the Lone Star and drawing in good crowds. Except for the red hair, everything the man had said made the woman sound just like Opal from San Antonio.

Dan was tempted to barge right into the saloon and start asking questions, but he had learned his lesson. He was going to take a room at the hotel and stay there until it was almost time for her performance. If this was Crystal, he didn't want to risk her catching sight of him ahead of time and escaping him again.

Ken was disappointed. Ruby had been gone from the Lone Star for little more than a week, and already there had been a dropoff in business. Some of his customers had been downright angry when they'd learned she had quit. He wasn't angry, but he did miss her and the excitement she'd brought to the place. Her beauty and singing talent and the way she'd charmed all the boys had made him smile every night.

Of course, Ken didn't blame her for quitting—not after that shoot-out. Nobody had died, thank God, but it had been a rough night. Ken hoped he didn't have another one like that for a long time to come.

"Evening, friend, what can I get you?" Ken asked as a stranger came in and approached the bar.

"Whiskey," the man replied.

Ken served him and took the money he shoved across the bar in payment. "You're new in these parts, aren't you?"

"Just passing through. I heard talk in San Miguel that this was the place to stop if you wanted to play poker, have a good drink, and enjoy some fine entertainment."

"That's right. Enjoy yourself."

According to what Dan had been told, the woman named Ruby performed her first show at eight o'clock. It was almost that now, so he took his whiskey and went to sit at a deserted table in the far back corner of the room.

Dan lingered there anxiously, waiting and watching for some sign of Crystal.

"Ready for another drink?" a saloon girl asked as she came to flirt with him.

"No, I'm fine, thanks." He dismissed her without a thought. He didn't want to be distracted. He had only Crystal on his mind right now.

"Is there anything else I can get you?" The girl's question and voice were suggestive.

If Dan hadn't been so determined to find his sister that very night, he might have let himself relax and enjoy a bit of female company. But the weeks of fruitless searching had left him tense and on edge. She had escaped him once in San Antonio. If this was Crystal, she wasn't going to escape him again.

"Not now."

The girl looked disappointed by his rejection. She moved off to try her luck with some of the other customers.

Dan checked his pocket watch and saw that it was now after eight. He grew even edgier, waiting for the moment when the entertainer would finally appear onstage.

The piano player made his way over to the piano a short time later and began playing a raucous tune, but no singer appeared onstage. Curious and growing a bit angry, Dan got up and returned to the bar.

"The talk in San Miguel said you had a singer

named Ruby working here. I was looking forward to hearing her tonight. Is she going to come out later?"

Ken was ready for his question. He'd answered the same one numerous times this past week. "I hate to tell you this, but our Ruby left us."

"She's gone?"

Ken quickly went on to explain how she'd quit the week before.

"That's too bad. And she's been gone for a whole week?" Dan asked, his mind racing as he tried to figure out where Crystal might have fled next.

"Oh, Ruby's not gone in the sense that she's left town. No, our little Ruby got lucky. She married Brent Hunter, one of the local ranchers. His spread, the Half-Moon, is one of the biggest around these parts."

Dan used his best poker face to keep from betraying his turbulent emotions. One moment he'd been ready to scream in rage, and now he was suddenly filled with hope again.

"Well, it's too bad she's gone. I heard she was good."

"Oh, Ruby was good, all right—real good. A lot of the boys are mad because she quit, but we'll find somebody else to take her place in time. Of course, it'll be hard to find anybody as good as Ruby. She was special."

Dan got a refill on his whiskey and went to join a poker game. He wanted to learn everything he could about the Half-Moon, but he had to be subtle. He would see what he could find out from the other gamblers. He just hoped he was on the trail of the right woman.

It was after midnight when Dan returned to his hotel room. He'd won a nice sum that night, and he'd also gotten all the information he needed. First thing in the morning, he'd be heading to the Half-Moon.

Dan didn't sleep well. He was too tense, too excited. He lay in bed remembering all that had happened the last time he and Crystal were together.

Soon—very soon—he would see her again.

Frances was the only one at the house when she saw a strange man riding in the next morning. No one ever just happened by the Half-Moon, so she guessed he was there for a reason, and she went out to meet him.

"Good morning," Dan called out as he dismounted in front of the house and tied up his horse.

"Morning," she returned. "Can I help you with anything?"

"I'm hoping you can. My name is Dan Stewart, and I'm looking for my sister. Folks in town told me she's married Brent Hunter and is living here at the Half-Moon."

"You're Crystal's brother? That's wonderful! We didn't even know she had any kin," Frances said.

"Crystal and I haven't seen each other in a while.

Is she here? I wanted to talk to her." He did not move any closer to the woman, for he didn't want to seem too anxious or in any way threatening.

"Crystal doesn't live here at the main house. She and Brent are living down at the cabin. She's probably there now." Frances gave him directions to the cabin.

"Thanks."

"You're welcome. It was nice to meet you, Dan, and I'm Frances, by the way."

"I'll see you later, Frances."

He mounted up again and rode off.

Frances felt quite happy that Crystal's brother had come. She was sure Crystal would be thrilled to see him.

It took all of Dan's considerable willpower not to race at full speed toward Crystal's cabin. He wasn't quite sure yet how to handle their reunion, but he knew he'd think of something when the time came. He wondered if she was going to be at the cabin alone, or if her new husband would be with her.

He hoped she would be alone. That would make everything much simpler.

Dan took care to ride up to the cabin quietly. He didn't see anyone around and suddenly feared Crystal might not be there. When he reined in before the house and no one came out to greet him, he went up on the porch and looked inside. The cabin was empty. Dan resigned himself to waiting for Crystal's return. Certainly he had nowhere else to go—not until he'd seen his sister and resolved things with her.

Brent had decided to put up an outbuilding near the corral behind the cabin, and Hank had been there helping him for the past few days.

Crystal had remained at the cabin, for there was something she desperately wanted to do that day. Frances had given her a few lemons, thinking Brent might want lemonade, but she had a better use for them. Crystal was tired of her hair being red. She no longer had to pretend to be Ruby, and lemon juice was just what she needed to regain her true identity. After combing the juice through her hair, she went to sit in the sun for an hour. She washed her hair thoroughly when the time had passed and was pleased with the results. As midday drew near, she started to fix lunch for the men.

For the first few days after she'd come to live with Brent, her husband had ridden out at sunup and hadn't returned until almost dusk. Since he'd started working on the building, though, he'd been nearby all day, and she loved every minute of having him around. Their life together was peaceful and loving. He had not pressured her for an answer about speaking to the lawyer yet, and she was glad. She wasn't ready to put this wonderful life they had together at risk yet. She wanted to enjoy the beauty of being a new bride for as long as she could.

When lunch was ready, Crystal took the food out

to Brent and Hank where they were working, a good distance behind the cabin.

Brent saw her coming and smiled broadly. He had loved her with red hair, but was thrilled to see that she was back to her natural blond color.

"I think you're the prettiest waitress I've ever had," Brent told her as she reached them. "What about you, Hank?"

"Well, I liked the pretty redhead who used to be around here," Hank said, grinning.

Crystal laughed. "You two are just charmers."

Hank dug hungrily into the food she'd given him. "Our new waitress makes a good lunch, too, though."

"Do you expect a tip for waiting on us this way?" Brent asked.

"Hank is company, so he doesn't have to tip me, but you do," she challenged.

"What kind of tip are you looking for?"

"I think a kiss would be just about right."

Brent gave her a quick kiss in spite of the other man's presence.

"Call me if you need anything else," she told them with a smile.

"You're a lucky man, Brent," Hank said after Crystal had moved away.

"I know," he agreed, watching her go. He'd been thinking the same thing.

Crystal thought it was a wonderful day. The sun was shining and a soft breeze was blowing. She was relaxed and at ease as she came around the side of the cabin.

"Hello, Crystal."

Crystal froze. There before her stood her brother.

"Dan!" Instant terror jarred her. "What are you doing here?"

"I've been looking for you for months."

Panic set in. Crystal turned and started to run from him, to scream for help, but Dan reacted too quickly for her. He grabbed her and covered her mouth with his hand. He held her pinned against his chest as she fought wildly to get away.

"Don't scream!" Dan ordered, trying to control her. "Crystal, stop it! I'm not going to hurt you! I came here to help you!"

Crystal went still at his words, and she was relieved when Dan immediately let her go.

"You want to help me?" She gasped, turning on him.

"That's right."

"After what you did to me?" she challenged.

"What I did to you?" Dan was shocked by her charge. "Crystal, I don't know what you mean. What are you talking about?"

Crystal stared up at her brother, seeing his very real confusion. She suddenly felt a bit unsure of herself.

"Hall told me what you did! He told me you sent him to me to take care of your debts! He said I was supposed to 'work it off' for you. That's why I—"

"He lied to you, Crystal," Dan interrupted, furious to discover what Hall had done. "I paid him back what cash I could when I met with him that night. I promised to pay him the full amount in time, but he was angry. He beat me up so bad, I was unconscious for several hours. He left me tied up in my room when he went after you."

"He beat you and tied you up?" She was completely taken aback by this news.

"Yes, and then after you got away, Hall came back to my room and—"

"What?" Crystal gasped as she went completely and utterly still. "He went to your room? But how? I killed him!"

Now it was Dan's turn to be shocked. "You killed him?"

Crystal told him about the gambler's attack that night. "He tried to rape me, and I hit him with a lamp. I killed him, Dan. He's dead. That's why I ran away. I knew no one would believe me if I told the truth—that I had been defending myself. I had to get away. I had to save myself."

Dan went to his sister and tried to take her in his arms. He wanted to calm her; he wanted to reassure her. But Crystal was still caught up in the power of her memories. She held herself stiffly and resisted his embrace.

"Crystal, John Hall is not dead," Dan told her slowly, wanting the words to sink in, wanting her to know she wasn't a murderer.

"No—I hit him on the head. There was blood everywhere, and he wasn't breathing."

"He's alive. Crystal listen to me!" Dan grabbed her by the shoulders, wanting to get through to her.

A cold, deadly voice froze him in place. "I don't know who the hell you are, but get your hands off my wife!"

Chapter Twenty-six

Chapter Twenty-six

Brent had been on his way up to the cabin when he'd heard Crystal arguing with someone. Brent hadn't recognized the man's voice, and he'd been immediately concerned for her safety. He was glad now that he'd followed her when he had. There was no telling what might have happened to her if he hadn't shown up.

Dan let Crystal go as ordered. He hurried to try to explain. "I'm Crystal's brother, Dan, and—"

He got no further. At the confirmation of the stranger's identity, Brent attacked. He swung at the man he believed had treated Crystal so badly and hit him full-force in the jaw.

Dan was not a fighter. The power of Brent's blow sent him sprawling backward on the porch. He lay there, dazed, rubbing his aching jaw and looking up at the man his sister had married.

Brent started to go after Dan again, this time with deadly intent. This was the man who had tried to prostitute his own sister! Fury and outrage burned within Brent.

"Brent! *No!*" Crystal saw the look in his eyes and threw herself at Brent to stop him before he could hit Dan again. "Wait!"

"Wait? For what?" He looked down at her puzzled. "Why are you defending him? He's the one who—"

"Dan didn't send Hall to me that night." She hurried to tell him what she'd learned. She could see Brent visibly relax as he heard the truth from her. "And Dan just told me Hall's not dead! I didn't kill him!"

Relief unlike anything Brent had ever known swept through him. He grabbed Crystal and hugged her tight "Thank God."

He actually felt tears burn in his eyes, but somehow he managed to fight them back.

"I know," she agreed, elated.

They remained wrapped in each other's arms. The hidden fear that had haunted their love was gone, and they savored the glory of the moment.

"So you're my brother-in-law," Dan said, watching them together and seeing that Crystal had found true happiness. He tried to give a wry smile, but it hurt too badly and ended up being more of a grimace.

At his remark, Brent gave Crystal a sweet kiss and put her from him. He went and offered Dan a hand up, helping him to stand.

"I'm Brent Hunter, and yes, I'm your brother-in-law."

They stared at each other for a moment, sizing each other up.

"Let's go inside," Crystal suggested. "I'll get you a wet cloth, Dan." She could see that his mouth was bloody.

"Is everything all right?" Hank asked as he came around the side of the cabin. He'd been waiting for Brent by the corral and had gotten worried at his long absence. He was surprised to see a stranger there, one who looked like he'd just been hit in the mouth.

"Everything's fine, Hank," Brent answered quickly. "This is Crystal's brother, Dan. He just stopped by to see her."

"Nice to meet you," Hank said. He was curious about what had happened, but he knew he'd find out later from Brent. "I'll go on back to work."

"I'll be along in a few minutes."

They went indoors, and Dan sat down at the table across from Brent.

"I've been searching for you ever since that night to warn you that Hall is out for revenge against you," Dan told Crystal.

"Revenge against me?" she asked.

"That's right. When you hit him with the lamp, you cut his face up real bad," Dan went on. "After he regained consciousness in your room, he came after me again. He thought I would know where you were hiding. He beat me some more, but when I didn't tell him anything, he left and went looking for you. I finally managed to get myself loose, and I went to check your room. I saw all the glass and blood. I didn't know if you'd been hurt or not, and I was desperate to find you. I went to Sheriff Spiller there in Long Horn and explained to him all that had happened. I told him I fully intended to pay my gambling debt to Hall and that there was no reason for the violence. He arrested Hall and kept him locked up overnight to try to calm him down. Even locked up, though, Hall kept yelling that he was going to get even with you. I made arrangements with the sheriff to send payments to Hall to reimburse him what I owed him. Then I left and set out to find you, but you'd already disappeared."

"I was long gone by that time. I ran as far away as I could. I thought the law would be after me for Hall's murder, and I thought you would be coming after me because you were angry with me."

"I did come after you, but it was to save you, not hurt you," Dan said gently. "I'd never hurt you, Crystal. I'm sorry any of this happened."

"So am I."

"I'm glad you're safe here with Brent, but I have

to warn you to keep watch. As furious as Hall was, I'm afraid he hasn't given up. I think he's still after you."

"How do you know?" Brent asked.

"The first time I wired a payment to Sheriff Spiller, he sent me a telegram back letting me know that Hall had still been vengeful when he'd released him the following day. He swore he wasn't going to rest until you'd paid for what you'd done to him. Sheriff Spiller said he hadn't seen much of him since then, but he was holding on to the money, in case Hall did return. Hall lives in Long Horn, and the sheriff thought it strange that he'd just taken off that way. But I think I know where he went—I think he's trying to find you. That's why I've been real careful, tracking you down. I didn't want to risk leading Hall to you. I just hope now that I've found you . . ."

Brent understood his concern and reassured him. "It's all right."

Crystal swallowed tightly as she looked from her brother to her husband. "What are we going to do?"

"Do you have enough money to pay off the rest of your gambling debt to him?" Brent asked Dan.

"Yes. I've got it now."

"Good. Wire it to the sheriff in Long Horn first thing tomorrow. That way at least the lawman will know that the debt has been paid back in full."

"I'll do it, but it's Crystal he's after, and as mean as he is, I wouldn't put anything past him. That's why I had to come and find you." He looked at his sister. "I couldn't rest until I had warned you."

Dan had had time to do a lot of serious thinking during these last months of searching for Crystal. The realization that she might be in very real danger had made him realize how selfish he'd been all these years. He hadn't cared about his sister's welfare. He had only used her to further his own fortunes. He regretted that deeply now.

Crystal looked up at Dan and smiled gently. Tears were shining in her eyes as she went to him and put her arms around him. "Thank you, Dan."

"For what?" He was taken aback by her display of emotion.

"For caring about me."

Dan gave her a hug. "I love you, Crystal. I'm sorry I haven't always been the brother I should have been to you. I'll try to make it up to you somehow."

"You already have."

"I have?"

"Yes, by coming here to warn me." Her words were heartfelt. "But what are you going to do about your own life? Are you going to find a way to earn an honest living?"

"I'm not sure what I'm going to do."

"You're welcome to stay on here at the Half-Moon," Brent offered. "I can always use another ranch hand."

Dan chuckled, his mood growing a bit lighter as he thought of himself on horseback all day, working stock or trying to saddle-break a wild horse. "I'm not exactly the world's best horseman. I was thinking more along the lines of getting a job at the saloon in town and maybe tending bar."

Crystal was thrilled by this change in her brother. In his heart, she realized, he truly was a good man.

Brent went back to work with Hank, while Dan stayed on to visit longer with Crystal. It was late in the afternoon when he rode for town. He was going to wire the last of the money he owed Hall to Sheriff Spiller in Long Horn the next day and ask if there had been any news about the missing man. He promised to let Crystal know what he heard back from the lawman.

A short time later, Hank left for the day as well, and Brent was alone with Crystal. He finally broached the subject of the threat against her.

"I don't know how much we should be worried about this Hall showing up here, but I want you to be prepared to defend yourself, just in case," he told her.

"I've got my derringer," she reassured him.

"Have you ever handled a six-gun?"

"Once or twice."

"That's not good enough. I'm going to give you shooting lessons—now, tonight." His tone was fierce. "I want you to be ready if there is trouble."

Crystal didn't want to think about that frightening scenario, but there could be no hiding from it. "All right. I'm as ready as I'll ever be."

Brent got his six-gun and took her out behind the

cabin for some target practice. He handed the re-
volver to her and pointed toward a tree stump some
distance away.

"See if you can hit that stump," he told her.

Crystal lifted the gun and tried to take aim. The
gun was heavy and a bit awkward for her to handle
compared with her derringer. She missed the tree
by a wide margin.

"Try again. We're going to stay here and keep at
it until you get it right."

"I hope you're a patient man. That could take a
while," she said with a pained grin, taking aim once
more. This time her shot went wide on the other
side of the tree stump.

Crystal was determined, if nothing else. She tried
again—and missed again.

"I think I like shooting my derringer better," she
said with a nervous laugh, disappointed with her
own performance.

"Your derringer is fine, but it's only a two-shot,"
Brent reminded her.

"I know, and if I'm this bad at hitting a target as
big as that tree stump, those two shots aren't going
to do me much good."

He laughed at her. "You'll get better. It's just going
to take some time, that's all. Let's try it again, but
this time I'll help you."

Brent came to stand behind Crystal. He put his
arms around her to steady the gun as she took careful aim.

Crystal enjoyed the warmth and excitement of having Brent standing so near her. She would have liked to just turn around and hug him, but she knew this was serious. She concentrated on his directions and got off another round.

"I did it!" Crystal shouted when the shot actually hit the tree stump.

"All right, now try it again, on your own," he directed, stepping back to watch.

With great care and precision, Crystal held the gun steady and fired. This time she only grazed the stump, but it was the best she'd done yet on her own.

"There is hope," she told Brent, her confidence growing. "I just wish we didn't have to worry about any of this."

"So do I, but it's important you learn how to shoot."

"Maybe women aren't supposed to be good with a gun."

He grinned. "Don't talk like that around Abby. She's a real good shot."

"Yes, but she's a Hunter."

"Hey, darling, you're a Hunter now, too."

She returned his grin. "I guess I'd better keep practicing. I have a standard to uphold. I don't want Abby to disapprove of me."

"That's right."

Brent pulled her close for a quick kiss, then let her go so she could continue to practice.

He didn't say anything more as she made slow but steady progress. When they finally quit and returned to the cabin for the night, Brent offered up a silent prayer that they would never have to find out just how good Crystal could be with a gun.

It was late in the day when John Hall rode into Diablo. He was cautious, yet alert. He didn't want to draw any undue attention to himself, but he also wanted to keep a look out for Dan Stewart. He didn't want the gambler to know he was so close on his trail.

The Lone Star Saloon beckoned. John hoped this was the end of his search. He'd heard in San Miguel about a pretty singer who was performing here. He had a gut feeling it was Crystal, and it looked like Dan felt that way, too. He'd been following the low-life, card-cheating worm for quite some time, and he hoped this was the end of the trail.

Soon, very soon, Crystal would be his.

John didn't rein in before the saloon, but chose to tie up his mount on a side street, just in case Dan was in town. He wanted the element of surprise on his side. He strode up to the swinging doors and took a quick glance inside to make sure Dan wasn't there before going in.

"Whiskey," he ordered gruffly at the bar.

"Evening," Ken said easily when he came over to wait on him. It wasn't easy to faze the bartender, but he couldn't help staring at the stranger's face.

He'd never seen anyone so disfigured before.

"What are you looking at?" John challenged.

"A paying customer," Ken managed quickly, taking the money that had been shoved across the bar at him. "Enjoy."

Ken moved away, leaving the man alone.

John took his tumbler of whiskey and went to sit at a table near the back. He wanted to be able to watch what was going on and to listen to all the talk in the bar.

"I'm Violet. Would you like some company tonight?" a saloon girl asked as she stopped by his table. He wasn't the most attractive man around, but sometimes his kind was willing to pay more for a woman.

"I sure would," John said, motioning for her to sit down. "You want a drink?"

"No, I want a man." She smiled at him, running her tongue over her lips in a suggestive way.

"You came to the right table, darling." John wasn't averse to a little recreation.

"Let's go upstairs," Violet invited.

"In a while. I want to hear the singer perform first. I heard she's real good," he answered.

"I hate to disappoint you, but Ruby ain't singing here anymore. She quit."

"Where did she go? Who'd she run off with?" John demanded quickly.

Violet was tired of all the men asking about Ruby

and wanting Ruby. "What does it matter? You got me instead."

John realized his mistake and forced himself to sit back. He smiled at her. "You're right, Violet. I do have you, and you are the best-looking woman in the Lone Star."

She smiled and purred at him. "I'm the most talented, too. I can't wait to show you how I can entertain you."

"Let's go on upstairs then, Violet. I could use a little entertaining right now."

John drained his whiskey and followed her up the steps to her room.

Violet closed and locked the door behind them, then began to slowly undress, wanting to be alluring.

"Don't waste time, woman. Get naked and lay yourself down," John ordered.

Violet had dealt with all kinds of men in the time she'd worked at the Lone Star, so his crudeness didn't surprise her or bother her. She did as he asked, expecting to be paid handsomely for obeying him so quickly.

John freed himself from his pants and fell on top of her without another word.

Violet gritted her teeth against his painful possession. It was bad enough he was ugly, but he was rough, too. Only the thought of the money he would be paying her, held her still. She was relieved when he finished quickly. She started to squirm out from underneath him, eager to get away.

"Where do you think you're going?" John demanded.

"You're done, aren't you?" Violet retorted.

"I'll let you know when I'm done," he said in a snarl, and he started moving again. This time he shut his eyes and pretended she was Crystal. His hands were harsh upon her soft flesh, and when she made protesting noises, he smiled to himself. That was what he wanted to do—cause Crystal Stewart a lot of pain. The thought of hurting Crystal brought him to satisfaction again quickly. He collapsed on top of Violet. He lay still for a moment, glad that she didn't try to get away from him again. Finally he rose up over her.

"All right, Violet, baby, where did your little singer go? Did she run off with some man who came in from out of town?"

"I don't know why you care so much about her," Violet said, pouting a bit. She had given him what he wanted, and yet he still was thinking about Ruby. "She wouldn't have taken care of you like I just did."

"I'm paying you to please me," he said tersely. "So please me some more, and tell me what you know about her and where she went."

Her eyes lit up at the thought of making more money just for telling him all about Ruby. She quickly told him how the singer had married Brent Hunter, and then she filled him in on the latest gossip about the Hunter family. They had been the talk of the town for years.

John listened with interest. "So where is this ranch?"

She told him, then added the talk she'd heard about Brent living in the cabin by the creek.

"Ruby sure is lucky. Brent not only has a big ranch; he's handsome, too," Violet finished with envy.

She hadn't realized how her remark about Brent's looks would affect this man. She immediately regretted her words when his hands moved cruelly upon her again.

"So looks are important to you, are they?" he asked coldly, glaring down at her.

Violet trembled with fear. He truly looked like the devil incarnate as he began to thrust within her again. Trying to be brave, she managed a smile for him. "No, looks mean nothing. I like money."

Before John had finished with her that night, he had directions to the Hunter ranch. When he was finally through, he left the bed and straightened his clothing before throwing money on the bed where she lay.

Violet was sore and exhausted, but she grabbed up the cash without hesitation. She was pleased with the amount. "Will you be back?"

"No," John answered, and he walked out. He was as sure as he could be that he'd finally located Crystal. He knew where he was going, and he knew what he was going to do.

Chapter Twenty-seven

Brent did not sleep soundly that night. He tossed and turned, worried about the threat to Crystal. He gave up the effort just before dawn. Going to stand at the window, he stared out across the darkened land. He used to think the view was beautiful and peaceful, but he now he saw only potential danger. They had no close neighbors, and there were many places where someone could hide. Not one to turn from any challenge, Brent tried to decide the best way to keep Crystal safe.

"You're awake already?" Crystal asked as she opened her eyes.

"It's almost light," he said, returning to the bed and sitting down beside her. "I was thinking we should ride over and talk to Pa and Abby today. We need to tell them everything that's happened, so they can help us watch for Hall. Then we need to go into town and talk to Sheriff Dawson. The more people we have watching for Hall, the better our chances of catching him before anything happens."

"How soon do you want to leave?" she asked, coming fully awake.

"As soon as you can get ready. If we reach the house early enough, I can catch Hank before he heads over here, expecting to work with me again."

"Brent?"

He met her gaze.

"Do you want to tell them about the baby today?"

"Do you?"

"Yes. I want your pa and Abby to know."

He nodded, bowing to her wishes.

Crystal wasted no time getting ready. She got her purse and took her derringer, too. Brent brought the buckboard around to pick her up. He had tied Storm to the back, in case he needed to ride out for any reason while they were at the house. When they arrived, Brent stopped at the bunkhouse to let Hank know he wouldn't need him until they returned from town; then they drove on up to the main house.

Abby and Jack both came out on the porch when they saw the buckboard approaching.

"I see you've made some changes," Jack said, looking at her hair. "I like it better."

"Thank you," Crystal said with a smile.

"Me, too," Abby added.

"It's my natural color. I feel more like myself now," she explained.

"So, to what do we owe this honor?" Jack asked.

"We've got to go into Diablo today, but we wanted to stop and talk with you first," Brent told them.

"Come on in," Abby said. "Crystal, Frances told us that your brother came looking for you."

"Yes, he did. Dan and I had a nice visit yesterday."

"I'm sorry I missed him."

"He's going to be staying on in Diablo, at least for a while, so I'm sure you'll get the chance to meet him eventually."

"Good."

Brent tied up the team and helped Crystal down. They all went inside. Frances came out of the kitchen, smiling in welcome.

"It's so good that you're here. Breakfast is almost ready," she announced. "Crystal, your hair looks lovely. Go on and sit down. I take it your brother found you all right?"

"Yes, thanks, Frances. It was wonderful to see him again."

"What's on your mind?" Jack asked bluntly, not interested in making small talk.

"A lot has happened, and we need to tell you about it," Brent began.

Crystal spoke up, wanting them to know everything. They were her family now, and they deserved the truth.

"There was a lot about me Brent didn't know when he asked me to marry him," she began.

Jack and Abby listened intently as she explained what had brought her to Diablo.

"Oh, Crystal—that's terrible!" Abby interrupted when Crystal revealed why John Hall had appeared in her room. Abby cast a quick glance at Brent. She was surprised to see that he was watching her. Abby suddenly realized how blessed she'd been to have her brothers—especially Brent. "How dreadful for you."

"Yes, but there's more." Crystal went on with her story, telling them how she had thought she was wanted for murder and how Dan had just come to reveal the real truth of what had happened that night.

"Well, you're safe now," Jack said.

"Yes, I am." She looked at Brent and smiled. "I told Brent the truth before we got married. I didn't want to marry him with any lies between us, but he loved me enough to marry me anyway."

"I told her at the time I thought she'd acted in self-defense. I knew she couldn't have killed anyone," he said supportively.

Jack's expression was serious during Crystal's revelations and grew even grimmer as he listened to Brent's words. He knew what prison life was like and couldn't imagine Crystal surviving it. "So what of this man Hall?"

"That's what we wanted to tell you, so you and

the hands could keep a lookout for him," Brent said.

"You mean he might show up here?" Jack asked sharply.

"According to Dan, Hall is still after Crystal. When she hit him with the lamp she cut his face, and he wants revenge against her," Brent told them. "If the scarring is as bad as Dan says it must be, Hall won't be hard to recognize."

"He's tall and dark-haired, but that's about all I remember about him."

"I'll tell the hands," Jack said. "The more we've got watching, the better."

"Brent gave me my first shooting lesson last night, Abby," Crystal said. "He said I have a long way to go to live up to your standards."

Abby was surprised by Brent's compliment. He had always been after her to be more ladylike, so it pleased her that he appreciated her shooting ability. "Practice is all it takes. You'll do it."

"I hope so."

Frances served them breakfast, and they ate the delicious fare hungrily.

"Did you say you were going into town this morning?" Abby asked as they finished up the meal.

"Yes, do you want to go with us?" Brent asked.

"Yes. Frances was saying we needed some supplies, so I can get them while we're there."

Abby went to ask the housekeeper for a list of what she wanted from town.

"I'm ready whenever you are," Abby told them when she returned from the kitchen.

"There is one more thing I need to tell you," Crystal began, looking over at her husband as she spoke. "Brent and I want you to be the first to know— we're going to have a baby."

Abby couldn't speak for a moment. She looked from her brother to his wife. Then she smiled and took Crystal's hand. "What wonderful news. I'm so happy for you." She hugged her sister-in-law, then went to her brother to be enfolded in his arms. "I already know you'll be a good father."

Jack's expression was guarded as he said, "You make sure you take good care of her."

"I will."

They started off for Diablo then. Jack remained on the porch watching them go. Only when they'd disappeared from sight did he go back inside. He stopped before the portrait of Beth and stood there gazing up at her for a long moment before going to get his bottle where he had it hidden in his room. He needed a drink.

When they reached Diablo, they stopped first at the hotel to find Dan.

"I didn't know you were coming into town today," Dan said, surprised to see them when he answered the knock at his hotel room door.

"We were worried, and we wanted to find out if you'd heard anything back yet from the sheriff in

Long Horn," Brent explained. Then, realizing Dan hadn't met Abby yet, he quickly made the introductions. "Dan, this is my sister, Abby. Abby, this is Dan."

Dan managed to hide his surprise at seeing a woman wearing pants and boots as they exchanged greetings.

"I sent the wire first thing this morning," Dan said. "The man at the telegraph office told me he'd let me know just as soon as he got a reply from Sheriff Spiller."

"Well, we're on our way over to warn Sheriff Dawson about Hall."

"I'll come with you."

They left the hotel and made their way through Diablo toward the sheriff's office.

"Are you really planning on staying on here?" Crystal asked her brother. She knew how restless he could be, and how he liked to move around a lot.

"I think so," Dan answered. He was so glad to have found Crystal that he wasn't ready to think about leaving her yet.

"Then you have to take a room at the boarding-house. I stayed there until Brent and I were married, and I know you'd like it. The owner is Anne Pals, and she's a wonderful cook."

"I'll do that," he promised. A home-cooked meal sounded mighty good to him.

Sheriff Dawson was at his desk in his office, and he looked up when they came in.

"Brent, is something wrong?" he asked, concerned.

"I hope not—but that's what we wanted to talk to you about. Have you heard yet that Crystal and I are married?"

"Crystal?" he asked. "I thought your name was Ruby."

"That was my stage name," she answered.

"Well, congratulations."

"Thanks," Brent replied. "And this is Crystal's brother, Dan. He came to Diablo looking for Crystal to let her know there's a man named John Hall who's hunting her." He explained all that had happened.

"I'm pretty sure he wants revenge," Dan added, telling the lawman about the threats Hall had made at the jail in Long Horn and how the sheriff there hadn't seen him in a while. "I've repaid my debt to him in full, and we're waiting now to hear from Sheriff Spiller to see if he's got any new information on Hall's whereabouts."

"What's Hall look like?"

Dan described him as best he could, including his scarred face.

"I'll tell my deputies. If anybody reports anything, I'll let you know right away."

"We'd appreciate it," Brent told him.

When they left his office, Crystal took Dan to the boardinghouse to meet Anne, while Brent and Abby went to the mercantile to get the supplies they needed.

Edmund had come out of his office to speak with someone in the bank lobby when he'd glanced out the window and seen Abby across the street with Brent and the others. He didn't know what had brought her to town, but he was glad she was there. He feasted his gaze on her for a long moment, until the customer he'd been talking with spoke up and interrupted his reverie. He'd concluded their business quickly and then gone to take a better look outside. He'd been shocked to find that they were going into the sheriff's office, and wondered what was wrong. The thought that there might be trouble at the Half-Moon pleased him, but he didn't let his reaction show.

Curiosity ate at Edmund as he watched and waited for them to come out. When he finally saw them emerge, he told the teller he'd be right back and went outside.

"Brent! Abby!" Edmund called out, hurrying down the street to join them.

Brent stiffened at the sight of the banker.

"You all right?" Abby asked, noticing the immediate change in her brother.

"Not when Edmund's around, I'm not."

"Oh."

"Brent, congratulations on your marriage," Edmund said smoothly as he joined them.

"What do you want, Edmund?" Brent knew Edmund must have an ulterior motive for coming out to speak with him. The man certainly hadn't approached them to offer his best wishes.

"I saw you come out of the sheriff's office," Edmund said. "Is there trouble out at the ranch?" His gaze lingered on Abby, taking in the sweet curve of her hips in her pants.

"What goes on at the Half-Moon is none of your damned business, Edmund," Brent told him coldly.

Abby was surprised by his reaction to Edmund. She took his arm. "Let's go."

"Well, I just wanted to help," the banker said.

"The only way you can help me right now is by getting the hell out of my way," Brent said in a growl as he walked quickly on, taking Abby with him.

Edmund stood back and watched them go.

"Give your bride my best," Edmund called after him sarcastically.

Brent did not respond. He just kept walking.

Fury ate at Edmund. No one treated him this way! No one!

Brent Hunter was an arrogant bastard, and Edmund was looking forward to the day when he got what was coming to him—him and his pa and their whole damned family.

Except Abby, of course.

He would never want anything bad to happen to Abby. He wanted her for himself.

* * *

325

"Brent, why did you talk to Edmund that way?" Abby asked when they were out of earshot.

Brent glanced down at her, his expression still grim. "I didn't tell you what happened when I confronted him about the loan he made to Pa for the Sullivan land."

"No, you didn't. What did he do?"

"He pulled a gun on me."

"What?" Abby was completely shocked. "Why?"

"I was furious with him for making the loan. I told him to cancel the sale. He refused and said it was already completed and there was nothing he could do. He actually seemed quite pleased about the deal—even though I had specifically asked him not to make any more loans to Pa."

"But why was he going to shoot you?" she repeated.

"I was so angry that I was ready to hit him. I didn't, but I wanted to. He pulled a gun out of his desk drawer and held it on me."

"I've always felt uneasy around him, but I never expected him to do anything like this. Thank God he didn't shoot you."

"I don't trust Edmund. Watch yourself around him," he advised her. "No matter what he might say, he is no friend to our family—not to us or to Pa."

Chapter Twenty-eight

Dan and Crystal had just left the boardinghouse, where Dan had rented a room from Anne, when Mr. Bryant, the telegraph operator, chased him down.

"Mr. Stewart? I got the wire you've been waiting for," he called out.

Dan and Crystal stopped to wait for him to catch up.

"Thanks for coming to find me," Dan said as he took the wire.

"I was just glad to finally get a response."

When Mr. Bryant left them, Dan opened the envelope and read Sheriff Spiller's message. Crystal was watching his expression, and she could tell immediately that the news was not what he'd hoped for.

"What is it?"

Dan looked up at her. "Sheriff Spiller hasn't seen or heard from Hall since before the last time I wired him money. He's holding on to what I sent him in case he does show up."

Their gazes met in understanding. There was nothing they could do now but wait and pray that nothing came of Hall's threats.

"We'd better go tell Brent," Dan said.

When Crystal and Dan reached the mercantile, they sought out Brent and Abby so they could tell them the news.

"Until this Hall shows up someplace, we'll just have to be careful, that's all," Brent said. He tried not to sound too worried, but he was already planning ways to keep Crystal safe.

"I'm staying on," Dan told him. He wasn't going anywhere until he was sure his sister was safe. "I'll keep an eye out here in town."

"Have you asked Ken over at the Lone Star about a job yet?" Brent asked.

"I plan to talk to him later today."

Crystal, Abby, and Brent went on with their shopping, while Dan decided to wait outside for them.

Melinda had just started into the mercantile when she found herself facing a handsome young man she'd never seen before.

"Why, thank you," she said sweetly as he held the door for her. "You're new in town, aren't you?"

"Yes, I am. My name's Dan Stewart. What's yours?" he asked appreciatively.

"I'm Melinda Barton. It's nice to meet you." She smiled up at him.

"Dan . . ." Crystal had realized she'd forgotten to tell Dan something, and she had come after him.

"You!" Melinda looked past Dan to see Crystal. She was stunned for a moment by the change in her hair color, and then her expression turned to one of loathing. She still hadn't recovered from the devastating news that Brent had married the saloon girl. She'd heard the talk of their elopement at church and had cried for an entire day.

"Hello, Melinda. I see you've already met my brother," Crystal said calmly.

"Your brother? Oh, how nice." Without another word, she walked past them both. She was disgusted. She'd finally found a good-looking man and he turned out to be Crystal's brother.

"You know each other?" Dan looked at Crystal.

"Oh, yes." She didn't want to elaborate. "I'll explain later."

Melinda caught sight of Brent at the back of the store, and she made her way toward him. She had a few things she wanted to say to him.

"Hello, Brent," she said, cornering him and ignoring Abby, who stood at his side.

"Why, Melinda, hello," Brent said. He suddenly wondered if his day could get any more complicated—first the run-in with Edmund, and now

Melinda. The thought of staying out at the cabin permanently—just him and Crystal—held great appeal at that moment.

"Melinda," Abby said politely.

Melinda had eyes only for Brent.

"I just saw your lovely bride." Melinda couldn't keep the sneer out of her voice. "Crystal is her name, right? Or is it really Ruby? The woman uses so many aliases, I wasn't sure."

"Crystal is my wife's name," he ground out, deliberately using the word "wife."

"Oh, Brent. It was so cruel the way you led me on. I thought what we shared was special."

Brent wanted only to get away from Melinda.

"I'm sorry if you were hurt, Melinda, but we both know I didn't lead you anywhere. If you'll excuse me." Brent moved past her, leaving Abby to follow him.

"Enjoy your life with your dance-hall-slut wife," Melinda said under her breath in a snarl, just loud enough for them to hear.

Brent heard her hateful remark, and his temper flared. He almost went back to confront her, but Abby stopped him.

"Let's leave. You don't want to cause any trouble here."

"I know," he said in a growl, "but I don't like anyone talking about Crystal that way."

They settled the bill, then went outside to where Crystal and Dan were waiting. After loading up the buckboard, they were ready to go. Brent mounted Storm and, after bidding Dan good-bye, they started back to the Half-Moon. Brent was looking forward to some peace and quiet once they got there.

After leaving the Lone Star the night before, John Hall had ridden out of Diablo and camped in the countryside. He had made the trek to the cabin without seeing anyone, and he was glad. He wanted to find Crystal, take his revenge, and disappear without anyone ever knowing he'd been there. He waited patiently now, hiding in the trees a distance away, watching for some sign of Crystal. The place seemed deserted, but that didn't matter. He would bide his time. All that mattered was finding her and seeing the look on her face when she realized she couldn't escape.

Hall smiled to himself. He was going to enjoy their reunion.

Edmund was restless in his office.

He couldn't stop thinking of Abby—of how pretty she looked and how those pants fit her hips.

Damn, but he wanted her. Heat burned within him. He wanted to lay her down and strip those pants off of her and bury himself deep inside her.

Edmund fought back a groan of pure desire. He reminded himself he was at work, but it didn't temper his need. He knew there was only one thing that would help. He would have to go pay Violet a visit—right now.

"I'm going to lunch. I'll be back," Edmund announced as he left the bank.

It was midday, so none of the bank tellers thought anything of his sudden departure.

Edmund was on his way to the Lone Star when he saw the sheriff coming out of his office. He deliberately detoured toward him, hoping to find out what Brent had been doing there that morning.

"Sheriff Dawson—good to see you."

"Hello, Edmund."

"How are things going?"

"All's quiet right now, and I like it that way."

"I was worried that there might have been some trouble when I saw Brent go into your office today. Is everything all right out at the Half-Moon?"

"Things are fine at the ranch, but Brent's new wife is in some trouble."

"What's wrong?"

"There's a man who's trying to harm Crystal. He's been chasing her for a while and might be coming to Diablo to look for her. I was just heading out to spread the word around town so we can be watching for him, in case he does show up."

"What do you know about him?" Edmund wanted to find out all he could about the Hunter family's troubles.

"His name is John Hall. They said he's dark-haired and has some bad scars on his face."

"He should be easy to spot."

"I hope. Actually, I hope he doesn't show up at all."

"I'm sure you don't, but I'll keep an eye out for him." Edmund moved off, smiling in satisfaction.

So Brent's darling Crystal might be in trouble. That's just too bad. . . .

Edmund had to make certain that no one saw him as he entered the saloon. He casually made his way to the rear alley and then let himself into the building. The back hall was deserted, as he'd expected, and he made his way up the rear staircase. He had done this before and knew the safest way to get to Violet's room unseen.

Edmund was eager to ease the burning ache in his loins. He knocked softly on the door.

"Come on in," she called out.

He let himself into the room silently. Violet was still in bed, wearing only a filmy gown that left little to his imagination.

"Edmund! This is a surprise," Violet said in purring tones.

He immediately began to strip off his clothes. She did the same, tossing her gown to the floor. When he came to her she welcomed him with open arms. He always paid her very generously, for he knew it guaranteed her silence. It wouldn't do for word to get out around town that he enjoyed himself with a saloon girl.

Edmund lay with her and had started to kiss her when he got a good look at her body.

"What happened to you?" He was shocked by the bruises on her pale flesh.

"I had a rough customer last night," she answered.

"I'll say you did."

"He wasn't only mean, but he was damned ugly, too. He had the most horrible scars on his face."

"He was scarred?" Edmund repeated, instantly alert.

"Yes," Violet said. "Why?"

"No reason," he answered coolly. She obviously hadn't heard yet that the sheriff was looking for just such a man, and he wasn't about to tell her—or anyone else, for that matter. The more misery Brent Hunter had in his life, the better.

"I think he was just passing through. He didn't stick around long after he left me."

"Did you enjoy all his rough stuff?" he asked, a wicked gleam coming into his eyes.

"The only thing I enjoyed was the money he gave me."

Edmund was tempted to be brutal with Violet, too. If he pretended she was Iona, he wouldn't have any trouble being violent with her, but the last person he wanted to think about was his drunken, useless wife. No, Abby was the woman he wanted. He wanted to close his eyes and pretend Violet was the younger woman.

At that thought, the lust within him flared even hotter. He wasted no time taking his pleasure of Violet several times over. Only knowing that he had to return to the bank drove him from her bed nearly an hour later.

Violet watched Edmund as he dressed and then left her room. She said nothing, but she wondered what had inspired such a fiery display of passion from him. She got up to count the money he'd left on the dresser for her, and when she'd finished counting, she was very glad that he'd come to see her.

Chapter Twenty-nine

The day passed slowly for Hall. As it got later in the afternoon and still no one showed up at the cabin, he began to wonder if anyone really lived there at all. Gun in hand, he left his hiding place and made his way on foot down to the cabin. He looked in a window to make certain there was no one inside, then let himself in.

He stood just inside the door, looking around. There was no doubt that someone lived there. The place was too clean to have been abandoned. He holstered his gun as he moved farther in and closed the door behind him. Whoever lived here wasn't home now, so he slowly and methodically made his way through the house, searching for some clue that would prove this truly was Crystal's home—that he was in the right place.

Hall went into the bedroom and paused to look at the bed. It had not been made, and he wondered if Crystal had been the last one sleeping in it.

An evil sneer curved his mouth. He imagined her lying there, waiting for him, wanting him, welcoming him, instead of fighting him.

He went to the small bureau and opened the drawer to go through the clothing, wanting proof that this was Crystal's home.

He found the proof he'd wanted in the bottom drawer. There, folded carefully, was her red satin gown, the same gown she'd been wearing at the saloon in Long Horn that fateful night.

Hall picked up the dress and ran his hands over it, caressing it. It was as sleek and soft as he'd believed it would be.

He felt triumphant. All his hard work had finally paid off. He had found her!

Hall started from the bedroom, the red dress still in hand. It was then that he caught sight of himself in the mirror over the washstand. He stared at his hated visage, seeing the horrible scars she'd inflicted upon him. The rage he'd kept tempered for a time now flared back to full life. In one powerful move, he tore the red dress apart and threw it on the floor.

Hall only regretted that Crystal hadn't been wearing it.

He wanted to get his hands on her. He grew aroused as he imagined what he would do to her.

He was going to teach her a lesson she would never forget.

Brent had dropped off Abby and picked up Hank at the main house. They were drawing close to the cabin when Brent noticed that a post was down on the far side of the pasture.

"We'd better fix it now. I don't want to risk losing any stock," Brent told Hank.

"Will it take you very long?" Crystal asked.

"No, we should be done in a few minutes," Brent assured her. "Just leave the team tied up out front and don't try to carry anything heavy inside. I'll take care of it when I get there."

Crystal drove on alone. It was still daylight, so she wasn't concerned about returning to the cabin by herself, and Brent and Hank would be close behind her. She was getting tired, though. The thought of a quiet evening alone with Brent held great appeal.

Hall was still in the bedroom when he heard the sound of the buckboard coming up the road. For a moment panic threatened. He wanted to flee the house—to make a run for the cover of the trees—but he controlled the urge.

He told himself to wait. He had the element of surprise on his side. The thought made him smile.

When he drew his gun, his touch upon it was almost a caress.

Hall had hoped to trap Crystal alone, but now it

no longer mattered. If she did have her husband with her, he would simply shoot him first, and then have his way with Crystal. He had waited too long for this moment to care about anything but revenge.

Hall went to stand to the side of one of the front windows. He stayed out of sight as he tried to get a look at who was driving up. He held himself in tense expectation as he waited for the buckboard to come into view. When it finally did, elation unlike anything he'd ever experienced before surged through him.

It was Crystal. And she was alone.

Hall didn't know where Brent Hunter was, and he didn't care. All that mattered was that Crystal would be walking right into his trap, just as he'd always hoped she would.

He moved carefully to hide behind the door. The moment she came into the house, she would be his. She would be helpless before him—his to do with as he pleased.

Crystal reined in and climbed down to tie up the team. She was carrying her purse as she opened the door and stepped inside.

Hall attacked so quickly that Crystal had no time to scream or react. With savage intent, he grabbed her from behind and clamped his hand tightly over her mouth.

"I've got you now, bitch!" He laughed in her ear.

Crystal fought back as best she could, struggling desperately against his brutal hold. Though Brent would come soon, she feared it wouldn't be soon enough. Her only hope was to get her gun from her purse.

Hall kicked the door shut, then dragged her farther into the room as she continued to kick and twist and try to break free of him.

"You can fight all you want, but this time you're not getting away from me. You're mine."

Crystal had thought she'd experienced terror before, but nothing compared to the cold chill that filled her soul now. As hard as she was fighting him, she still couldn't get a hand into her purse. She tried to swing at him, but he pinned her arms and then yanked the purse from her hand and tossed it aside.

Her gun was her only hope! Crystal knew it was up to her to save herself. She pretended to faint, praying that her limpness would cause Hall to ease his grip on her. Only then would she be able to tear herself away from him long enough to get to her gun.

Hall was surprised when Crystal suddenly collapsed against him, but he was also glad. He hadn't thought she was the fainting type, but if she wasn't fighting him, he could enjoy himself with her more. His hold on her slipped a little as he struggled to lift her deadweight.

Crystal saw her opportunity and took it. As Hall tried to take her up in his arms, she tore herself from him with all the force she could muster.

Her plan worked—for a moment.

She managed to break free, but Hall was too quick for her. He was right there behind her. He gave a maniacal laugh as he grabbed her savagely by one arm and spun her around.

"You ain't getting away from me!"

Hall backhanded her fiercely and laughed again when she cried out in pain.

"Did that hurt? Good!"

He slapped her another time, liking the fear he was seeing in her eyes.

"I'm glad it hurts. I want you to know exactly what real pain is—what it feels like to have your face cut like mine was. You're going to be real pretty when I get done with you."

Unable to wait any longer to begin his torture, he pushed her to the floor and pinned her there with his body.

"You're not repaying your brother's debt to me this time, Crystal, honey. This time you're paying your own debt."

"No! Let me go! I don't owe you anything. Brent's coming. He'll be here soon, and he's got other men with him."

At that moment Hall didn't care if the sheriff and an entire posse showed up. He had Crystal right where he wanted her—beneath him and helpless.

"I'll be gone long before anybody comes to save you." He leered down at her, enjoying her struggles, enjoying her terror. He took both of her wrists in one hand and drew them up above her head. With his free hand he grabbed the neckline of her day gown and ripped it forcefully downward.

Crystal screamed at his attack. She didn't know how close Brent was, but she hoped he might be able to hear her.

"You can yell all you want, but there's nobody around who cares." He chuckled. The power he had over her made him feel invincible. Heat settled in his loins. He groped Crystal as she twisted and bucked beneath him.

"No! Let me go!"

He paid her no mind. He was intent only on his own pleasure, his own need. Reaching down, he pulled up her skirt and tore at her underclothes.

Crystal was kicking at him as best she could, but her efforts did little to deter him. She could see her purse on the floor, but it was too far away to reach. She would never be able to get to it in time to get her derringer. His hands upon her were viler than anything she'd ever known. Tears blurred her vision as she continued her struggle to save herself.

Brent!

She needed him desperately. He had saved her before. Surely Brent would save her again.

But Hall kept on with his attack, ripping her clothing, fondling her.

Crystal was shocked when suddenly he released her hands. Any thought that she was being freed vanished when she saw that he had let her go only so he could unbuckle his gun belt and free himself from his pants.

"You can't do this! I'm pregnant!" Terror seized her at the thought of what was to come.

She had to save herself! But how?!

Hall only laughed again at her fear as he tossed his gun belt aside and opened his pants. "And whose little bastard are you having?"

In a frenzy, Crystal attacked. She clawed at his already scarred face, drawing blood.

He let out a scream of pain as he stopped what he'd been doing and drew back to hit her again.

Crystal saw her chance. His gun belt was within reach, and she grabbed for it.

Chapter Thirty

The sound of a gunshot split the quiet of the afternoon.

Brent and Hank were riding in when they heard it.

"Crystal!"

Instant terror pounded through Brent. It couldn't be . . . Not again . . .

"Dear God! No!" The words were torn from him as he spurred Storm to a full gallop and charged toward the cabin, leaving Hank to follow.

Memories haunted Brent as he raced on. Was Crystal all right? Would he reach her in time? He hadn't been able to save his mother. Could he save Crystal?

Brent drew his gun, ready for trouble. He was furious with himself for having allowed Crystal to go on alone. He should have stayed with her.

Brent didn't think about the possibility of any danger to himself as he rode up to the cabin. He was thinking only of Crystal.

Brent threw himself from Storm as he reined in and then made a run for the front door.

Hall had been stunned when Crystal made the grab for his gun. He thought he'd beaten her enough that she wouldn't fight him anymore, but he'd been wrong. As she'd tried to take aim at him, he'd knocked the gun from her grasp and then slapped her again as fury raged within him. Now he grabbed her by the shoulders, giving her a violent shake.

It was then that Hall heard the riders coming in.

"It's Brent!" Crystal cried out in joy. He had come for her! She began to fight Hall even harder.

He snarled in outrage. Keeping a tight hold on her, he dragged her along as he tried to get his gun.

"Brent!" Crystal kept struggling, wanting to stop Hall from reaching the gun, but he was too strong for her.

Hall's hand closed on the weapon just as Brent reached the porch and kicked in the door. Hall stood, holding Crystal as best he could as he tried to take aim.

Brent charged inside the cabin, gun in hand. Driven by fear and desperation, he was going to save Crystal or die trying.

Brent had feared he would find Hall standing over

Crystal's body. He had feared he would face the same horror he'd discovered ten years ago. He had feared he would be too late.

As he came through the door, the sight of Crystal alive and fighting fiercely to free herself gave him hope.

Hall realized he was caught in a deadly situation. He shoved Crystal away from him as he lifted his gun to shoot Brent.

But Brent reacted first. He got off a shot at Hall the instant he knew Crystal was out of the line of fire.

The bullet took Hall squarely in the chest, and the force of it flung him backward. He crashed to the floor and lay still.

Crystal had been frozen in place for a moment. Then she gave a small cry as she got to her feet and ran to Brent.

"I knew you'd come! I knew you would!"

Brent took her in his arms and held her close. He could feel how fiercely she was trembling.

"It's all right now. He's never going to hurt you again," he declared.

"Are you two all right?" Hank asked as he came running inside, his gun in hand.

"Yes. It was Hall. I got him," Brent answered quietly.

Drawing Crystal with him, Brent went outside on the porch. When he gazed down at her and saw her bruised face, he hated Hall even more.

"He hurt you." He lifted one hand to gently touch her cheek, where a bruise was beginning to discolor her pale complexion.

Crystal saw the rage within him and sought to calm him. "I'm only bruised."

"Thank God I reached you in time." Brent drew her back into the circle of his arms and leaned down to kiss her ever so tenderly.

Brent found he was trembling, too, from the force of all his turbulent emotions. His violent rage had been replaced now by an incredible sense of relief. He held Crystal to his heart, knowing he never wanted to let her go.

She was his life—his love.

One week later

Brent stood silently over his mother's grave for a long moment, then bent down and laid the single blossom he'd brought with him next to her tombstone.

"I saved Crystal," Brent said quietly. "I got to her in time, and I saved her."

A sense of peace stole over him as he stood back up.

"Brent?"

He hadn't heard anyone approaching, but when he turned, Crystal and Abby were coming toward him.

"I had a feeling you might be here," Abby said.

"Frances said to tell you dinner is almost ready."

"All right." Brent had been working at the main house that day, and Crystal had driven over to visit Abby. They had decided to stay on for dinner. It wasn't easy for him to be around his pa, but he wanted to spend some time with Abby.

"So this is your mother's grave." Crystal paused, staring down at the tombstone. "I wish I'd known her."

"I wish you had, too. You would have loved her," he said.

"I'm sure I would have. She must have been wonderful. She raised you and Abby," she told them both with a smile.

"And Quince and Matt," Abby said as they left the grave site and made their way back to the house. "I'm starting to get worried about them."

"You shouldn't, especially where Quince is concerned. He can take care of himself," Brent said. His tone turned cold as he spoke of his brother. "He'll show up here when he's good and ready, and not a minute before. As for Matt, it's anyone's guess whether he'll come home."

"You're right," Abby agreed.

Brent was about to tell his sister that Quince didn't care about anyone but himself, but he didn't. She'd have to figure their brother out on her own.

They reached the house, and Abby went in ahead of them.

Brent and Crystal had just started to go inside when Crystal suddenly stopped.

"Oh," she said, startled. She put a hand on her stomach as she looked at Brent.

"What is it? Is something wrong?" Brent was instantly concerned.

Crystal stood still for a moment longer, a look of wonder on her face. "No. No, there's nothing wrong. In fact, I think everything is very right. I just felt the baby move."

"You did?" Brent was stunned.

"Yes."

Brent stood, gazing down at Crystal. He had come so close to losing her that he now cherished every minute they had together. "I love you, Crystal."

"And I love you."

He kissed her sweetly before they started to follow Abby into the house.

Brent paused at the door and looked back out across the ranch. The sun was sinking lower in the western sky, bathing the lush land in a golden glow.

For the moment, he could forget the cloud hanging over the Half-Moon—his father's venture back into debt. From this vantage, the land looked like paradise, and Brent knew that as long as he had Crystal by his side, it would be heaven.

Epilogue

Edmund dismounted in front of the secluded cabin. It was late, but he didn't care. He had business to take care of. As he drew near, the door to the cabin opened and a disreputable-looking man came out, gun in hand.

"Oh, it's you." The man lowered his gun when he saw that it was Edmund.

"Yes, Kane, it's me," Edmund said with a confident smile. He had been there many times before to see this man and knew what to expect. Kane was a loner, a man without principles, but he was also both efficient and dependable about accomplishing any job he was hired to do—for the right price. And Edmund always paid him handsomely.

"Come on in."

Kane led the way inside. Edmund followed him,

but didn't say anything until the other man had closed the door behind them.

"Here." He handed him an envelope.

Kane opened it to check the contents.

"Don't worry; your money's all there."

He ignored him and started to count out the bills.

"I said—"

"I heard you." Kane looked up at him and smiled coldly. "But your reputation as an honest man doesn't impress me, Edmund. I know better."

Edmund fought to conceal his irritation. As filthy and arrogant as Kane was, he had still proven invaluable to him in the past, and he'd be even more valuable in the future. Forcing himself to remember that, Edmund said, "You did a good job handling things at the Sullivan ranch."

"Rustling is my specialty," Kane answered with a grin.

"I've already foreclosed and sold off the property to someone else, so you won't need to do anything more there until I let you know. In the meantime, I have another job for you."

"Good." Kane looked at him with interest.

Edmund knew this man loved his work. He continued, "You've done work on the Half-Moon Ranch before, but things have changed since Jack Hunter returned from prison. You're going to have to be careful. Do you think you can handle it?"

Kane's expression was contemptuous. "What do you think?"

"Don't get cocky with me, Kane. I can't afford any mistakes."

"Just tell me what you want me to do."

Edmund paused, then smiled coldly. Yes, Kane would do anything for a price.

Edmund started to speak.

A short time later, Edmund rode back to Diablo. He was satisfied with the outcome of his meeting with Kane. Things were going his way.

An image of Beth Hunter flashed in his mind, and his satisfaction faded. It had been ten years since Beth had died, but his rage was still as powerful as ever.

Edmund knew he had Jack in the palm of his hand. He had set his plans into motion, and he was confident everything would fall into place. But no matter how successful his scheme was, he could never possess Beth.

It was Jack's fault Beth was dead. It was Jack's fault that he had never known her intimate touch. It was Jack's fault that he would never hear her admit she had made a mistake when she'd refused him. It was Jack's fault that he would never hear Beth plead for his forgiveness.

Edmund's expression grew resolute. Jack was responsible for the one great failure in his life, and for that, he would pay.

For that, all the Hunters would pay—all of them.

He would see to it.

Chapter One

Texas

The mid-morning sun burned hotly into his back as Quince guided his mount carefully along the narrow trail. He surveyed the familiar terrain with bitter-sweet feelings. The last of the season's bluebonnets still tinted the ground with a haze of color, but the bright green of spring had all but faded. The knowledge that summer would soon bleach the landscape a paler hue as long, dry days settled in brought memories of the many times he had used this particular shortcut on his way home while growing up. He knew the advantage as well as the danger in taking it. It hadn't mattered to him when he was younger that he was crossing Old Man Potter's land, or that the crabby old coot would be riled if he knew. The truth was, it didn't matter to him now, either.

The thought flashed across his mind that he hadn't changed much, but Quince revised it instantly. He *had* changed. At three inches over the mark of six feet, he had always been tall, but five years on the Arizona frontier had added a formidable breadth of muscle and sinew to his formerly lanky frame. Still wearing buckskins, fully bearded, with his dark hair having gone uncut longer than it should, he bore little resemblance to the youthful, clean-shaven wrangler he had once been. Yet the greatest change in him wasn't physical. It was reflected in startling green eyes that were now coldly assessing, in an intimidating demeanor that discouraged all challengers, and in a silent, occasionally dangerous resolve that was conveyed without words. Having had no recourse but to leave the family ranch five years earlier, he had ridden away an angry, frustrated young man. He was returning now, mature, ready to face all problems squarely, and determined that no one would ever drive him away again.

Quince's jaw hardened.

No one.

Abby's letter flashed to mind again. He had read it many times during the endless journey home. He had felt the deep emotion and panic in her words when she had written:

"Dear Quince,

I haven't received a letter from you in a long time, but I know you think about me like I always think about you. I know you wouldn't have left the Half-Moon if you didn't have to, and I know you wish you could be here right now. In my last letter I said things had settled down and were going all right, but everything's changed now.

Papa's coming home.

I don't know what to do, Quince. Brent still won't talk to me about what really happened that day, and Matt and Brent did nothing but argue about Papa the last time Matt came home. All I know is that Brent's determined to meet Papa at the prison and bring him here.

I'm not sure what Matt will do when he finds out.

I'm not sure what I should do.

I need you here, Quince. Please come home.

> *Your loving sister,*
> *Abby"*

Matt and Brent arguing.

Nothing had changed there.

Quince frowned. He had been at odds with his brother, Brent, as long as he could remember. Only a year older than he, Brent had taken the role of elder more seriously than Quince felt he had right to. Conservative and serious, Brent had disapproved of him, of his humor and spirit of adventure, and of his willingness to take risks to achieve his goals. Brent had been unable to comprehend the special bond that existed between their mother and her second son—a son whose rough, masculine features and strong-willed personality so resembled the father she had adored.

Sadness stirred when he thought of Eizabeth Quincy Hunter—beautiful, gentle, soft-spoken, loving, and so undeserving of her violent, premature, and meaningless death.

A familiar resentment brought back thoughts of Quince's younger brother, Matt. Always wild and rebellious, Matt had been a source of constant grief to Beth Hunter. Yet Quince knew that same quality in Matt had somehow earned him a unique place in their mother's heart—making even more painful Quince's conviction that Beth Hunter might still have been alive if not for her youngest son.

The image of a slight, dark-haired sprite appeared suddenly before Quince's mind, ejecting all negative thoughts. Her skin tanned a golden hue and her green eyes dancing, Abby had always made him smile. Eleven years younger than he and determined not to let him leave her behind, she had trailed at his heels from the time she took her first step. She had imitated his every move and had been on her way to becoming as skillful a wrangler as any man. He had been proud of her. Left motherless at the age of eight, Abby had turned to him when the resulting turmoil at the ranch became too hard. Leaving her behind had been the hardest thing he had ever done.

As for Pa—

His thoughts interrupted by a screeching whinny in the distance, Quince was suddenly alert. The whinnying grew louder, more strained as Quince nudged his mount to a faster pace along the trail. He arrived at a familiar section of trail bordered by thick brush and heard a soft cursing join the frantic whinnies. Proceeding cautiously, he nudged his mount into an area where a stream fed into a depression in the terrain, creating a swampy expanse that was both unexpected and treacherous. Almost thirty feet in circumference, the quicksand had grown larger during his five-year absence. Caught in the middle of the sucking mud, fighting frantically to escape its relentless downward tow, was a panicked mare with a furious young woman still mounted on its back.

Annoyed by the rider's lack of control over the frenzied animal, Quince ordered abruptly, "Hold that mare still, damn it! All that thrashing about is only making matters worse."

Her head jerking up toward him, the rider revealed a small-featured face flushed with frustration and angry dark eyes that burned as she spat back, "Don't you curse at me!"

"Use your head, then." Quince's reply was curt. "The more that animal struggles, the faster it's going to sink."

"You're not telling me anything I don't know!" Fiery tendrils of hair protruded from underneath the brim of her hat as she glared at him. "Well, are you going to get us out of here or not?"

"I don't know." Goaded by her arrogance, Quince returned coldly, "Maybe not."

The woman muttered under her breath as Quince dismounted to assess the situation more closely. The mare was still out of control. At the rate she was sinking, her legs would soon be totally engulfed.

He stated flatly, "You're going to have to calm your horse down. If you don't, there's no way I'll be able to get her out."

The young woman grew livid. "Just stop preaching and get us out of here!"

Right.

Ignoring his inclination to leave the red-haired witch exactly where he had found her, Quince reached for the rope on his saddle, then said, "Grab the line when I toss it to you. I'll pull you out first."

"No. I can do a better job of controlling the situation if I stay where I am."

Quince's jaw hardened. "You mean like you're doing now?"

"Look . . ." The young woman seethed, "I don't have time for your macho attitude."

360

"Look . . ." Quince retorted, "It's my way or no way. *Comprende?*"

"*Comprendo*. Now get us out of here, damn it, or I warn you, you'll be sorry!"

"Really?" Quince's gaze turned to ice. "There isn't too much you'd be able to do from underneath a few yards of mud, *ma'am*."

Allowing the witch to stew over that thought for a few seconds, Quince then ordered, "Grab the rope when I throw it to you and I'll drag you out."

"My horse—"

"Grab the rope."

"All right!"

Throwing his loop with a practiced eye, Quince grunted with satisfaction when it settled around the stiff-faced female's shoulders. He waited until she adjusted it around her waist and gripped it firmly, then said, "All right, now let yourself slip down onto the mud, lying flat on your stomach so I can pull you out."

"That isn't necessary. I can walk out if you have a rope on me."

"I said—"

"All right!"

With a quick twist, Quince secured the rope over his saddle horn, gave his mount a few swift commands, and guided the line as the woman slipped belly down onto the mud and was towed gradually nearer. Grasping her arms when she reached him, he pulled her to her feet.

The young woman turned on him, ignoring the slimy grit that plastered her riding clothes to her body, and said without a word of thanks, "My horse is still sinking."

"I don't know if I'll be able to get her out."

The woman went momentarily still, then said, "You don't mean that."

"Look at her." Sober and hard-eyed, Quince indicated the frenzied animal, which had sunk to its belly into the mud, "I can loop her around the neck and try having my horse pull her out, but—"

"No buts! Let's do it!"

Gritting his teeth, Quince looped the mare with the first throw. He clenched his jaw tighter as his horse attempted to tow the mired animal out. He lent his own weight to the effort, making no comment when the woman joined in.

The woman released the rope without a word when the mare, still whinnying frantically, was engulfed to her shoulders. She muttered, "We're not going to get Cinnamon out." Turning on him abruptly, dark eyes direct, she pressed, "Are we?"

"No."

Her voice devoid of emotion, she said, "My rifle is on the saddle."

Which was rapidly sinking out of sight.

Quince reached for his own gun. Out of the corner of his eye he saw the woman take off her muddied hat and slap it down onto the ground with disgust before she turned and walked away. She did not react when a single gunshot shattered the silence and the mare's struggles ceased. Instead, she continued walking directly toward the sun, which was rapidly rising toward its zenith.

Moving with slow deliberation, Quince retrieved his rope and secured it on his saddle. He stared for long moments at the slight figure silhouetted against the brilliant sunlight as the young woman continued trudging eastward. Narrow shoulders held painfully erect, her fiery hair blazing in the sun, she did not look back as she walked with silent resolution, ignoring him as easily as she did the mud already baking hard on her skin in the heat of the day.

She was as tough as they came.

Studying her more closely, Quince frowned. Yet for an instant he thought he had seen—

Quince mounted abruptly. Silently cursing, he took off after her, then rode at her side for a few moments before asking, "Where are you going?"

After ignoring him briefly, the young woman replied with a touch of belligerence, "Home."

"Where's that?"

"The Diamond C ranch house."

"The Diamond C?"

She glanced up at him with disdain. "You're on Diamond C land."

"This is Old Man Potter's land."

"He's dead. It's the Diamond C now."

Quince nodded. Old Man Potter's ranch house

was approximately three rough, desolate miles from where they were.

He said, "I'll take you there."

"I can walk."

Right.

He should let her do it, too.

But there was something about the little witch's determination, the set of her chin . . . and the vulnerability he had glimpsed in the almost imperceptible twitch of her cheek a moment earlier.

Ignoring her protest as well as her muddied state, he reached down, scooped her up, and set her down across the saddle in front of him.

"I said—"

"I heard you."

The silence between them deepened as Quince's arm closed securely around her waist and he nudged his mount into motion.

Things just went from bad to worse.

Sitting rigidly, intensely aware of the strong chest supporting her and the brawny arm draped loosely across her waist as the stranger's mount plodded forward, Glory Townsend closed her eyes in pure despair. She snapped them open again when the image of her mare's fear-crazed eyes flashed before her. Cinnamon had been prized by her father and her since the first day they arrived at the Diamond C four years earlier. Pa and she had been stunned to see so valuable a young horse in one of the dilapidated stable stalls, almost as stunned as they had been a few months earlier when they received a letter informing them that Mr. Elijah Potter had deeded his Texas horse ranch to Pa in his will.

Mr. Elijah Potter.

It had taken Pa a few minutes to remember the name. When he did, his eyes had filled. Will and Henry Potter, Elijah's only sons, had been in her father's company during the war. Pa had told her they were good men—boys, really—who had fought valiantly for the Confederacy. He had grown close to them, and when they were both killed only minutes apart, he had suffered their deaths keenly. He had not realized, however, that the simple act of writing their father a letter when the war ended, telling of his personal, affectionate regard for the old man's sons and describing in detail their bravery in battle, would bring him such a reward.

It had taken the letter detailing his inheritance several months to trace their travels, but it couldn't have arrived at a better time. His plantation devastated by the war and the land usurped by carpetbaggers years earlier, Byron Nathaniel Townsend had piled his wife, six-year-old daughter, and their remaining belongings into a wagon and had driven west, vowing to restore to his family everything they had lost.

It hadn't happened. Instead, nine years of failures had left her father more frustrated with each passing day. Her dear mother, Evangeline Parks Townsend, had died in the interim, still believing in her husband. That belief had been passed on to Glory, and when her father and she reached the Diamond C and saw its potential, she had believed her faith would prove justified.

The story did not have the happy ending she had anticipated. Elijah Potter's ranch had been mortgaged to the hilt and foreclosure had been imminent. The last of her father's savings had halted the process, but they had been struggling ever since.

Nor had Glory anticipated that her father would be thrown from his horse in a freak accident two years later—never to walk again.

Having assumed her father's responsibilities on the ranch, Glory had sworn to restore the Diamond C to financial stability, but that wasn't happening, either. Instead, costly mishaps had become a common occurrence over the past years. Now, in another freak accident for which she could not account, Cinnamon had bolted unexpectedly when they neared the bog that morning and had plunged deeply into the deadly mud before Glory was able to regain control—bringing a heartbreaking end to dreams of breeding the most valuable mare on the ranch.

Glory needed no one to tell her that her father's health had deteriorated badly in the past year, that he was facing his last chance to see his dream realized—or that she had failed him miserably. That fact would be only too evident to everyone on the ranch, too, when she returned covered with mud, seated across the saddle of a shabby, arrogant, itinerant wrangler who did not bother to conceal his assessment of her ineptitude.

Glory silently seethed.

She was angry at herself for not having controlled Cinnamon when the mare bolted.

She was irate that fate seemed somehow set against her.

She was incensed at being made to appear less than she was, when she knew in her heart she was as capable as any man.

But most of all, she was furious with the obnoxious, cold-eyed stranger who'd had no qualms about letting her know he had done everything right—while she seemed to have done everything wrong.

Her back stiffened as the Diamond C ranch house came into view in the distance, Glory felt a familiar determination rise. She had worked hard to convince the Diamond C wranglers that she was worthy of their confidence after her father's accident. To arrive back at the ranch now and have an egotistical saddle bum describe in mortifying detail the story of her costly mishap was a defeat and a humiliation she could not allow.

"Stop this horse," Glory ordered sharply.

The arm across her waist tensed, but the horse plodded on.

Infuriated, Glory demanded, "I said, stop this horse!"

The stranger reined his mount to a sudden halt. Turning toward him when his grip across her waist inexplicably tightened, she met his gaze and said, "Let me down. I'll walk the rest of the way."

No reaction.

She grated, "Did you hear me?"

The stranger searched her face with his penetrating, green-eyed stare, then replied unexpectedly, "Accidents happen. There's no shame in it."

Did he read minds, too?

Glory snapped, "I don't owe you any explanations for my behavior. Just do what I said!"

The stranger's gaze went frigid. "No, you don't owe me anything at all."

The fine line of Glory's lips twitched, "I could've gotten out of that quicksand any time I wanted to."

His silence spoke volumes.

"You give yourself too much credit."

"I was thinking the same thing about you."

"I said, let me dow—"

Releasing her abruptly, the stranger did not react when Glory slipped from the saddle and hit the ground with a thump. Standing up, refusing to rub her throbbing backside, she said, "I should've expected that from you."

"No, but I'd say you earned it."

A movement in the distance caught her eye, and Glory recognized her foreman's distinctive Appaloosa starting out from behind the ranch house. Suddenly desperate to be rid of the arrogant stranger, Glory relented. "All right, I suppose I do owe you something for your help. You'll probably be in town for a few days. If you're there this weekend, I'll come in and see to it that you receive some compensation."

The silence between them grew deafening.

She knew what he was waiting for. Somehow unable to say the words, Glory turned and started toward the ranch house. She felt his gaze burning into her back but she kept walking. She refused to react when his deep voice sounded coldly behind her.

"You're welcome, *ma'am*."

Bastard.

Relieved when she heard his horse turn, when the sound of the animal's hoofbeats gradually faded, Glory realized belatedly that she hadn't even asked the stranger's name.

Half-Moon Ranch

Somewhere in the lush grasslands of the Texas hill country is a place where the sun once shone on love and prosperity, while the night hid murder and mistrust. There, three brothers and a sister fight to hold their family together, struggle to keep their ranch solvent, while they await the return of the one person who can shed light on the secrets of the past.

From the bestselling authors
who brought you the *Secret Fires* series comes . . .

BOBBI SMITH

Rapture's Rage. Renee Fontaine's cascading black hair and soft, full curves draw suitors like bees to spring's first flower, but the dazzling beauty has eyes only for the handsome lawyer who scorns love. The innocent young woman can't get him out of her mind—and she knows that he is the one man she will ever want.

___52238-1 $5.99 US/$6.99 CAN

Renegade's Lady. Sheridan St. John sets out for the Wild West in search of the perfect hero for her new book. The man she finds fulfills every requirement for a fantasy lover—half Apache, all dark dangerous male. And the wildfire attraction between them destroys her reservations, leaving her with one burning need—to become the renegade's lady.

___4250-9 $5.99 US/$6.99 CAN

Dorchester Publishing Co., Inc.
P.O. Box 6640
Wayne, PA 19087-8640

Please add $1.75 for shipping and handling for the first book and $.50 for each book thereafter. NY, NYC, and PA residents, please add appropriate sales tax. No cash, stamps, or C.O.D.s. All orders shipped within 6 weeks via postal service book rate. Canadian orders require $2.00 extra postage and must be paid in U.S. dollars through a U.S. banking facility.

Name_____
Address_____
City_____State_____Zip_____
I have enclosed $_____ in payment for the checked book(s).
Payment <u>must</u> accompany all orders. ☐ Please send a free catalog.